Books by Liz Crowe

I0663108

Brewing Passion

Tapped

Tapped

ISBN # 978-1-78686-117-7

©Copyright Liz Crowe 2017

Cover Art by Posh Gosh ©Copyright 2017

Interior text design by Claire Siemaszkiewicz

Totally Bound Publishing

Published in 2017 by Totally Bound Publishing, Newland House, The Point, Weaver Road, Lincoln, LN6 3QN, United Kingdom.

Brewing Passion

TAPPED

LIZ CROWE

Dedication

To Desiree Holt, who never, ever, ever let me give up.

Chapter One

The man must be out of his ever-loving mind.

Evelyn tried hard not to yell, or otherwise overreact, ever aware of her reputation as one of the sole females in this testosterone-soaked world of beer sales. But she simply could not stand for this sort of manipulation.

She rose to her feet. "I won't do it."

From his position behind the desk, her boss, Grant Taylor, president of Tri-City Distribution, tipped back in his chair and appraised her from head to toe. "He asked for you specifically. And I am certain I don't have to remind a professional such as yourself that Fitzgerald is our best craft beer brand — one of our *only* craft beer brands and the one I hope to use to build a better beer portfolio." He feigned a pitiful look.

"You look like a constipated crocodile when you do that." Even as she accepted that her day had just grown that much worse, if it were cosmically possible, she slumped back into the chair on the other side of his desk.

"Evelyn, honey, it's not that bad. He's a good guy, really."

The foul liquid that passed for coffee at the Tri-City offices polluted her throat, giving her a few seconds to think. After only two years in the beer and wine sales business, she'd found her niche, and she even had an incentive trip to Barbados from the Corona guys nearly within her grasp. A day spent — more like wasted — trying to shove hipster beer down the throats of savvy buyers at her best stores would not get her any closer to that goal. Evelyn stared out of the window at the annoyingly perfect blue sky.

"Grant, you know I need a heads-up longer than an hour.

Seriously, I have to shuffle the whole sales day. Jesus. I don't even know where — "

Grant held up a hand. "Spare me, please. I know you've already committed where Fitzgerald products are placed to that gorgeous, top-selling brain of yours. You sold more of their amber, IPA and Winter Spice bullshit than anybody. Don't kid a kidder." He grinned at her.

Stress bloomed in her chest and spread, bringing a familiar anxious mantra to the forefront of her mind.

This stupid job is the only thing between me and the homeless shelter.

Nothing would make her jeopardize what she'd built out of, essentially, nothing. A two-year associate's degree was all she'd been able to afford before she'd started working in a trendy downtown craft beer and cocktail bar. When a Tri-City sales rep had mentioned they were hiring and how much she could make in commission, she'd jumped at it.

Who knew she'd be a sales star?

"Fine. But if you think I'm gonna suck up to the Chosen Son of the Fitzgerald fortune, you are sadly mistaken. He can ride in my car and go on calls with me, but he'd better understand that I have a full day already set and I won't be giving him any special attention." She drained the last of the caffeine then set the mug down on Grant's desk with what she hoped sounded like a decisive bang. A sudden puff of air blew past her, ruffling the papers on Grant's desk.

Her boss's eyes widened. He pointed to something behind her and started to open his mouth.

"No," she cut him off. "Don't say another word. You know I'm right. Everybody knows he's just a trust-fund baby, opening a brewery with his daddy's money, then gallivanting around the world, getting his degree" — she hooked her fingers in the air around the word — "in brewing science. Jesus. Who needs a degree in that? He should just stick to improving his golf handicap and deflowering debutantes."

The petulant sound of her own voice annoyed her, but

stories like Austin Fitzgerald's made her the maddest. She'd been raised by a single mother who'd waitressed by day and, she'd later learned, turned tricks at night while the young Evelyn had done homework and watched TV at her aunt's house. Her mother had died during Evelyn's second year of college, forcing her to quit after she'd figured out that the modest funeral would eat up every cent her mother had managed to save.

Grant cleared his throat and stood, buttoning his suit coat. She watched him, her brain still on fire with helpless frustration. Even if she'd agreed to haul Fitzgerald around, she had no plans to sell craft beer that day.

"I *need* to schmooze my wine buyers today, Grant. I can't be babysitting this guy." The back of her neck tingled when the ends of her hair fluttered in another sudden breeze. She frowned, observing her boss stick his hand out as if about to shake hers, a big smile pasted on his face.

"Well, if I weren't deathly allergic to both golf and debutantes, that might have been a career choice," came a low, raspy voice from right behind her.

Evelyn's entire body broke out in goosebumps.

"Grant, good to see you again," the voice continued.

She gritted her teeth and rose, giving Grant what she hoped was a sufficiently withering look before turning around. Deep green eyes met hers. She was struck dumb by their depth and humorous sparkle. Dark jeans and a simple navy blue crew-neck—undoubtedly cashmere—sweater, brown box-toe loafers and a camel-colored dress jacket completed the look. He would have been at home on a *GQ* model as easily as he navigated a brewery floor. Close-cut dark-brown hair topped a clean-shaven, angular face.

A face that seemed pretty amused by her at that moment.

"And you must be Evelyn Benedict, saleswoman extraordinaire." His smile lit up the room, rendering Evelyn speechless. Grant nudged her arm until she stuck out her hand. Austin's warm, firm grip lingered long enough to make her uncomfortable.

"I see she's mesmerized by the size of my...trust fund already." He glanced over her shoulder at Grant then at her, pinning her in place again with that intense, still amused gaze. "Austin Fitzgerald, the albatross around your neck for the day." He gave her palm a friendly squeeze before letting go. "At your service."

Austin's gaze remained squarely on hers. She had on her best thrift store designer suit over a silk blouse open at the neck. Used to men eyeballing her from tip to toe, she found it refreshing for one not to automatically zero in on her cleavage.

"Never had such a lovely babysitter before, Grant. Thanks."

She swallowed when his eyes narrowed, then frowned as he gazed quickly up and down her front, lighting an unwanted and unexpected fire in her belly. Since when did she like it when some guy checked her out in such an obvious way?

He shrugged, sidestepping as if to get out of her way, the moment between them over. "Ready to go when you are. Rumor has it you have a big day ahead," he said, the expression on his handsome face suddenly neutral.

"Yes. I do." She strode past him, needing to regain her composure. Loud, masculine laughter echoed in her ears all the way to the ladies' room. She splashed water on her face and stared in the mirror while her heart took up a loud drumbeat in her ears.

He is nothing but a spoiled-rotten trust-fund brat. No matter if he wears it like a stockbroker-slash-daytime drama hero. I do not need this distraction right now.

* * * *

Austin tried to focus on the guy behind the desk as they stood in the claustrophobic office. But his brain spun with a combination of fresh perfume and sudden, kneejerk lust for the woman who'd just stalked out of the room.

The day suddenly looked a lot better—less 'annoying ride-along crap' and more 'honest to God, get to know a beautiful woman.' He had countless headaches back at his brewery to deal with. Didn't need the time away any more than she seemed to want him around, but he grinned at the sight of her rich golden-blonde hair and deep blue eyes when she emerged from around the corner. Her expression was flat. He sensed her determination to resist whatever had occurred between them earlier.

Yeah. Not if I have anything to do with it.

"After you." He held out a hand and followed her down the narrow hall toward the parking lot door, adjusting himself behind the zipper of the stupid jeans he'd grabbed off the rack yesterday, desperate for something to wear that was suitable for selling and not brewing.

Good Lord, but she's hot.

Alarmed at his instant, adolescent response to her, he held the door open. She breezed past him. He had to shut his eyes against the quick breath of light, clean scent that invaded his nose again.

He helped put his sample bottles in the trunk of her one-step-from-the-graveyard car, then climbed into the immaculate interior, watching as Evelyn pulled out her itinerary for the day and studied it, a frown marring her perfect face.

"Okay, so I'm trashing this, I guess." She tossed the papers into her briefcase with a sigh. "Let's hit it, shall we? By the seat of our pants? Not the way I usually like to approach a work day."

"Yeah, good plan." Without even realizing he was doing it, he touched the hand she had resting on the gear shift between them. It was meant as a 'we're in this together' sort of gesture. Nothing more. She stared at it, then up at him. Utterly unprepared for the spark that leapt from her skin to his, he swallowed hard and jerked his arm back.

"Sorry," he muttered, grabbing his own thigh while she backed out of the parking space. Trying to quell the alarm rising in his chest, he risked a glance at her while they waited at a light. Her angry stare made him smile and hold up both hands. "Don't nail me for harassment, okay? My mommy and daddy won't bail me out anymore, or so they claim."

Her quick laughter was music to his ears.

"I'm sorry. I was just…" Her jaw clenched and he had to force away the urge to run his finger over it if only to get her to relax. Such a beautiful woman should not be so uptight. A surge of protectiveness nearly suffocated him.

Wow, Fitzgerald. Get a hold of yourself.

For a guy who'd never worried about where his next meal—or his next pair of designer sunglasses—would come from, Austin remained fairly introspective. He was well aware of his reputation, but hearing it tumble from Evelyn's mouth earlier had pissed him off, making him want to prove something to her.

The fact that he'd finally given in to his mother's harping on about marrying the Masterson girl had honestly slipped his mind since laying eyes on the gorgeous creature behind the wheel. He suppressed an inward groan at his dilemma. But couldn't resist encouraging the connection between them. He somehow sensed she'd love to play along. Some light flirting, nothing more or less. Harmless, really.

"It's okay. Really. Just an awkward moment we'll laugh about with our kids someday."

She snorted. "Sure we will. Just before you dump me and the brats for the trophy wife your mommy always wanted for you."

He narrowed his eyes, hoping she didn't realize how close to the truth she'd gotten about the mother-approved arrangements. When she grinned at him, two amazing dimples appeared on her cheeks, making him grateful he was sitting, since his knees had officially turned to jelly.

He looked away from her. Staring straight ahead, making a mental count to ten, he calmed his breathing, reminded himself he was there to work. Evelyn cleared her throat at that moment, effectively ending the internal break-up monologue he'd begun with his almost-fiancée.

Valerie, a girl who would have been a debutante — had such things existed in Grand Rapids, Michigan — as heir to the Masterson restaurant empire. She was an interior designer of some repute, pretty, bossy, and desperate for the Mrs. Fitzgerald designation. He liked her well enough and was so sick of the nagging about his continual reluctance to put a ring on her finger that he'd been ready to close the deal.

He put a hand over his eyes and muffled a groan at the mess he was about to make. All over this one, single, first impression.

But what *an impression.*

"All right, we'll swing north and hit the big chain stores first." She spoke as she drove, and Austin used every ounce of his willpower not to stare at the leg exposed by her short skirt, at the way her thigh muscle flexed when she worked the clutch, gunning the engine too high every time. "I'm close to getting the winter lager placement alongside your amber. Then I know the boys at Beer Baron and Hop Town would love to see your rock-star face, so we'll stop in there."

He glanced over to gauge her level of seriousness. The tingling sensation in his scalp at her ironic smile alarmed him all over again. Every single memory and thought of the woman he'd been half-heartedly screwing for years had gone in the blink of Evelyn's amazing blue eyes. He swallowed hard and listened to her talk business.

"Also, I'd like to drop in on a couple of new boutique beer and wine stores that opened last month. Your esteemed presence gives me the excuse I need."

"Uh, okay. You're in charge. Just give me the high sign when I'm supposed to speak."

"Oh, don't worry, you'll figure it out. I'll have to do some inventory stuff at most of these places, so there will be time for you to bond with whatever management is on hand. A few of them are ladies — you'll make their day, I'm sure."

Unable to stop himself, he touched her again, this time letting himself own the heat that passed between them. "Don't be jealous, honey. I'd never cheat on you."

"Ha! I'll farm you out in a heartbeat, *sweetie*. You'll do whatever it takes to increase our bottom line. Hope you took your vitamins." She yanked her hand out from under his.

Smiling at her once more, he shifted in his seat to relieve the pressure building under his zipper.

He'd been damn close to asking Valerie to marry him, willing to leave her and her bitch of a mother to the wedding arrangements, ready to nod in agreement at what he hoped were the proper intervals. His mother had finally stopped haranguing him, left him to run his brewery in peace and he'd made a similar peace within himself, realizing the Faustian bargain he'd struck.

But now, as he sat in the passenger's seat of Evelyn's car staring out the windshield without seeing anything, a long-buried urge almost blinded him. And he knew Valerie was history.

Chapter Two

As if on autopilot, Evelyn pulled into one of her biggest retailers — The Beer Barn — a store that took up half a strip mall on the north-east side of town. During the ride from her office, she'd resisted the extreme impulse to flick her gaze over to him and felt smug about that victory. But now they were parked, and she made the crucial error of looking straight into his eyes. The intensity of his gaze made her whole body tingle in a way she'd not felt in her entire life. It also brought a flicker of resentment to the confusion roiling in her gut.

The moment sizzled, etching a groove in her psyche so deep she could sense its contours. By way of self-defense, she glared at him until realizing she still had a grip of death on the steering wheel.

Yeah, a grip, Benedict, get one.

She ground her teeth and forced her gaze away, nearly tumbling out onto the asphalt in her haste to put some distance between them.

Austin got out of the car and stayed quiet, merely holding out his hand to receive the samples of his two best-selling brews she shoved at him. "Good choice," he remarked, as she slammed the trunk and squared her shoulders. "This place is pretty mainstream."

"No, it's not actually." She grabbed her smart phone and fired up the ordering program. Might as well make a few bucks while she let him do his dog-and-pony show. The owner of this joint was a self-described beer snob who'd happily throw young Mr. Fitzgerald out on his ear, she knew.

She grinned to herself, realizing why she'd come here first. This guy needed to learn his place in the real-world pecking order. She'd toss him to the wolves right up front, take some orders for the store's higher-gravity section of beers and be on her way. "Your problem is you don't really have a good sense of what to make beyond these." She gave the two bottles in his hand a glance. "Those are fine, but I think you should expand your offerings beyond the basics. Of course, what do I know?"

He raised an eyebrow at her, which she ignored as she made her way to the glass front door, walking through as he opened it for her.

"Evelyn! My gorgeous girl!" Hal Granger came out from behind the counter, a huge smile on his face. "To what do I owe the honor of two visits in a week, hmm?" He kissed her square on the lips and folded her into a bear hug.

She sensed Austin's gaze on her, but she continued ignoring him as she flirted and small-talked with one of her best retailers for another ten minutes. To his credit, Austin didn't butt in.

Finally, Hal broke the ice. "Did you bring your new boyfriend to carry samples, my love, or just to make me jealous?"

She flushed and mentally acknowledged her childishness for making the guy stand there like a third wheel.

"Oh, God, no, you know you're my one and only." She winked at Austin and he took a step forward. "This is Austin Fitzgerald. Owner and…"

Hal stepped right in front of her and held out a huge paw of a hand, forcing Evelyn to move out of their way.

"Why, of course! I wondered when you'd be stopping by my little store, Mr. Fitz—"

"Austin. Please," he said. "And this is hardly a little store, Hal. Don't be so modest."

She stared as the huge man practically squirmed with delight. *What the hell?* Austin's loose-limbed stance never changed, his casual yet in-charge manner shifting into high gear as he gripped the two bottles by their necks in one hand and gave his pitch.

Hal gushed, preened and stopped just short of falling on the floor and letting the guy scratch his exposed belly. Evelyn's ears buzzed with fury and something she now recognized as bright white jealousy. They flat-out ignored her for a solid twenty minutes, exchanging industry and local gossip, before Austin segued into one of the cleanest sell jobs she'd ever observed in her life. She leaned back against a shelf and watched Austin work, unable to resist the need to devour him with her gaze.

Without even glancing her way, he held out the two bottles and she grabbed them, found cups behind the counter, and popped the caps off the beers. Trying to remain angry but letting a small bud of admiration blossom, she poured and handed them first the IPA then the wheat ale.

This was where Hal would nail him, she felt certain. Both of these beers were solid but nondescript, and this guy loved his 'out there' beers — giant Imperials and heavy stouts alternating with weird, sour Belgians. These two would never make his cut and would never see shelf space in this store. Resuming her position where she could keep an eye on Austin's ass, she waited for the inevitable.

"Wow!" said Hal.

She shook her head, trying to clear the hazy fuzz of horniness that had crept over her because she obviously had misunderstood that response.

"Austin, I had no idea!" Hal clapped the man on the back while Austin turned and shot her a look so full of 'told you so' she nearly choked on her own tongue. "Evelyn, you've been holding out on me, you naughty girl." He downed the sample and held out his cup so she could take it.

She bit back the urge to remind him the last time she'd brought this beer in he'd declared it 'swill for the masses'. The buyer was always right. Even when said buyer was a proverbial liar. She gave him a weak smile and refused to meet Austin's eyes.

Back in the car, once again trapped in a small, confined space with a man who was making her breathless with aggravation and no small measure of lust, she entered the embarrassingly large order for the Fitzgerald 420 IPA, the Santa's Bag Spiced Ale and even the odd winter wheat lager.

"You're welcome." His rough voice grated on her nerves and stoked her libido at the same time. She didn't reply. He sighed and seemed to re-focus on his phone as she threw the car into gear and backed out of the lot, already picturing their next stop at a major Michigan-based chain grocery store. The general manager would be around today. She had dated the guy last year and remembered he had no patience for bullshit salesmen. Let Austin try to pull that again.

* * * *

"Look." Her jaw ached from all the teeth clenching. "I don't know what you did in there..." She gestured to the gigantic store where the damnable man had just made yet another huge sale to not one but three of their flagship stores, elbowing out a fake craft beer from Bud and a well-established regional micro represented by one of her company's biggest rivals. "But you have to know I've tried with both those guys... I mean, it's not like... Oh, never mind."

She didn't owe Austin Fitzgerald an explanation. She huffed and puffed her way to the next three stops, all of which resulted in slam dunks for Austin, significant increases in her craft beer sales and more delicious crow-flavored bile for her.

* * * *

During the twenty-minute drive between their stops, Austin tried to calm the spinning in his brain. He'd been on hyperdrive with the famous Hal Granger, realizing the moment he'd laid eyes on the guy what she'd done—put him smack in front of the hardest sell in a city full of beer snobs, one that had the power to make or break his company. Impressive, and ballsy on her part.

But setting herself up to fail just to prove he couldn't sell his own beer?

Not today.

After sneaking a glance at her legs again, he looked back at his phone screen by way of diverting his attention. But all he could envision was the color of her flesh, the smooth line of her thigh. In the big grocery he'd been in an inner frenzy of irrational jealousy as he'd watched the smarmy asshole of a manager keep an arm around her waist about two minutes longer than was absolutely necessary.

The strange jolt of possessiveness struck him in the chest once again.

That pretentious asshole had been with her.

His *Evelyn.*

He shook his head.

Get a grip, Fitzgerald. She's a lot of things, but yours is not one of them.

He'd channeled one hundred percent of the blinding jealousy into making a huge sale, surprising himself with how easily it had come. By the time they'd waltzed out of the store, his whole body had hummed like a tuning fork. The jumpiness wouldn't calm, even as she'd tried to convince him she knew how to do her job. Afraid he'd blurt out something utterly inappropriate, he'd just nodded at her, smiled like an idiot, and said something innocuous he didn't even remember. He needed to get away from her, or he risked disaster. She obviously despised him and the more he sold, the madder she got, in some perverse reversal of logic.

After she'd screeched to a halt in front of another local beer and wine store where he had to strap on the sales hat once more, he took a breath. Staring straight ahead, letting the shimmering energy in the car propel him toward stupidity, he spoke. "You still sleeping with him?" He shut his eyes, wishing to suck the words back down his windpipe.

Without hesitation, she responded. "That would be in the 'none of your business' category, I'd say. C'mon, Fitzgerald, gird your show-off sales loins. The lady manager in here is a ballbuster."

He groaned and ran a hand over his eyes then climbed out, grabbing sample bottles out of her hands without speaking. Within minutes, he honestly believed the fifty-plus battleaxe of a woman who'd glared at him when he walked in would gladly either bear his love child or make him dinner, whichever he desired.

Sensing the heat of Evelyn's fury as he finalized another large order, he excused himself and made his way toward the restroom. The tuning-fork sensation had morphed into a dull ache centered in his gut, which steadily made its way down to his balls.

When he emerged — after splashing water on his face enough times to calm the hardening in his jeans — he almost plowed straight into her. He gripped her arms to keep her from falling and the impulses that had bounced around in his brain since the morning nearly brought him to his knees. He dropped his hands and looked away, swallowing back the urge to say something, anything, to convince her he wasn't such a bad guy.

"Sorry."

Her voice was flat. He took a step back, stopped only when his butt hit the wall. The space between them filled with near-visible silence, but he didn't move.

"I don't know how I'm doing it, but the longer we work together, the more sales I make, and the more you hate me. Clue me in here, Benedict. I thought sales were the goal of the day." He crossed his arms, holding them close to his chest so she couldn't gauge how shaky his hands had gotten.

She swallowed, and he watched the exquisite warm peach hue of her skin redden. Admiring the line of her neck, her jaw, the plump fullness of her lower lip as she bit it, a nervous tic he'd love to come to love, if she'd let him, Austin sensed himself falling deeper into a very scary hole. Her ongoing silence took on a life of its own.

"Well? I left my secret-sales-goal decoder ring at home. You obviously have a different agenda for today. I get it. 'Prove to the rich boy he doesn't have what it takes' is fine, but we could have saved some time if you'd just told me first."

She opened her lips, then pressed them together and shouldered past him. He watched, fascinated, as his hand reached out of its own accord and snagged her arm. She stopped, stared at it, then up at him. When he realized the blue of her eyes was brighter because of tears, he hesitated. Female tears always unnerved him, but his chest tightened in a thoroughly alarming way at the thought of having caused her unhappiness.

He let go. "Sorry. I didn't mean to..."

In a split second, her beautiful face was within inches of his. "Don't flatter yourself. I'm just pissed off. You've had that effect on me since I first laid eyes on you, so yeah, I guess I set you up. But apparently, all your country-club, private-school time has been worth it. Bullshitting comes naturally to you. And that's all this job is. A whole barrel of bullshit."

She stomped away before he could speak or, even better, grab her and kiss her. The space she vacated quivered with anger. But her crisp perfume stayed in his nose and he had to clench his hands into fists to keep from shoving her up against the wall and kissing her until she saw it his way.

Evelyn leaned against the bathroom's metal door, turning her head so she felt the ice-cold surface against her face. She closed her eyes, but when all she saw behind her lids were a dark denim-covered ass, large hands, just-shy-of-perfectly-handsome face and deep-green eyes, she groaned. She had no business whatsoever obsessing over this guy. He was so far out of her league he could be on another planet.

Besides, she had no time for a quick roll in the hay, although her thighs tightened at the prospect. Her goals were set for the year. She'd be independent, free of her mother's debts if she met them. No time to hassle with the playboy owner of a brewery, no matter how drop-dead, movie-star compelling he was.

So, yeah, snap out it.

She splashed water on her face, then flushed the toilet to make it sound as if she'd come in here for a reason other than to hide. Opening the door, she frowned at the sight of his annoyingly attractive self, still leaning back against the wall, staring at her in that infuriating, skin-pebbling way he had.

"Let's go," she said, hoping she didn't sound as wobbly as she felt. "One more stop then we'll eat." But she stopped in front of him. "Unless we need to clear the air now." She matched his stance, crossing her arms but keeping less than a foot between them. "Do we?" She refused to break their eye contact. The grin that broke out across his face, somehow igniting the green in his eyes, made her want to weep, throw things, and launch herself into his arms. "Guess not." She turned and walked back into the store, blinking in the sudden glare of her own need.

Chapter Three

By the time they dropped into a semicircular booth across from each other for a late lunch, Evelyn was convinced she was either madly in love with the guy or sick with jealousy over any woman who had her claws into him. He'd sold—and sold and sold—increasing her craft beer profit dramatically in just three hours. All with an easygoing attitude, clever but precise brewing chatter and self-deprecating charm that left her breathless.

She listened as he regaled her with stories of his life in the brewing institute in Munich.

"No, no really, I'm serious. You should see how we minions literally have to haul giant hot boulders from the forge with these old iron tongs and keep putting them under the brew kettles. And God help you if you let the fucker get a half-degree cooler than it's supposed to be—or warmer for that matter. Frankly I'm surprised I survived it." He smiled at the waitress.

Evelyn repressed a rush of anger at the girl's simper. "Well, you did what you loved. You were lucky." She bit the inside of her cheek at the self-pity that surged out with that comment.

Stop it! He doesn't give a crap about your sad-sack story. Just eat, get through the day, and drop him off at his Maserati or wherever.

"Yeah, I did." He ordered and handed the menu to the girl.

Evelyn looked away, then back at him. A zing flew from her scalp to her toes before nestling in around the vicinity of her panties at the intensity of his gaze.

"And I am lucky. But I work hard, contrary to popular opinion."

"I know. I can see that now."

He'd regaled the beer shop owners with stories of late nights spent babying batches of brew, poring over the books and brewing logs, trying to match supply to demand without going too far into the red.

Something between them had snapped, crackled and popped its way into a strange camaraderie by the time they'd left the last stop. It was a relief to talk, *really* talk, and not spend so much energy being pissed off at him. She sipped her water, knowing she was giving away her nervousness, but had to put the glass back down her hands shook so hard. She clutched them together in her lap.

"So, lovely Evelyn, I'm gonna attempt to start over. You ready?"

She nodded, not trusting her voice.

"Boyfriend? Fiancé Does a guy have a chance or will I get flattened by the former-NHL-star-turned-CEO who surely claims you as his?" His eyes were guileless, open and twinkling.

She swallowed hard. "Uh, no. None of the above. But, why, I mean..." She lowered her gaze, mortified by her flustered state. Without a word, he slid closer, never taking his eyes from hers, his arm draping over the back of the worn leather of the booth.

"Say no more." His lips were dangerously close to her ear.

Her scalp prickled and she glanced around, hoping no one was watching, but suddenly unable to care. His body felt so warm, so solid. And so completely utterly wrong on some level. She moved a few inches away from him, anger returning in a sudden wave of self-protection.

"I don't need this." She grabbed the beer the waitress plunked down in front of her.

"Need what?" He sat back and sipped his own amber-colored brew, his face impassive.

"I don't appreciate you thinking I'll jump in the sack with you just because you turn some kind of magic, rich-boy charm on me, that's what."

He raised an eyebrow. "Didn't know I had rich-boy charm." He moved away, leaving her strangely bereft. "And for the record, you were the one who said 'jump in the sack'. I only asked if you had a boyfriend who would beat me up. Nothing more, nothing less."

She had to stop herself from begging him to come back around to her side of the table. But she'd started down this path, so she figured she stay on it. "I'm not your type, Fitzgerald."

"I'm pretty sure I know my type better than you do, Benedict."

His calm voice irritated her. He turned his killer smile on the stupid girl bringing them their lunch and Evelyn cursed herself for being such a bitch.

But the guy was most likely after only one thing from her. One thing she was not about to give him. This was heartbreak on two designer-denim-covered legs, waiting to pounce.

"Look, Evelyn." He held out a hand. She stared at it for a few seconds before realizing what he wanted. She regretted it the second their palms met.

Oh God.

She tried not to close her eyes against the chemistry between them.

He kept talking.

Which didn't help.

"I'm sorry. I didn't mean to give you the wrong idea. You are an amazingly beautiful woman, and an incredible salesperson. I, um, didn't really anticipate...oh hell." He grinned and shrugged, giving her a friendly squeeze before releasing her. "Let's just pretend that never happened, shall we? I'm out of line. Enjoy your lunch. Tell me about your life while I stuff my inner alpha male back in his cage."

She smiled, happy to break the moment, but willing it

back just the same.

In spite of the lust running rampant through him, Austin managed to choke down his burger and fries, slamming back one more beer to try to calm his rattled nerves.

She was his type.

She was definitely going to be, anyway.

He shook his head, needing to clear it of the foggy, possessive thoughts that had rolled through him all day.

Yeah, and how the hell do you really expect to end your current relationship, smart guy?

Valerie Masterson might be a beautiful, spoiled rich girl, but she was stubborn. She and his mother had worn him down. Valerie's slightly dramatic talents between the sheets hadn't hurt. But he had the impression it was a lot of show. It felt fine, physically, but at that precise moment, he acknowledged he had nothing in his heart for her. He owed it to her to cut it off.

Shaking his head at his own self-justifying inner dialogue, he paid — something that was expected on ride-along days — and spent a few minutes in the men's room, staring in the mirror.

What in the hell had him so worked up over Evelyn Benedict, anyway? Nearly thirty-six years old, with the equivalent of a doctoral degree in brewing from Germany under his belt, he could now call himself president of one of the fastest-growing new microbreweries in Michigan.

He'd had his fair share of life's adventures. His time in Germany had been well spent — not only becoming a legit Master Brewer but also screwing his way through as many lovely, willing *Fräuleins* as possible. But when faced with the ample determination of his mother, combined with the seemingly obvious connection with a woman who matched his means and upbringing, he'd caved like a beta male and he knew it.

He was a trust-fund baby, yes, but determined to make this one dream of his come true in spite of his father's overwhelming disapproval. His goal of not taking another cent from the man after five years of business had seemed improbable at first, but he'd managed it.

Fitzgerald Brewing already operated in the black. His products were distributed throughout the entire state of Michigan, in Chicago, and down into Ohio. They were on track to expand and he'd cut the financial cord by signing a loan application that would no doubt give his father a heart attack but would allow him to continue the expansion his parents wouldn't support.

He knew on some level he'd agreed to marry Valerie in exchange for his mother to stop haranguing him about his 'obligation' to their family company.

A quick flash of anger at his long-lost brother brought a flush to his face.

Maybe I should just drop off the face of the earth too. That seemed to have worked for him.

Then visions of the tall, blond German man who'd been his friend and fellow lady-killer in Germany at the brewing institute invaded his brain, shoving thoughts of his twin, his one-time best friend, out.

He and Ross Hoffman been fellow rookies his first year in Munich and the strong friendship that had sprung up between them had taken them both by surprise. Austin's easygoing, relaxed manner had been a perfect foil to Ross, who was high-strung and driven to the point of obsession with his own brewing perfection. They'd ended up roommates and many a morning had woken with a lovely woman wedged between them.

Though he'd dabbled with threesomes in college, Austin had never encountered anyone more eager to engage in them than Ross. They used to enter a bar or party, take one look around and hold up fingers to each other indicating the number of minutes it would take to find a willing female, peel her away from the throng, and fulfill her every fantasy between them. He'd told Ross everything about his family and his parents' ongoing belief that he'd get his little brewing obsession out of his system on their dime and return to Michigan prepared to take his rightful place at the head of the family business.

Ross hadn't said much about himself, but had been a great listener and an amazing study and brewing partner — his first true friend since his brother. Even though he'd kept himself emotionally aloof — so aloof at times he was almost unapproachable — as long as he was willing to continue the threesome fun, Austin hadn't minded, much.

He let a chill of memory pass through him, wishing he knew how to proceed. What had happened with Ross had had time to progress, become a deep friendship of the sort Austin had never dreamed possible, although they hadn't stayed in touch like he'd thought they would.

Mental images of the beautiful woman waiting for him, no doubt tapping her patent-leather toes in impatience, forced him to pause. The crotch of his too-tight jeans had become decidedly uncomfortable as the images of her, gloriously naked beneath him, paraded around in his lizard brain.

Ross would know how to handle this.

Whenever there'd been a woman who'd needed a bit more convincing than their usual flirty banter, or the one-two punch of the handsome dark-haired American and the smoking-hot blond German brewer hadn't convinced her, Austin had tended to drift away, lose interest. Then Ross used to move in and close the deal alone, give him a high sign, and the fun would commence. It was the 'Ross Superpower', they used to joke the morning after as they drank espressos and relaxed before a day of brewing or study.

Austin would admit that he'd never felt this way about a female, at least not this quickly. Women peopled his life, no doubt. Women thrust into his face by his meddling mother. An over-abundance of women during his years in Munich. And finally, the current one, the Chosen One, at this moment likely spending a small fortune on God knew what in Paris. This woman, this Evelyn, completely and utterly confident of her own independence — and of his predator status — would not normally appeal. Typically, he'd write her off.

This has the potential to be way too much trouble. You already have enough to worry about.

And yet...

He groaned and willed his cock to soften, without much luck. Shouldering his way back out to the noisy restaurant, he pulled up short at the vision of Evelyn seated in a chair in the hallway outside the women's room. She was bent forward, adjusting her shoe, the strong line of her calf and thigh drawing his gaze like a magnet. He blinked as the fall of her thick blonde hair tumbled over her face, the ever-present phone held to her ear.

She laughed at whatever she heard and Austin jumped right into it, wanting more than anything to sleep and wake with that honey-rich sound in his ears. Every easygoing, go-slow bone in his body screeched to a halt and ushered in a need so deep he nearly choked on it.

Mine.

Without a single thought for the possible consequences, he squared his shoulders and pulled her to her feet.

"I'm on the phone," Evelyn hiss-whispered, shocked, but he took it, touched the screen to end the call, and tucked it in his pocket, at the same time covering her mouth with his. His firm, forceful lips gave her a clear message. Her entire universe shifted under her feet when she met his tongue's demand, let him sweep inside her mouth, thread his fingers into her hair, and push her back against the wall.

Holy hell, the guy sure knows how to kiss.

She made a noise in her throat when he moved his amazing lips from hers and traced a line down her neck. Against all logic, she wrapped her arms around him, angled her body so she could feel every inch of him, including the obvious erection straining his zipper. He moved one hand down her back, cupping her ass and pulling her tighter and higher up his body. To her utter shock, she parted her thighs, let him slip one of his between them. The restaurant noise faded, leaving nothing but the sound of their breathing in her ears.

He released her ass and reached up to cradle her face between his palms.

"Evelyn, you are —"

Flustered beyond imagining, she pushed him away. "Horny now, thanks to you." He burst out laughing. She shook her head. "Sorry. I'm a little blunt. It's a failing."

He pulled her close again. "Not to me, it's not. Let's go."

She frowned, disentangled herself and stared at him. "Oh, okay. Yeah." She readjusted the skirt that had slid up her thighs, and forced the lusty mist clouding her brain to dissipate.

Not your type, remember? Work to do, remember? This trust-fund jerk only wants to notch his bedpost.

He still hadn't moved out of her space. Placing her hands on his too-close chest, she cleared her throat and pushed him back once more. "You're right. Let's go. Work to do." She grabbed her purse and marched out on wobbly heels, assuming he would follow.

By the time she'd made it to her car, a cold wind had picked up. She shivered, regretting leaving her threadbare dress coat at home. Tears of anger at herself threatened to spill over as she wrenched the door open, gasping when hands gripped her shoulders and span her around. He was so close she could see his square jaw clenching.

"Work is over," he ground out.

"Are you nuts? Some of us have to put in a whole day, Fitzgerald. You know, bills to pay and all that?" Elbowing him aside, she climbed into the car, slammed the door, and prayed she hadn't shut his hand in it.

She had to get away from him. Either that, or lose all control and prove herself a desperate, poor salesgirl, willing to let the rich boy between her legs after just one kiss. He slid into the passenger seat, slid his hand around the back of her neck, and brought his impossibly handsome face up to hers.

"Don't." She heard her voice, papery, thin, and shut her eyes against the temptation to let him do whatever he wanted.

"Open your eyes."

That now familiar rasp in his voice made her whimper. When he kissed her again, it was gentle, taking his time, exploring her lips and tongue with his. She clutched at him over the console, gasping.

"You are perfect," he said. "And I need to touch you more. Now. So let's go. I'll give you directions." He gave her a soft kiss at the juncture of her collarbones, then sat back, keeping his fingers in her hair. She gulped and shook her head, turning to grip the steering wheel so hard her knuckles ached with the effort.

He pried her loose and put her hand against his chest. "Do you feel that?" His heart beat hard and fast under her palm. "I'm terrified of this. I can't explain it. And I'll excuse you from work. I know your boss." He grinned.

Reality smacked her hard in the face, reminding her exactly what must be happening. Horny men were no new concept to her. Time to nip this in the bud before she did something she really regretted. She trailed her fingers down to the impressive bulge between his legs.

He squirmed when she cupped his balls. "I know what you want, Fitzgerald. It's pretty fucking obvious. So keep your bullshit heartbeat-romance lines to yourself." She turned to put her hands back on the wheel, her own heart whamming around in her chest.

How had this man, who'd been nothing but a name to scoff at, turn into something her every nerve ending cried out for — clamoring in her brain to give in, drive him home, and dive between his expensive sheets. Why couldn't she just do that?

"I have work to do." She hated how weak she sounded. "Sorry you don't understand." Turning the key, she jerked the car into gear. "I'm not some freebie that comes with the ride-along." She tried to stop the words tumbling from her lips but couldn't. "You can't have me, Austin. Got it? I am not part of today's deal."

She glared at him when they stopped for a traffic light. The combination of unhappiness, desperation and regret on his face nearly unhinged her, made her want to turn into the nearest parking lot and jump him in broad daylight. But, surely, he knew how to put on such a face, used to coaxing stupid co-eds into his bed in the middle of the day while the rest of the world worked for a living.

No. I will not go there. He can find some other gullible girl. Surely a line of them exists somewhere.

Chapter Four

Austin stared at his computer screen, willing Evelyn's face to stop dancing across his brain. But every time he thought he had her good and banished, her eyes, legs, the curve of her hip, or something funny — or even smartass — she'd said would surface, sending him into a spiral of longing. After a solid hour of battling his inner horny guy, he stood and stretched, groaning at the tension in his jaw.

Figuring that a bit of quality time in the brewery would clear his head, he started to pull off his sweater, still fighting the urge to call her, text her — hell, to jump in his car and drive to her place and kiss her again...and again.

The soft ping of an incoming Skype message paused him mid-strip. He frowned at the name that popped up, then sat back down. Shocked at the bizarre timing, he leaned on his elbows and contemplated the small photo alongside the name Ross.

Ignoring a text from his mother, he dropped into his chair and read the message from the man who'd turned his young life inside out during the three years learning how to do what he loved — brewing beer.

Memories assaulted him, taking him back to his early days at the brewing institute. Long days of grunt work — lugging hot rocks to place beneath the copper boiling kettles, being berated in German and other mind- and ego-numbing activity had taken their toll. One night, about eight months into the first year, Austin had collapsed on their couch after a particularly hot and miserable shift. As he'd sat trying to work the kinks out of his aching arms he'd heard Ross come in, then head for the kitchen.

When a fresh, cool, brown bottle of brew had appeared beside his neck, he'd taken it. Then strong hands had been on his shoulders, kneading out pressure. He'd flinched, then given into the deep-tissue manipulation Ross had offered, groaning as his body had released long-held stress.

"I got us a present," Ross had whispered, making Austin's entire body tingle. "Open your eyes, Austin, and take a look."

Not one, not two, but three incredibly gorgeous women had met his gaze when he did. Austin had blinked, then turned slightly to find Ross still standing over him, hands resting on Austin's shoulders. His deep blue eyes had been dark with lust as he'd watched the women file into the apartment. "I figured it was time to change up the odds a little. See what might happen."

"Holy shit." Austin had said, relishing the erotic energy in the room. "How did you...? Never mind," he'd said as two of the women had begun undressing each other, slow and sexy, their full red lips touching then releasing, then grazing nipples and firm flesh. Austin had felt completely limp with exhaustion, but his dick had been raring to go after a few minutes of the girl-on-girl show.

As he'd watched, Ross had inserted himself between the two now-naked hotties and had let them do their undress dance on him. The guy had been a match to them, physical-perfection-wise with his broad shoulders and sculpted arms and abs. And while Austin had known his own dick was larger than average, he'd also known from seeing it enough that Ross had been one of those rare, super-huge dudes. Most women would have gasped at the sight of it and this day he had three women staring in happy shock at its fully erect state.

"Lick her pussy," Ross had demanded of one of them, as he'd pointed to another, hands on his hips. "My friend wants to watch." He'd winked at Austin, then given one girl — a full-hipped, chesty type Austin knew from experience Ross preferred — a quick slap on her ass as she'd settled herself between girl number one's legs and got to work.

Girl number three had moved around the sexy tableau on the rug in front of him and dropped to her knees in front of Austin. The whole thing had had an air of the surreal. While he'd never been a huge fan of porn, watching his friend finger one chick as she ate out her friend right in front of him had made him feel...strange. Chalking it up to his exhausted state, he'd watched as if from far away as number three had unzipped his jeans and taken his rigid cock between her lips.

The sounds, smells, and sights of their impromptu orgy had filled all Austin's senses and he'd closed his eyes as the very talented young woman licked and sucked him. The one lying on the floor had begun to moan, then sigh then she'd cried out, which had made Austin open his heavy lids and take in the view of Ross' giant, now-condom-covered dick entering her from behind. He'd had his hand tangled in her long black hair as he'd pounded into her, making her ample tits bounce and jiggle over the girl number one.

The sensation of being caught in some kind of weird, experimental dream had never left him as he'd let go and allowed himself to come down girl number three's throat. Spent, he'd sat sprawled and gasping on the couch. She'd stood, wiped her lips, pecked his cheek, and ambled into the kitchen while Ross had fucked her friend on the floor so hard a lamp on a table she'd been hanging on to crashed to the floor.

Austin had let himself drift while his friend had finished up, risen and beaten his bare chest with his fists like Tarzan. Dazed and wishing he could curl up on the couch and sleep for twelve hours, Austin had smiled and given a thumbs-up, knowing his friend required validation of his appreciation of the present he'd presented. The two girls had coiled up together on the floor, still writhing around, kissing and licking and sucking.

His blow-job buddy had emerged from the kitchen holding a beer, handed it to him, then dropped into the fray of long hair, red lips, tits and pussy. That had been the moment Austin had realized that Ross Hoffman had more game than he likely would ever approach, but he would always be grateful for the man's friendship and willingness to share in the female bounty.

He'd rallied that night after a nap, a shower, and a great meal prepared by Ross himself. While the females had chattered away in German, Austin had observed them and his friend, and had marveled at the strange, wonderful turn his life had taken. One by one, he'd sampled the riches, and by the end of the night had gone down on two of them, fucked another by himself and sandwiched the hot, busty brunette with Ross in an epic double penetration move that had taught him a fair bit about the mechanics of doing such a thing with a guy as well-endowed as his friend.

The girls had been gone the next morning when they'd risen, glassy-eyed and sore in all the right places, which had been a-okay with Austin.

The next few years had been a blur of challenging classroom and on-site work and some of the most erotic moments of his life. They'd clashed a fair bit as Ross had tended to overreact to nearly every obstacle while Austin had been able to see them merely as one more thing to overcome, one more skill to master. Their rep with women had preceded them and by the end of the three-year program, Austin had honestly believed that he'd done or tried to do pretty much every position, every configuration, and every damn thing his kinky heart had desired. All thanks to his buddy, the super-alpha male, Ross Hoffman.

In the process, Austin had believed he'd found his calling and the best friend he'd ever had, but had known it was on borrowed time. He'd go back and run the brewery he planned to open in Michigan. Ross would stay in Germany or perhaps work on the west coast. His skill had been that of a musician, a true artisan, innate and sometimes over the top, while Austin had studied, learned, and filed it away as part of his master plan to open and run the most successful brewery in the Midwest.

As he sat, staring at Ross' name, the memories came at Austin fast and proved too much after the turmoil of the day. He considered ignoring the note, unsure of where his head was anymore with regard to his friend. He'd been trying like hell to get him to come and be his brew master. But Ross' seeming aloofness and unwillingness to consider coming to work with him pissed him off in ways he didn't really understand. They'd never, ever had a nasty, jealous moment between them. To them, during those wild, erotically charged years, women had been interchangeable. No emotion had been attached to any of them.

Now that he had a totally new outlook on his life thanks to a chance meeting with the incredible Evelyn, getting Ross there seemed somehow less urgent. So when he absorbed the message, he exhaled with relief.

Sorry, Austin. I can't. Although I am flattered that you keep asking. Stay in touch, Ross.

Realizing that required no response, he closed the laptop and stared at it a minute. By the time he hit the door of the brewery, the familiar smells and sights of his successful venture enveloping him, he managed to shove memories of Ross Hoffman and all they'd experienced together out of his head.

Which meant he could make room for the sexy loop that starred one Evelyn Benedict.

After some satisfying hours spent checking on fermenting batches, reading brewery floor reports for the day, studying the pick sheet and inventories, and mentally calculating the outgo for the sales he'd made that day, exhaustion settled over him like a thick, warm blanket. It made him groggy and snappish with the few staff members remaining. They ran a twenty-four-hour shop and the night shift had just clocked in as he made his way up to the office overlooking the brewery floor.

Without giving himself time to think, he fired up the computer, signed into his email and sent two messages, the first to Grant at Tri-City.

Had a great day with Evelyn. Can you put me back on her schedule for Friday? We need to do some follow-up work and hit some places in Muskegon and Manistee, cheers, Austin.

He knew the guy would shuffle whatever needed shuffling to make this work and experienced a small twinge of guilt for manipulating the situation to suit himself, until he recalled how perfect she had felt, how soft and amazing her lips had been. And how very much he wanted to convince her they should take it one step further.

Willing himself back from fantasy land, he wrote the second email to Valerie. She was spending two weeks in Europe for work, ostensibly, but he knew most of her time was taken up with shopping.

Hey. When you get home we need to talk. Alone.

Austin had broken up with his fair share of girlfriends, but this one promised to be a real doozy, even though it had to happen. There was no way in hell he would be with anyone else while Evelyn Benedict existed in the universe. Realizing he was literally counting the hours until Friday, he turned off the computer and the lights and headed home.

* * * *

Evelyn lay awake into the early hours, staring at the ceiling and willing her tired brain to sleep. After an hour or so, she gave up trying to find a comfortable position and hauled out her trusty vibrator to take some of her edge off.

Even that didn't work.

She clenched her eyes shut as she sat on the side of her bed, trying to force Austin's compelling green eyes, firm lips and strong hands out of her consciousness.

Pushy asshole had practically jumped her in that smelly back hallway. He really had some nerve.

She checked her phone for texts or email, hoping — like a lovesick teenager waiting for a prom invite — to see his name there. But of course nothing appeared other than the usual reminders to pay her credit card on time this month please and to renew her health club membership at the low-low rate of nine dollars and ninety-nine cents for one month. She tossed the stupid thing onto the dresser and glared at herself in the mirror.

You are not his type. He might try to grope you, but he's probably all snuggled up right now with Debutante Barbie. Get a grip. You did the right thing cutting him off.

But her chest ached as if she'd run several miles and her breathing wouldn't slow at the thought of him. No man had had this effect on her, ever. It was unsettling in the extreme. And Evelyn was determined to conquer it. She had no time to spend being moony over the one guy every woman in Michigan was after.

A glance at the clock confirmed the hour of four a.m. had come and gone. She pulled on her worn-down running shoes and stuck buds in her ears. Cranking the hard rock up to a level that would hopefully drown out everything, including the gravelly, sexy memory of his voice, she headed out into the cool dawn air.

By the time she hit the office, her brain had kept up its weird schizophrenic leapfrogging between her to-do list for the rest of the week and intense memories of Austin's lips on hers. She was already sick of herself. She grabbed coffee and passed by Grant's door, heard him laughing and suppressed a shiver of déjà vu. The 'before Austin' and 'after Austin' parts of her life were now permanently separated. And that damned place would never feel the same to her again.

Oh for Christ's sake, Benedict! Stop being so melodramatic.

"Evelyn!"

She stopped at the sound of Grant's voice and forced her

legs to carry her back to it, halting at the doorway, unwilling to enter.

"Nice work yesterday." Grant leaned back in his leather chair, grinning at her. She summoned a weak smile. "So good, as a matter of fact, it seems Mr. Fitzgerald is a fan and wants another day in your august presence. As soon as possible, like Friday."

Evelyn sputtered and nearly choked on the sip of coffee she'd taken in an attempt to be casual. Grant held out a tissue as she stumbled over to his desk to look at a message he'd pulled up on the computer monitor. There it sat, glowing and real, like the kernel of lust she'd nurtured in her core since yesterday.

She fell into the chair, hand over her eyes.

"Beat it, chick. There's beer and wine to sell." Grant's voice broke through the haze that threatened to overtake her. She looked up at him. His shrewd, handsome face was pensive as he looked at her. "Be careful." He waved a hand to dismiss her.

"Careful of what?" She stood, still clutching the tissue and coffee mug.

"Oh, you know. Predatory country-club boys looking to score. I'm forwarding you this, so you can answer yourself. But it's fine with me if you want another selling day with him."

She frowned at him, but her heart leapt into her chest yet again, making her breathless as she hustled down to her cubicle. Stopping herself from mentally flipping through the meager options in her business-wear closet, she clenched her hands together and watched the email drop into her inbox.

There it sat, his words as real as day. Typing her name, requesting more time with her, for 'follow-ups' and some other shit about going up the coast to sell. Nothing they had actually discussed, but, of course, their parting had been a bit strained.

She squared her shoulders, read it for the hundredth time,

then started to respond and politely decline his request. But her fingers would not cooperate and she found herself typing out the words — *Sure. See you then. Same time, same place. Evelyn* — then hitting Send before her inner smart person won the battle raging inside her.

The thing about email, she reflected as she put her aching head on the desk, was that once you sent, it couldn't get called back.

"Hey, what up?" Her friend Melody Rodriguez appeared at her cubicle. They'd been chatting over lunches lately and Evelyn had found herself liking the extraordinarily striking woman. Melody had an accounting degree from the local community college, worked in the logistics department at Tri City and lived with her widowed mother and three younger siblings three floors down from Evelyn's apartment — they'd discovered to their amused delight. They'd spent a few late nights sampling beers and exchanging crappy relationship stories — or rather, Evelyn had shared her crappy stories and Melody had listened to them.

"My life is over," Evelyn groaned into her arms.

"What happened?"

"I have to sell with Austin Fitzgerald again."

"You're so full of shit it's leaking out your ears," Melody said.

When Evelyn didn't reply, her friend snorted and smacked her shoulder. "Girl, you need to get a grip. That man is fine." She made a kissy noise. Evelyn glared at her, not quite ready to admit just how fine Austin was, based on her direct lip-to-lip experience with him.

Within a minute, she heard the little *ding* of an incoming message and knew before she raised her eyes to the screen who it would be from. The words seared into her brain.

Great! Looking forward to it. I promise to behave if you will. Austin.

Chapter Five

Evelyn smoothed her linen skirt once more, nervously creating wrinkles in the too-expensive material as she waited for Austin to show up. She'd made a quick credit card payment, running the damn thing back up again with a new suit, shoes, hair color session and, in a fit of bizarre optimism, a Brazilian bikini wax. All in the name of presenting a professional front, she justified with every swipe of the card.

By the time she'd arrived at the office Friday morning she had worked herself into a regular state, unable to eat or choke down coffee. The twin combination of anticipation and anger fought for control in her brain.

She ignored the rest of the salesmen in the break room, flipped off a few of them at their asinine commentary about fancy clothes and fancy boy toy for the day. Once she figured out Mr. Boy Toy himself was going to be fashionably late, she let anger win the arm-wrestling match in her head.

Melody wasn't in her office when Evelyn checked and one of the admins told Evelyn she'd called in sick.

Pissed that she couldn't vent to her friend, Evelyn sent Melody a quick text to check on her, then opened her laptop and starting banging out the weekly reports she'd normally be doing anyway were she not nearly two hundred dollars further in debt thanks to Austin-fucking-Fitzgerald.

Her ears buzzed and her gut churned every time she heard the front doorbell chime, indicating someone else had walked into their front office. She glanced at the phone when it buzzed with a text.

Sorry! Running late! B there in twenty.

She stared at the unfamiliar number, shrugged, entered him as a contact, and tried to tame the butterfly parade marching around her stomach. Visions of him, memorized from earlier in the week, had danced in and around her libido for hours at a time, making her nearly insane with lust.

He doesn't want anything more from you than a quick lay. Don't do it. Unless you think you can handle it.

She bit her lip, willing herself calm when the doorbell sounded and she knew before she even heard the deep rumble of his voice that he'd arrived.

She sat, frozen in place, white-knuckling her own fingers. He made his way back, greeting everyone as he came toward her small space. She stared up at the ceiling, then down, and met his gaze. He leaned on the opening to her cubicle, grinning, eyes twinkling. Clad this time in expensive-looking tan trousers and a blue button-down open at the neck, the man was as delectable as she remembered.

More so, if that were possible.

His essence filled her space, her very pores seeming to open and accept him. Odors of rich malt and piney hops filled her nose.

Evelyn sucked in a breath.

I am so totally screwed.

The words tumbled around in her head as she stood, knocking her coffee cup onto the keyboard of her laptop in the process. He jumped forward to grab it at the same time she did, his nose colliding with the top of her head. "Ow," he muttered as he threw tissues from the box on her desk down on the spreading brown stain.

"Here." She handed him some for his nose. "Sorry. I'm a klutz." Her hair draped her face, hopefully hiding the extreme flush that had spread over her skin as she sopped up the mess and wiped the computer down, praying she hadn't ruined it.

The sight of him holding a tissue to his perfect nose, one eyebrow raised at her nervous activity, made her giggle. His smile grew, which made her snort with laughter.

"Glad I can entertain you," he mumbled behind the tissue. "I aim to serve." He stood and made his way toward the bathroom as tears streamed down her face and her gut ached from laughing so hard. By the time he'd returned, a smile still playing around the corners of his full lips, she'd calmed to hiccups. She grabbed her keys and phone and led the way down the back hall toward the parking lot.

Austin's ears felt hot and his pulsed raced as he followed her, mesmerized by the sway of her hips and the sound of her earlier laughter. All the anticipated stress he had ahead of him as he broke off the relationship with Valerie and dealt with parental fallout faded as he let the fuzziness of time with Evelyn wash over him. They tucked samples into the trunk of her crappy car and he slid into the passenger seat. She nodded toward an obnoxious black sports car two slots down from hers. "That must be yours."

He shrugged, suddenly at a loss for words. Even the smell of her set his nerves dancing. The clean linen and slightly floral notes of her perfume curled around his brain and settled in for the long haul.

He gripped his knees.

Perhaps this was a bad idea, after all.

The distinct sensation of his control slipping away from him, giving way to base urges and a near-painful need to have her in his arms unnerved him so much his legs shook and a headache took hold in his temples.

"Very alpha male. You overcompensating for something?" Her expression was one of pure evil. He had to physically restrain himself by hanging on to the door handle not to yank her close and kiss that look off her face.

"I don't have a single thing to overcompensate for with a car." He feigned nonchalance, not believing for a minute she bought it, wincing at the creaky, nervous sound of his voice.

As she started in on their selling itinerary for the day, he heard nothing but the buzzing in his ears that had ramped up to nearly deafening decibels. But he settled himself in, focused on his goal, and turned to her as she pulled into the early morning traffic heading north toward the resort areas along Lake Michigan. "Thanks," he said simply.

She glanced over her shoulder and merged onto the busy highway. It took her nearly five minutes to acknowledge him. He spent the time well, studying the angles of her face, her high cheekbones, bright blue eyes and God help him — that glorious fall of honey-blonde hair that fairly begged for his hands.

When she spoke, it startled him, so absorbed was he in the future fantasy. Of her, him, together, with kids of all things, running the brewery, happy forever.

Jesus, Fitzgerald, you've gone full female on yourself.

"You're welcome." She glanced over and smiled. His heard pounded so hard he was surprised she didn't see it move his shirt. "For..."

"Huh? Oh, well, you know, for taking me out again." He watched as his hand moved, breached the distance between them, hovered, then retreated when she frowned at him. "I know, I promised to behave. And I will. So —" He shifted, attempting to find a comfortable position. Even the constant state of arousal he experienced around her felt familiar. "Repeat the agenda for me, would you? I was, ah, distracted earlier."

She cleared her throat and did so, as he attempted to concentrate on her words and not just the cadence of her voice. One way or another, he had to get his hands on her again, today, soon, now, even. He experienced a small thrill of worry. Maybe that was all he wanted from her. But one thing he knew for certain — he'd never felt this way about Valerie. Their various sexual exploits consisted of her trying to prove how good she was at blow jobs or how quickly she could orgasm. Boring. Predictable. And unsatisfying. He licked his lips and snuck another glance at Evelyn just as she was doing the same to him. He grinned and she glanced away first, her face flushing a delightful shade of red.

* * * *

By one o'clock, Austin had worked his flirtatious sales magic at all seven of the stops they'd made, charming one lady bar manager into ordering six cases in anticipation of the upcoming holiday weekend. Evelyn had even admitted her irritation at his ease with women, and how every single one of them ended up doe-eyed and slack-jawed by the time he was done.

She tamped down the jealousy, reminding herself he was making money for her after all. The moment in the car when he'd almost touched her then stopped still made her quiver. Which was so sappy even she could barely acknowledge it.

She'd done her best to give off a 'stay away' vibe. And it seemed to be working. He'd gone full-frontal business the minute they'd hit the first store. The big test would come after they'd had lunch at the Grand Traverse Resort. Fitzgerald already had a permanent tap handle there, so no selling was required, just checking in, having a good meal and relaxing a little. But her nerve endings were zinging around with the sort of twitchy, flat-out horny energy she'd never experienced in her life, relaxation seemed like a distant, unobtainable goal. And thoughts of the three large beer stores they needed to nail after lunch made fatigue hover on her horizon.

"Holy shit, my jaw hurts from talking so much." Austin groaned and stretched.

She kept her eyes averted to avoid the temptation of staring at the way his shirt stretched across his shoulders. He rubbed the ache in question and she had to clench her fists under the table to keep from doing the same thing — she could practically feel the roughness of his stubbled face under her fingertips.

"How the hell do you do this every day?"

She gulped some water. They'd had some great conversation in the car between stops. Talking about the business, his process, her need for him to be more in tune to what the salesmen told him. *'We're the front lines, you know. We know what people are buying, thanks to the retailers who place the orders.'*

He'd laughed at her tale of touring a large brewery in Detroit. She'd been wearing high heels and had slipped on a puddle of glycol and landed on her ass, resulting in a bruise that had taken weeks to heal.

But now, facing him once more across a small table overlooking the pristine golf course at the resort, her nervousness was all-consuming. The urge to protect herself as phrases such as *out of your league* and *looking for a quick lay* dashed across her brain made her dizzy.

But he kept talking and she kept nodding, trying not to stare at the way his lips moved and how much she wished he'd shut up and kiss her again. What was wrong with a simple physical relationship anyway? Her last boyfriend hadn't been that good. She'd gone out with him the second and third times for the companionship and had been bored silly. And the chemistry that rolled between her and Austin Fitzgerald now was obvious to her — and to him, she felt certain.

She smiled at him, shifted her shoulders, and tossed her hair. He hesitated, seeming to lose his train of thought in a very satisfying way. His next words made her blink in surprise.

"Where'd you come from, anyway?"

"Huh?" She sipped the Fitzgerald 420 IPA to hide her confusion.

"Did you just spring in all your fully formed beauty into my world from nowhere? I mean, did you grow up here? How have I never seen you before?

"Oh, well, I didn't exactly belong to the country club. I doubt you even know where the crime-riddled high school was that I attended. Not to mention the public pool where

I used to lifeguard."

He reached over and grabbed her hand before she realized what he was doing. His skin was warm, perfect, and she let him hold on to her, discovering her sudden spike of pique at his question had faded away.

"Evelyn," he said as he ran his thumb across the top of her hand. "I didn't mean to upset you. Let me try again." He leaned in and took her other hand, making her nearly choke on the stone-fired pizza bite she'd just taken. "Tell me your story. I want to know all about you. Including the crappy school, the public pool, and whatever else."

"I assure you it's boring." Her face burned and she pulled away, but he wouldn't let go. His dark-emerald gaze mesmerized her as she cleared her throat. "Uh, let's see. I was an original latch-key kid. My single mom worked at a bowling alley bar. I wore second-hand clothes and fixed crappy, unhealthy meals for myself. But I made decent grades and had a few friends. And I got into Western Michigan, but my mom died of what I'm pretty sure is AIDS when I was a sophomore. She was turning tricks in her car after hours in the bowling alley parking lot, it seems."

Why in God's name she was telling him all of this, she had no idea. The concept that he'd be put off by her background, offended or disgusted by her sad-sack backstory had occurred to her. But he kept staring at her. Making her want nothing more than for him to lay one of those toe-curling kisses on her again.

"I had some money saved from being a lifeguard and got a fair bit of financial aid, but once Mom died, well, I just lost interest...or something." Her voice faded when she realized how incredibly lame the whole thing sounded. She tugged out of his grip, pissed at him for making her say so much.

He leaned back, sipped his beer and kept quiet.

"So, now that I've impressed you with my pedigree, I guess we can agree that anything that happens between us" — she pointed to him then to herself, determined to get this shit out in the open once and for all—"is purely physical. I mean, I'm not your type, as I said. Other than for a quick lay, I guess."

Anger shot across Austin's face as he leaned forward. "I said it once and I'll say it again. You don't have the first idea what my type is. So stop putting words in my mouth. It's annoying."

She shrugged, attempting to keep her expression casual. But the burning sensation in her face had traveled down her spinal cord, lighting a fire in her core, then going even farther south, settling in her now unquestionably damp panties.

She watched his hands, imagined how they would feel against her bare skin. Saw his lips moving, remembered exactly how they'd felt on hers. When he reached out and ran his finger over her cheek, she jerked back, shocked when she saw the wetness on his fingertip. She swiped at her face. Angry tears had been her downfall her entire life. But she was shocked that she'd been crying in front of him without even realizing it.

She stood, determined to put some distance between them before she made a complete fool of herself. "I'm going to the bathroom. Don't get up." She turned away before he could speak. Once inside, she collapsed against the stall door, breathless with lust and furious with herself for falling for Mr. Old Money Brewery Playboy.

Chapter Six

Austin forced himself to stay put, sipping his beer, with a lid clamped on his libido. But his new-found compulsion to save Evelyn Benedict, to plunk her into an expensive car, a house or condo, with designer clothes on her back, vacations to Europe, all the shit he took for granted had overwhelmed him. Even though something told him she'd balk at all of it.

Stubborn woman.

He smiled, watching her return to the table.

Stubborn, beautiful, smart and wholly unsuitable, according to his ingrained parental requirements for a life partner. Ignoring the small whisper of doubt about his motives, he rose, threw some money on the table and guided her back out to her car. His head was awash with images, all of them erotic and all starring her and him and the first of many long weekends together.

She stayed quiet, giving only monosyllabic responses to his questions for the next hour as they drove past the coastal Lake Michigan resort towns. Figuring now was not the time to invite her to pop in at his family's large house on a bluff in Manistee, he kept at it, trying to get her talk, to shake whatever funk had settled over her at lunch.

By the time they'd reached their destination, he had her laughing again at some anecdote about his time in Germany, leaving out some of the seedier exploits he'd gotten up to with Ross but making sure she knew that theirs had been a friendship built on a love of the brewing process.

Evelyn parked the car, turned it off then faced him, her smile genuine. "Sounds like you really had a good time there," she said, her voice free of any hint of irony. "And that you had a great friend in Ross. Where is he now?"

"Uh, west coast," he said, his voice shaky. "Listen, Evelyn, don't get the wrong idea. I'm... We were kind of, well, we fucked around while we were there. I mean, we worked hard but, um, played just as hard."

She frowned and tilted her head to the side. "Lots of girlfriends, huh?" Her voice was tight and unhappy.

"No, no nothing like that. We were...ah..."

"Oh, I see now." She leaned back and crossed her arms, her blue eyes taking on a darker hue. "You and Ross...were together?"

Austin felt his skin heat up. "Oh, no, not us. We just sort of enjoyed...sharing experiences, I guess."

God, you are lame.

"Ah, so you're double teamers, eh?" The corner of her lips turned up, giving him a small modicum of hope. "Those guys." Her voice and eyes reflected amusement, but it wasn't at all what he wanted her to think about him. He ran a hand down his face, closed his eyes, and mentally kissed his shot at her goodbye.

She parked and they sold, hitting three places and making three successful sales pitches together, learning to riff off each other, fill in the blanks, and impress some fairly recalcitrant bar and beer managers.

"Jesus," she sighed, stretching before getting back into the car, giving him a heart-stopping view of a small sliver of her skin between skirt and blouse. He had to step away from her before he did something stupid. "I'm exhausted." He climbed into the car before she saw the effect she had on him. "One more stop, then we'll head home, hopefully miss the worst of the traffic on ninety-six." She named the busy interstate around Grand Rapids.

He nodded and stayed quiet, trying to calm his newly raging lust and visceral desire to touch her.

She set her jaw as she started the car. He gulped and looked away. He had never had this weird, almost queasy feeling in his gut about anyone before. Ross had brought out something in him he'd embraced and enjoyed. But this…this was something different entirely and he wasn't sure he liked it. But realized he was willing to try — to go so far as to break off his long-running relationship with another woman if only to get this woman into his life.

The tension was back and now more palpable than ever. It shimmered in the air, suffused his every pore, made him twitchy, horny and pissed off all at once.

It was, in a word, perfect. He let it carry him along as he followed the luscious sway of her hips up to the entrance of the giant liquor store, their last stop before the long trek back down to Grand Rapids. He needed to make a move but for the first time in years had no idea how to go about it. It made him wish for about a second Ross were here to smooth his path, until he acknowledged there was no way in hell he'd be sharing this woman, not even with the man he'd shared pretty much everything with for so long.

"Evelyn!" A tall, handsome bald guy who vaguely resembled Dwayne Johnson came out from behind the counter and enveloped her in a hug, setting Austin's teeth on edge. He forced a smile and shook the man's hand. It took every ounce of self-control he had not to yank her back, tuck her under his arm, show this preening jerk whose woman she was. He gave himself a mental shake.

She is not yours…not yet.

She frowned at him and he realized he hadn't taken her cue. He shook his head and started in on the patter that had netted them so many sales today. At one point during their back-and-forth he studied her profile and made a vow to get her back to Grand Rapids tonight. To take her out, show her an amazing time, and cut to the chase once and for all.

He flinched when a sharp pain pierced his toe. When he realized she was stabbing the top of his foot with her heel he also realized that he'd gone moony again, lost the train of their collective thought on this last crucial stop.

Finally, she pushed herself off the counter where they were

leaning, chatting, tasting and trying to get the bald dude to place a large order. Austin noticed the guy eyeballing her cleavage in a way-too-familiar fashion, sending a lightning bolt of fury down his spine. He shoved his hands into his pockets and decided he no longer cared if this asshole bought a single beer from her. They were done here.

He stepped back, raised an eyebrow at her glare, and said no more. He was not begging for a sale—mainly because he didn't care for the way the muscle-bound dude was devouring Evelyn with his eyes.

Her jaw tightened but he kept his lips zipped, unwilling to rise to her bait and keep up the banter or to acknowledge how fucking furious he was at the man's reaction to her.

"So, um, Trent, why don't I just go back and check your stock real quick? You guys, you know, carry on." She brushed by him, mumbling under her breath, "Cut the shit, Fitzgerald. Close the damn deal."

He frowned at her, then over at the giant ass hat behind the counter, who eyeballed her perfection as she made her way toward the back of the warehouse-like store. The guy dragged his gaze from her backside over to Austin, grinned and shrugged.

Austin stared at him for about three seconds longer than he cared to, then spoke, "It's up to you, man. You know this beer will sell. I guess you can keep stringing her along so you can feel her up with your eyes a few more times or we can be out of your hair. Your choice."

The guy frowned, then his face broke into a perfectly natural smile, setting Austin back on his heels. "Dude." He came out from behind the counter, holding out a hand. "Sold. I like your style. And that one"—he nodded toward the swinging doors between the store and cold storage—"is back there waiting for you, best I can tell."

Austin opened his mouth to refute the charge. Trent slapped him on the shoulder. "Don't be a pussy, Fitzgerald. I can tell you from direct experience that she's worth the effort. But, if you'd rather I go back and check on her…"

Austin leapt out from under the guy's hand and strode back to the doors, focused on one thing only, every nerve ending he possessed on fire with anticipation.

* * * *

Fury pounded in Evelyn's ears as she glared around the giant cold-storage room. While she took notes on her phone on the various products Trent's store needed, the realization that Austin had decided to sabotage this last sale of the day kept her pulse racing.

What was his fucking problem? Was it that obvious she'd gone out with Trent? 'Gone out' and let the guy between her legs pretty damn fast. Not that she regretted it. He was hot as shit and great in bed but had way too much baggage, including an ex-wife, a daughter and bit of a bondage fetish she'd never quite gotten into.

And what about that thing Austin seemed so wigged out about with the German brewery guy? Ross, was it? Was he trying to tell her he preferred to have sex with girls *and* guys? *Jesus. Could this get any weirder?*

They'd been dancing around the edges of flirtation for hours, pulling away at the last minute. Maybe it was up to her to set this thing straight.

She set her shoulders and pressed her lips together. She had to get this last deal done, head home, and get the hell away from his charisma, his money and power and... hotness.

It was that or risk heartbreak, she just knew it. Guys like him didn't give two shits about girls like her. Once they got what they wanted, they were back to the country club and the skinny rich chicks.

When she took a deep breath, trying to clear the lusty cobwebs from her brain, and turned, Austin grabbed her arms and walked her backward toward a huge stack of wine bottle cases against the wall, his face mere inches from hers. She bit the inside of her cheek, tried to resist, to call on some reserve of sanity. But he was in her space, overwhelming her inner logic, and she loved every minute of it.

"You are amazingly frustrating," he whispered, trailing his fingers across her lips.

"No, I'm not. You're just obsessed by something you can't have."

He grinned, igniting the smoldering pile of lust she'd been nurturing all day. No man on the planet should look this good, be this rich and…smell so damn great.

She shut her eyes, loving the feel of his entire body pressed against hers. Lips touched her cheek, her jaw, her neck, making her gasp and reach for him. But he gripped her hands and held them over her head against the cardboard. Cold air swirled around them, but nothing would cool the heat now.

"Dear God, Evelyn, you are…"

She sighed as he kept her wrists captive overhead and cupped the back of her neck with his other hand.

"I need to kiss you more than I need to breathe."

"Then what are you waiting for?" She opened her eyes and let him pin her with that incredible green gaze. "An engraved invitation?"

"Mmm…no, not exactly." He caressed her face with his fingertips then trailed them down her neck, finally resting them lightly on the tops of her breasts.

Stop him, dammit. Don't be this girl, Evelyn. Remember? He only wants what you won't give him. When he gets it, he'll be history.

But God help her, his touch burned everywhere it landed, making her squirm with need. When he ran his thumb over the hard peak of her nipple through the thin bra and silk shirt, she shivered, a whimper escaping her lips. He kept his touch soft, light, borderline noncommittal, making her crazy, teasing in a way no one had ever done before.

He shifted, pressed a thigh between her legs, and she gave up in a burst of pulsing erotic energy, tugging her hands free of his grasp and grabbing his face.

"I see I have to make the first real move here," she said, her voice raspy with lust. "Fine. You rich boys are all alike." She smiled then touched her lips to his as he groaned and buried his hands in her hair and met her halfway in a tongue-tangling kiss that left her gasping for air. He pressed against her body, making his arousal clear. She broke from his lips, loving the sensation of his hands all over her, his sheer command of the moment, and her own seeming inability to resist.

She reached down, unzipped him, and gripped his hard, velvety flesh, relishing the smell and taste of his skin, the rasp of his stubble against her cheek.

"Fuck," he muttered as she moved her hand up and down his length. "You weren't kidding about first moves. Better not, unless you're...oh shit." He groaned as she swiped a thumb across his head, using the natural lubrication of his desire to make him shudder.

His next kiss had a life of its own, firm, in control, but wildly perfect. He lifted the edge of her too-expensive skirt and ran a hand along the lacy scrap of panty she'd managed to soak in the last few minutes. He found her clit and started stroking, keeping his lips and teeth on her neck. Without even realizing it, she raised one foot onto a nearby overturned beer keg, and thrust her hips into him.

"Yes," she hissed as he increased his speed and pressure. "I'm...oh my God." The orgasm shocked her with its speed and intensity, forcing her to let go of his cock and grip his shoulder as her entire body was engulfed in spasms. "Shit, Austin."

He raised his eyes to hers, held her captive as he put his hands on her waist, lifting her higher against the wall of boxes.

"I don't know what you've done to me but if I don't get inside you in the next few seconds I may kill myself." His voice was low, throaty, and made her ache for that very thing.

"We can't. Austin—we're in a goddamned beer cooler.

Oh," she gasped. "Make it...quick. Ah! Yes!"

With a single stroke, he filled her, shutting off her protests with the force of his body inside hers. He pressed in deep, his pubic bone grinding her clit, his hips moving slow and easy, as if there were all the time in the world for this one, perfect moment. He stared at her, burrowing into her soul. She clutched his shoulders as her world exploded around her in a shower of forbidden pleasure. He grabbed her leg and bent it up before whispering, "I'm coming, Evelyn. Come with me. Now."

Evelyn would count back in her life to pivotal moments, and this split second, when she gave in and let herself enjoy him, let him take her in a beer cooler while their client waited for them to emerge, would be the one that burned bright and clear forever.

Austin groaned and let his brain disconnect as his body took over. The nearly overwhelming urge he'd felt all day — hell, all week — then given in to as he'd followed her back here had spurred him on, made him do the kind of thing he usually avoided in public. But right now, he regretted nothing. The taste of her lips, her skin, the feel of her body under his hands and now, enveloped by her completely — it was worth all the getting-caught-in-the-act potential on the planet.

His vision darkened. He saw nothing but her as he dug his fingertips into her hips and experienced the sort of epic release they wrote about in books.

They quieted, his arms still propping them against the wall of cardboard, her breathing hot on his neck, the smell of her filling his nose. He sighed as she eased herself up and off him. He zipped up fast and tugged her into his arms, unwilling to let her go. Her whole body shook, but he kissed her hair, her forehead, whispering words not even he heard, anything to calm her and keep her with him, forever.

She looked up at him, her deep blue eyes shimmering with emotion. He gulped, afraid he'd messed it all up, taking her like this, in public like some kind of horny sailor on shore leave. "Evelyn, I'm…sorry. I mean, kind of…"

She smiled, shook her head, and disentangled herself from his embrace. He already felt bereft and alone, although she stood not a foot from him. A gnawing anxiety took hold in his chest. His head spun, clanged with warning bells, but he helped her rearrange her skirt and blouse.

He tilted her chin up to meet her eyes. "Not really sorry. Not in the slightest. Would do it again, if given the opportunity, actually."

She blushed. It was the moment he knew he loved her. And he'd do anything to make her understand that simple fact.

"Let go of me, dammit." She stepped away, lifting her hair off her neck.

Austin ran a hand down her cheek, unwilling to break the connection. "So, tonight. Dinner? Drinks? A movie? A baseball game? Opera? Sitting at the kitchen table and talking? Book club meeting? I'll do anything you want. You know, tonight." He tried not to grin like an idiot.

She shook her head and ran fingers through his hair. "You look like a guy who just got laid in a beer cooler." She arranged her shirt once more and turned away from him. His heart sank. But the tremor he felt passing through her when he pulled her back and kissed her one more time told him all he needed to know.

That whole tough-girl façade was just that. And, frankly, he liked it as long as he got to see the soft, mushy center every now and then. And as long as he was the only man who got to see it. Ever.

"I am that guy. And you are that girl. And I want to be these people some more."

She kissed him back but broke away, forcing him to release her. She gripped his biceps, her blue gaze piercing and serious, but the expression on her face was one he'd pay money to see again. "Okay, okay, back off a second. Give a girl some space." She tucked his shirttail in, ran her hand up his chest, cupped his chin. "I'll go out first. I need to find the bathroom. You stay back here and pretend...oh, whatever you want." The tough-girl inscrutable expression was back in place. He grinned and stepped back, running a hand across his lips, getting an intoxicating nose full of her all over again.

"Fine. But I mean it. About tonight."

She glanced over her shoulder. "I'll think about it." She turned then, crossed her arms and stared at him. "What makes you think I want you around, anyway? I mean, I got what I wanted, you know."

He laughed, stuck his hands into his pockets. "Yeah, but now I want more. And you don't seem like a fuck-and-run kind of girl to me."

"How would you know anything about me?" Her face flushed red. He stepped close and put his finger against the pulse beat of her throat. "Besides, last I checked, you prefer your girls that way."

"I don't know nearly enough about you, Evelyn Benedict. But I intend to find out, and soon. You game?"

She frowned. "Maybe. Maybe not. I'll let you know."

He smiled and held the door open for her, his whole body still pulsing with the aftermath of their encounter. Just as she was about to step out of the cold, he grabbed her arm and slanted his lips over hers, loving it when she molded against him once more. "Don't take your time. I don't like waiting." He nipped at her earlobe. She palmed his zipper, making him sigh into her skin.

"Like I said," she whispered back, "I'll let you know." She smacked his ass on the way out, leaving him to ponder the possibility that he might very well be in love with the most challenging woman in the universe.

Evelyn strode out, head high, shoulders squared. But the second the door swung shut behind her, she collapsed into a chair by a big metal desk. Her knees simply would not hold her another minute. Her ears were hot, her palms sweaty, her thighs slick from their hookup.

Je-sus H. Christ, Benedict, what have you done?

She put her head down on the cool surface and tried to calm herself.

Way to let the captain of the football team fuck you in the back seat of his sports car. And that even after he bragged to you that he and his co-captain had already double-teamed the entire cheerleading squad.

She groaned, shifted, and tried to deny how great she felt even after their quickie. How goddamned amazing Austin Fitzgerald was.

And how much she had to get the hell away from him.

But a small voice still tickled her brainstem.

This could be fine. A physical relationship with a great guy is allowed. You're single grown-ups. No one's getting hurt by enjoying each other's bodies.

She shivered, recalling how perfect he'd felt inside her.

She sat up, hearing a buzz near her ear. The store sounded busy, so she stayed put another few seconds, gathering her thoughts and emotions, or at least pretending to so she could stand the near two-hour drive back home with him. She smiled to herself, imagining pulling over, letting him do what he obviously did so well again. And again.

She pep-talked herself into a milder form of panic. One she could get her mind around. Her body was languid but somehow revved up, ready for more. She stood, looking for a bathroom so she could clean up, when the buzzing sounded again. She put her hands on the desk, feeling around for a phone once she figured out the buzz must be coming from one.

She picked it up and stared at it, trying to comprehend the photo on the screen.

Once she realized the device was not hers, it was too late.

The picture was of Austin. Undoubtedly. Smiling, his green eyes alight with his arm around a pretty, very skinny woman with long, dark brown hair. The name on the screen was, for some strange reason, *My Girl Valerie Masterson.*

Evelyn gasped and dropped the phone back on the desk top, hand to her mouth. Her face burned hot.

Holy shit. He has a girlfriend?

And she was Valerie fucking Masterson? As in Masterson's, the giant chain of national grocery stores. *And you just let him...* She whirled around at the sound of his footfall behind her. He ducked and barely missed getting brained by his own smart phone. It hit a box, and landed on the floor still intact.

She grabbed it and shoved it in his face. "You colossal asshole." She kept her voice low. The warm wetness coating her thighs now did nothing but piss her off. She grabbed tissues from a box nearby. "Stay the hell away from me."

He stared at the screen, put a hand over his eyes then looked at her. And God help her, she almost believed the remorse in them.

Yeah. Right. Rich boy getting whatever he wants, remember?

"Evelyn, this is..." He held out as if to touch her. She stepped back again, putting another couple of feet between them. Tears threatened, but she choked them down.

"Bad timing, on her part it seems." She pointed at the phone he had clutched in one hand. "But you know, I still hadn't made up my mind about you. Now" — she reached under her skirt, used the tissues to swipe at the moisture between her legs while staring at him — "I have." She tossed the damp paper into the trash and walked out without another look back.

The hole that had formed in her chest yawned, aching and empty. She gritted her teeth.

You are not in love with this guy. Get a grip.

But her head pounded as she breezed past Trent and out of the door, unwilling to speak lest she burst into lame-ass girlie tears.

She stopped by the car, realizing all her stuff was still inside, including her phone, keys and handheld ordering computer. Putting both hands on the top of the car, she shook with fury, remorse and missed opportunity. A touch on her shoulder made her jump.

Austin held out her keys, phone and computer. She took them without a word, unlocked the car door, and threw everything into the back seat. He stood, blocking her as she tried to shut the door after climbing in. Mortified horror mixed with sickening embarrassment, leaving her more furious at herself than she had ever been.

"Move, please," she ground out, not meeting his eyes. He stayed put. "I'm gonna shut this door on your leg in a minute." He crouched down, grabbed her arm, but she pulled out of his grip.

"Evelyn, please can you let me explain?"

"No." She stared straight ahead. To think she'd nearly convinced herself to get into some kind of…what? Fuck-buddy relationship with this jerk?

Oh God.

She pressed her aching forehead against the steering wheel.

"Look at me, dammit." His low voice buzzed through her brain, lighting weird little lusty fires she tried to jump on and tamp out.

"Why should I? So you can turn those pretty-boy eyes on me? Maybe I'll spread my legs for you again, before you head back home to Valerie?" she spat.

Heaving a teenager-worthy sigh, he stood. "Okay, well, not that you're gonna listen or anything, but here is the scoop. At this moment in time, yes, I have a girlfriend and her name is Valerie Masterson. But something happened to me exactly five days ago that solidified a decision I'd made already."

She scoffed, unwilling to even acknowledge him. Afraid for herself because she knew she was halfway to being in love with him.

"I've only stayed with her to placate my parents. My mother, actually, who would not get off my fucking back about running the brewery and not working with my father in our food supply business. It was a pact with the devil, and, trust me when I say breaking it will not be easy." He crouched back down and yanked her chin around so she had to face him. "But I'm going to. For you."

"Yeah, right. Nice try."

He frowned. "You are the most aggravating..." He sucked in a breath, then stared straight at her. Her heart lifted at the intense gleam in his eyes. But the picture ghosted across her brain again. Austin, and the skinny rich bitch *My Girl Valerie Masterson*.

He'd been with her.

And probably not in a beer cooler.

A combination of raw jealousy and embarrassment choked her, almost blocking out his next words.

"I want you. Not her." He kept his voice light, but she sensed his stress, could already read his body language. And that scared her more than anything.

"Get away from me," she ground out.

He shrugged and stood, stepping back. She slammed the door shut then turned the key so hard the engine screamed in protest.

She sighed when he rapped on the passenger-side window and rolled it down just enough to hear him. "Unlock this. I can't get in."

She smiled, but the pain in her chest paralyzed her. "That's the general idea."

"Evelyn, be reasonable. Even if you don't believe me, you can't leave me here."

"You said it yourself, Austin. I'm aggravating, frustrating, and I have the car keys. Goodbye." She started to roll up the window then stopped. "Call Valerie. I'm sure she's not too busy shopping to come pick up her asshole cheating boyfriend."

Austin frowned at her. "She's not here. She's..." He sighed. "In Europe."

The ugly laughter that burst from her gut hurt, but she let it fly. "Of course she is." She threw the car in reverse and left him there, a solid two hours from home. It took nearly an hour to stop sobbing and, by the time she pulled into her apartment parking lot, her whole body felt empty, reamed out and useless.

Chapter Seven

Austin swore under his breath one more time for good measure as he watched the complex play of emotions cross his father's face. Keeping his body loose and relaxed by the sheer force of his will, he wished for a cigarette for the first time in years.

His father tented his fingers in front of his nose, a classic, familiar Fitzgerald stalling mechanism. He kept quiet. Filling the air with unnecessary words was not his style.

Austin took in his father's large office, littered with photos of famous people and politicians posing with Maxwell Fitzgerald, on the golf course, inside large Fitzgerald warehouses, on Lake Michigan beaches, in tuxedoes at various high-profile fundraisers. All of the people in the photos were wealthy, conservative in their politics, and eager to get on the good side of the richest, most successful entrepreneur in the Midwest.

There was exactly one Fitzgerald family photo, a smallish one, on the credenza behind the large desk. He'd seen it plenty of times before, and, at that moment, it merely served to remind him of his own large responsibility, as the only child left to a man whose brothers' children had all gone in different career directions. There simply was no one left interested in running the family business. Austin knew that and guilt over it made his entire body hot with anxiety.

He tried not to sigh like an impatient little kid. His father had hated that, even when he'd been an impatient little kid.

"Son," he finally intoned, "I think you're making a mistake."

"Yeah, well, it wouldn't be the first time you thought that."

"No, it wouldn't be, but this—" He leaned on his elbows and stared Austin down, making him feel like the thirteen-year-old he'd been once who'd put frogs in his cousins' beds at the lake house. "Austin." The man's voice was deep with barely concealed anger. "Your mother isn't going to like it."

Austin sighed and leaned back. "She doesn't like anything I do. I want to know what you think for a change, not how you think she'll react."

"That's where you're dead wrong. Your mother only wants you to be happy. As do I. And life with Valerie would be…could be…"

"Miserable. And I refuse to subject either of us to it."

His father frowned at him. "She's a lovely girl. She cares for you. She'll make a fine mother."

"Dad, I don't love her. I never have. I don't plan to be forty years in a loveless marriage, her drunk every night by ten and me banging everything else on two legs in the meantime."

The man had the decency to look flustered and embarrassed at that dig.

His father stood, indicating the audience was over. Austin rose, shook his father's hand, wishing for the sort of relationship where he could get real advice and not a bunch of platitudes and excuses.

"It's your decision. But you're responsible for telling your mother."

Austin let a brief disquiet settle in his gut. His mother had dominated his and his brother's lives, without a doubt, taking her role as seriously as she did everything. But she'd been unable to let go of him, feeling a need to micromanage everything about him, especially once it became clear that she couldn't—or wouldn't—do the same for Brock. He'd experienced her displeasure plenty of times before and fully acknowledged it could be a force of nature.

He'd rebelled against her in every way he knew how, from smoking as a teenager and screwing of girls in the basement of their house to the moment he took off for the west coast and then Germany with her disapproval trailing after him like fog he couldn't outrun. Which left his twin brother behind to manage the fallout—something he'd managed, at least for a while, until…well, that was something Austin didn't want to ponder.

Not now. Not on top of all this other drama.

The urge to shock and still please his mother nestled together in his psyche like he and his twin brother had been inside her womb thirty-some years ago. But he knew the whole relationship with Valerie compromise with her had to end. The fact that Brock was likely never coming back to be the head of their family business was simply not Austin's problem anymore.

"I know, Dad. I always do."

His father put a hand on his shoulder. "Is there someone else?" His green eyes were searching. Austin decided to own up to it, even though he wondered if anything would ever come of the whole thing, especially after their disastrous second day together.

"Yes. There is. She doesn't know it yet, though."

His father's booming laugh eased some of the tension that had curled in Austin's gut at the thought of the next conversation he had to have, and the one after that, with the actual woman in question who was, no doubt, expecting that conversation to involve a large engagement ring.

Jesus, what a fucking mess.

At that moment, he missed his brother so intensely he had to stop on the way out of the front door and lean over, hands on his knees, gulping air in an attempt to dispel the urge to yell, or put his fist through the wall.

His heart was still pounding by the time he climbed behind the wheel of his car. He'd bought the stupid thing a few weeks ago, ditching the gas-guzzling SUV he'd been driving for a couple of years. This one was way worse on the show-off scale, but damn him if he didn't love the deep rumble of the German-engineered motor and the roar of the manual gearshift. He sat, windows down, willing his pulse to stop racing and reliving the moment two weeks ago when he'd known he was ass over teakettle in love with Evelyn Benedict.

Surprisingly, his brain reacted by hauling out an even older memory — that of the last conversation he'd had with his twin brother.

'Brock, dude, what the fuck are you doing? I thought you were clean.'

'What I should have done years ago. I'm sick of this shit, sick of pretending to be something I'm not. Sick of them interfering. Sick of...trying to be something they want but not from me, from you.'

The ghostly tendrils of this final encounter with his brother made Austin's heart clench. But he'd give a million dollars to talk to the guy right now. To bounce all this off him, listen to his advice — anything, really.

Even as he acknowledged it was likely a bad idea to go with an impulse, he grabbed his phone and typed out a quick text to Evelyn.

Hey. Can we talk?

It took all of thirty seconds to get his response.

No.

He smiled and composed a reply, relieved she hadn't ignored him.

Come on, I'm sorry. I mean, for whatever it was I did that pissed you off.

He waited another sixty seconds.

You know why I'm mad. Don't be obtuse. It's unattractive.

Trying to keep things easygoing, he typed out,

You're the attractive one. Not me.

Flattery gets you nowhere. Go on now, take your girlfriend out to lunch or something. I'm sure she has nothing better to do. I have to work.

Austin winced but made himself respond.

I told you. She won't be my girlfriend after tonight.

Well, if your ability to control yourself around other women is any indication, it's probably a good thing for her.

He could practically see her furiously typing out her responses on the phone. Could picture her biting her lower lip in angry concentration. He gripped the steering wheel, trying to come up with a decent response. But he couldn't, so he threw the phone in the passenger seat and squealed out onto the street, heading to his parents' house, and his date with a bout of maternal anger. The last step before he met Valerie herself. They had plans to attend some tuxedo-required fundraiser with his parents. He'd tried to convince her to skip it, but she'd insisted. Probably anticipating some sort of scene she could avoid by being dressed up and hanging on his arm.

* * * *

Austin ran a shaking hand through his hair and stared at the woman who clung to him like a barnacle—in spite of the fact that he'd started out the night by telling her their relationship was over. She'd merely smiled, patted his face and insisted they attend this obnoxious fundraiser together, anyway.

If there was a hell, he was most certainly smack in the middle of it. Knocking back yet another of his brewery's beers, he glanced around at the glittering crowd of rich assholes congratulating one another on being so rich by overbidding on lame-ass vacations and wine dinners for a charity he'd already forgotten.

He pulled his arm out of Valerie's clutches. The look she shot him would easily have floored a weaker man. But he kept his gaze flat and noncommittal. Only leaning in at the last minute. "I'm gonna find the bathroom, then I'll be at the bar."

She sucked in a breath and he congratulated himself once again on how amazingly smart he was to do this now, before they went any further with the charade and made each other miserable until death did them part. Even after six beers, he felt stone-cold sober. Which was the exact opposite of how he wanted to feel.

After getting abandoned in the parking lot up in Traverse City with Evelyn, he'd called a buddy from college who lived halfway between there and Grand Rapids. They guy had laughed his fool ass off at Austin all the way home. They'd gone out and gotten shit-faced after that, which had allowed Austin to force all memories of the amazing creature who'd fucked him, then left him high and dry two hours from home, out of his brain. At least until the crashing hangover had dissipated the next day and she'd filled his head again.

And with her, came with the sorts of memories of his twin brother. Which made him irrationally furious at her for opening up his mind to such un-fixable crap. It was as if accepting how he felt about her had exposed him to an emotional fire-hose, a deluge of personal issues he'd thought were firmly locked away in the corner of his psyche labeled *Brock*.

"Hey, Austin." Some random tool in a monkey suit identical to his slapped him on the back. "Great job with the new place."

"Yeah, thanks." He attempted to muster enthusiasm but couldn't. He looked for an out but ended up talking to the guy for nearly an hour, feigning interest in his chatter. He got a lot of advice from people and usually he could let it roll off his shoulders, ignoring the bulk of it as people ignorant of running a business wanting to hear themselves talk. But this guy grated on his nerves like a fork on an empty plate.

He drank another beer, waiting for the know-it-all to finish. But a feminine hand on his shoulder stopped him from rising to his feet and being insufferably rude. His foul mood had only deepened the longer he went without having some sort of resolution with Valerie. The sight of her well-manicured hand did nothing to dispel his frustration. He jerked out from under her palm and stomped away.

As he emerged from the bathroom, a bit calmer after splashing water on his face and giving himself a lecture, his mother pounced. Clutching his arm, she led him over to a bank of plants and whispered in his ear, "You simply cannot do this to Valerie, Austin. It's not right."

He glared at her. "Mother, it's not your business. We had this discussion. Stay out of it." He forced his natural urge to placate her while simultaneously rebelling under a thin layer of adult control. He took a breath. "I realize what you're saying. But you said you'd let me handle it my way, remember?"

She gave him the familiar, withering I'm-so-disappointed-in-you-son glare. He ignored her, took the phone from his pocket, and pretended to take a call. She narrowed her eyes then moved away, her gait regal, revealing nothing of the trouble underneath.

He had to get out of here before he imploded and made a scene. His discontent had rumbled around in his gut, kept him up late, and made him touchy and short with his staff. And he hated himself. Hated his inability to make Evelyn really listen to him and for being a weakling when it came to Valerie. Hated having ignored Ross all these past years. Hated his inability to help his brother when he'd been at such a low point.

Well, at least one thing he would solve right the fuck now.

He spotted Valerie across the lobby, her thin frame encased in designer black, her long hair swept up in an elegant pseudo-casual style. She was extraordinarily attractive—whip-thin and ethereal, compared to Evelyn's less complex, open-book, raw beauty.

Valerie had the pedigree. She'd no doubt take to the job of being Mrs. Austin Fitzgerald with all the gusto she put into her loud, over-the-top orgasms. But the thought of being married to her, having to be with her day in and day out, made him cringe. And it always had. Even if he never worked the damn thing out with Evelyn, at least she'd made him realize that. He gulped, knowing that 'never working the damn thing out with Evelyn' was simply not an option for him but unsure what to do about it.

He walked over to her, pulled her away from the crowd of similarly skeletal women, and sat her down on a couch as far from the crowd as he could get.

She lifted her chin. "You're drunk."

He narrowed his eyes. "No, I'm pretty sober, considering."

She leaned back, crossed her long, well-exercised legs, flashing him a glimpse of tan thigh. Valerie was no lightweight and he knew damn good and well she'd not go without a fight. He steeled himself for it. "I'm sorry, Valerie. Like I said, I probably should have done this months ago. Please try not to take it personally."

She sipped from her glass of wine, then pinned him with another withering glare. "'Personally' is the only way one can take being dumped, Austin. So, spare me your lame apologies." She put the glass on the table at her side.

He started to speak, but she stood, glaring down at him. "I repeat, spare me."

She moved gracefully away into the crowd. Austin sat back, amazed but relieved with a sudden urge to get the hell away from here and back in front of Evelyn. To make her understand how he felt, to appreciate the importance of what he'd done. He stood, sudden purpose lightening his soul. Ignoring everyone who stared, he strode out of the front door of the Women's Club and into the cold night.

He'd stayed silent once before when faced with a loved

one who'd needed his help. And that had netted him the sort of loss he honestly thought he'd never get over. This felt like a shot at redemption—a chance to act, to do the right thing—and change his life forever.

* * * *

Evelyn stared at the laptop screen, willing it to work faster so she could complete the day's report and take a shower. She pressed her fingers into her eyes, trying to take it all back. The flirtation, the temptation, the…sex in the damn beer cooler, all of it.

Austin Fitzgerald.

His scent, the feel of his body she'd gotten so briefly, made her shudder. Granted, it had been a long while since her last physical encounter; maybe she'd overreacted.

But he would not exit her brain. His essence had latched on to her psyche, giving it a nice shake, just enough to rattle her, make her pissed off at herself yet again. She glanced around her Spartan, tidy apartment.

And the fact that he'd been a self-admitted man-whore while in Germany only served to ramp up her lust in some kind of perverse, logic-defying fantasy world where she, Evelyn, might get to be the one who changed him.

Right. As if.

Along with the rest of her generation who'd grown up in Grand Rapids, she knew of his family and their fortune made in the food-supply business. Austin was their golden boy, one of a pair of fraternal twin sons. The other son, Brock, she thought she remembered was his name, had been the quieter one, less in the public eye. He'd dropped out of sight a few years ago, but since he'd not been as visible or show-offy as his brother, no one had noticed much. It had been Austin who'd displayed just enough overt rebellion as a teenager and now with his brewing dream to remain cool and dripping with women.

And apparently destined to be with a fellow silver-spoon

child of Grand Rapids royalty.

She paced, sipping one of her favorite beers. When she glanced at the label — Fitzgerald 420 IPA — she heaved the bottle across the room with a loud curse, smiling when it shattered against the wall, making a lovely liquid amber mess of glass down her wall.

A loud rap sounded at her door. "Hey, you okay in there?" When she peered through the grimy peephole, she had to stifle a groan of consternation.

Austin.

He was holding bags, more beer, and was dressed in — she squinted — a tuxedo. She turned away, leaned on the hard, wooden surface, and took a deep breath. Arranging her face into what felt like a neutral yet slightly annoyed look, she opened the door and stood, arms crossed.

"You again?" She wanted to protest, but the time she'd spent alone, pondering him, had worn her down.

He grinned, making her scalp tingle. "Sounds like you just brained a guy with a beer bottle in here. Need help burying the body? I'll get a shovel."

She shrugged and stood back, ignoring the way every cell and molecule of her being wanted to wrap itself around his long, lanky form. "Well, come on in. But I'll warn you I am in a shitty mood. I've had the most aggravating ride-along work days lately."

She stared, amazed at her own increasing capacity for stupidity as he stepped into her small kitchenette and set everything on the counter. Without a word, he stuck the six-pack in the fridge and pulled containers of delicious-smelling Indian food from a greasy bag.

She remained leaning against the front door, observing his busyness in her space, trying to calm her pounding heart. After he found forks and brought the food to the table in front of her couch, he popped the lids off two more Fitzgerald IPAs and smiled at her.

"Madam, we feast."

She grinned back, unable to resist. Then made herself find

paper towels and her Dustbuster, so she could clean up the mess she'd made.

"I love a girl with a healthy temper."

"No, you don't. You're trying to get into my pants again, sweet talker." She stayed bent to the task, trying to ignore him, berating herself for letting him in the door.

He slipped out of his jacket, draping it on one of her mismatched kitchen chairs. Finally, they stood, staring at each other long enough for it to feel awkward. "Why are you here?" She tried to sound strong, but it came out a weak whisper. "I'm not interested, remember? I'm the girl who left you without a ride in Traverse?"

He chuckled, running a hand across his jaw. She immediately picked up on the fatigue in his stance, his red-rimmed, tired eyes. She held on to the back of a chair to keep from closing the distance between them and gathering him in her arms.

The last week had been a sheer hell of remorse and emptiness. She'd missed him, amazingly enough, and not just his lips and hands, although those would be welcomed.

No, she missed his voice, his humor, his beer knowledge, his presence. It had soothed her in ways she'd not been willing to acknowledge until this minute as he stood, looking at her, misery etched in every line of his face.

"I broke up with her. I was going to, anyway. I promise. It was just..." He shrugged and stuck his hands into his trouser pockets, then slumped back against the wall. "A badly timed call from her, before I could erase that stupid picture and name in my contacts." He held out both hands to her. "I'm here because I wanted to see you. Why do you find that so hard to believe? I mean, you're a beautiful woman. I won't deny wanting a repeat of our cooler moment, slower, easier, and without the risk of someone walking in on us. But I'm here to see you, to talk. If you'll let me."

She frowned, trying to process this, still keeping her distance. "Okay, Fitzgerald. We can talk, but that's it. You are not allowed to get close enough to touch me."

He nodded and sat, offering her one of the beers. She took it, steeling herself against the whiff of his cologne that caught her off guard. She lowered herself into a chair, right as the brew went down the wrong way, making her cough and sputter and flail around like Kermit the frog.

He got up, smacking her back with a little too much enthusiasm. "Ow," she muttered. He kept his palm against her for a second longer than was necessary, removing it only when she glared at him. But her heart had resumed its now familiar Austin-proximity rhythm and she knew she would be a goner if he remained in her personal space much longer. "Go sit," she insisted, trying to keep her face neutral.

But he stayed put, finally kneeling next to her and catching a lock of her hair that had come loose from the utilitarian tie-back. Her skin pebbled, but she kept her eyes down, watching as he rubbed the strand between his fingers before tucking it behind her ear.

Trying not to bite her lip like a little kid, she chanced a peek at him and was shocked at the raw emotion on his too-handsome face. "Don't," she croaked out in what she intended to be a strong command that ended in a weird squeak.

He ran a rough fingertip down her cheek, along her jaw and neck, resting briefly along her exposed collarbone. She shut her eyes, but her body betrayed her by responding, as if on a weird sort of lusty autopilot. When his lips touched where his finger had been, she meant to push him away, but apparently, her hands had a mind of their own.

He leaned in, cupping her face with one hand, kissing his way along her shoulder and back up her neck as she threaded her fingers in his hair. Berating herself so loudly in her mind she was surprised he didn't hear it, she let him part her thighs and settle between her legs, run his hands down her arms and around her waist then back up again. The heat spread south and she gasped as he put a palm against the curve of her bra-less breast, arching into him as if attached to a live wire.

"Wait," she mumbled before he covered her mouth, silencing her with a kiss so intense the room actually got dark. "Wow," she whispered into his lips. "You're damn good at that."

"Hmm, yes, I've had some practice. And it was all for you." His voice sounded raw, rough. He smiled and her heart gave up the ghost, finally, forcing her into action. Panic nearly suffocated her when she realized what she was about to do. As if sensing it, he released her, keeping his hands on her knees but giving her some space. She sucked in a breath.

"Shame on you." Her voice shook. "Kissing me like some kind of gold-medal champion when all you want is a quick lay."

She put a hand out, meaning to push him, but he grabbed it and hauled her to her feet. Evelyn realized this moment could be life-changing but was unwilling to calculate the cost or regret. His voice struck a deep well of desire in her, not only to let him do it, but to never let him out of her sight again.

He spoke, rattling her nerves even further. "Guilty. But that's not all I want from you, Ms. Benedict."

She tried not to shiver and lost the battle the moment he brushed her lips with his once more. He held her close and the calm he exuded poured over her nerve endings like a warm waterfall. She kept her arms in front of her, knowing if she did anything else, she'd be lost forever.

"I don't like you." She spoke into his chest, taking deep breaths of his delicious scent. Every fiber of her being cried out with relief at being back in his arms. "Not at all. You're a bossy know-it-all braggart and too rich for your own good."

He smiled and led her back to the couch. "Maybe. But I like you. And my like beats your don't like by a lot. Just watch." He loomed over her then pushed her down, dropped to his knees and tugged the soft flannel pants to her feet in one quick motion. "Kissing isn't the only thing I medaled at."

"I'll be the judge of that, mister."

He shoved her knees apart.

"You're awfully pushy, you know that?"

With a wide grin, he lowered his lips to her sex.

She gasped. "Oh my God, don't stop!" She sighed as his lips closed around her clit. Fingers slipped inside her, reaching high, touching areas she didn't even know existed while keeping up his exquisite suction.

She lifted her hips, needing more, willing him deeper. He groaned against her, changed the angle of his fingers, and brushed something that made her squeal with delight and thrust against his mouth until the orgasm burst across her consciousness, making the room light, then dark, then perfect. Still gripping him with her thighs, she fell back on the couch, gasping and embarrassed.

"Holy Christ." She put a shaky hand over her face.

He lifted his gleaming eyes and shiny, wet lips and launched up her body without a word, plundering her mouth, pressing her down onto the couch. For the first time, she didn't mind the taste of her own sex, if it meant she could kiss him forever.

She sighed and parted her legs even wider, relishing everything about him. He broke the kiss, his smile crooked and endearing, his gaze full of meaning she wasn't ready to explore. "I'll take that as a compliment. But it's still just me. No gods in the room. Unless, of course, you want to worship me."

"Shut up about yourself, will you? You have too many clothes on," she muttered around his lips.

"Finally, something we can agree on."

She grinned and started popping the buttons on his shirt. She flicked at a copper-colored nipple, making him moan and thrust his hips against her.

The familiar velvety-smooth skin of his cock made her sigh with contentment. She brushed her thumb over it, felt fluid pearled at the tip. He shuddered then stood so he could slip his tux trousers all the way off.

"That's quite the impressive tool you have there." She put her arms behind her head. To her surprise, he reddened and shrugged. "Oh, damn. You're shy? How cute."

He knelt back between her legs, his own gaze dark and admiring. "No, not shy. Just worried." He licked his way up her body as he tugged her ratty sweatshirt over her head before getting down to work, sucking one nipple then the other into his mouth. Every touch of his lips sent tremors of pleasure and something resembling fear to the base of her brain.

"Worried?" she asked then gasped, threading her fingers through his hair, shoving fear aside in favor of more pleasant thoughts. "What about?"

Austin looked up from her breasts, propped his arms on either side of her head, and covered her mouth with his. The room spun from the force of his kiss.

She broke away, wondering how in the world she would ever be the same. This man would kill her, no doubt about it. He would use his many skills with her body, get what he wanted, and be on his way, leaving her heart in tiny pieces around her feet. "Austin…" She pushed him away but put no real effort behind it.

"I'm worried you won't respect me after this." He grinned and sat up, his beautiful eyes wide and dark with desire. The remains of her resolve melted inside their green depths.

"Worry about that after you fuck me silly, why don't ya?" She meant it, but left the words *And please don't ever leave me* unspoken. "I mean, you know, after you put a condom on that thing." Hiding her real emotions behind a wall of flippancy came easy. Nearly as easy as the tears forming behind her eyes. But she clamped down on that, unwilling to let him see how much these last weeks had affected her. How his very existence was blowing apart her senses and her strength and all the logic that had sustained her for so long.

"Happy to oblige," he whispered. "Hang on."

She couldn't hold back the giggle as she watched the handsomest, most successful and sought-after bachelor in the Midwest fumble around in his pocket for his wallet, then a condom, nearly tripping over his own feet in the process. She bit her lip as she watched him roll the latex over his impressive shaft, her body zinging from head to toe with anticipated pleasure.

This is a bad idea.

The voice spoke in her head before she silenced it by reaching for him, pulling him down on top of her as she shifted position on the couch. His lips hovered near her ear. "Glad I can entertain you," he said, low and growly before roaming down her neck and to her breasts once more, nuzzling, sucking, making her hips thrust and her back arch but keeping the one part of him she wanted separate from her.

Her entire body pulsed, thrummed, and her ears buzzed as he slid a hand down between her legs. She parted them, let him touch her, rub her clit until she begged him to do more, stop teasing and get serious. "Inside me," she gasped. "Now. Please."

He kissed her as he propped himself on his hands, teasing her with the head of his cock. She wrapped her legs around his waist, angled her hips, and stared into his eyes. "What are you waiting for?" Her voice sounded harsh, needy, and she hated it, let a small thrill of anger run through her mind. But his soft smile and the honest emotion in his eyes made her shiver. "I need you…inside me…now."

His face changed then and she saw in him the man she wanted. That realization made her hesitate. Needing a man was simply not on her agenda. Not even the amazing one poised between her legs. Poised to rip her world to shreds. She shut her eyes.

Chapter Eight

Austin wrestled around and yanked his inner grown-up control away from the horny cave man who wanted to simply fuck her. To own her, make her cry his name, and beg for more.

He clenched his jaw and stared at her as her huge blue eyes sent a different message from that of her lush, amazing body. Her legs held him tight—her nipples were hard peaks and he could smell her—the rich, heady pheromone of female desire swirled in his head, bringing that raving teenaged boy to a near-painful point of no return.

He broke away from her and sat, his legs shaking with the effort to maintain his distance. His cock throbbed and his balls ached, but he would not do this. Not after what he'd seen in her face.

She might want him, but she would not really be with him. Something in her would resist and fight him, making him insane, but, at the same time, driving him equally mad with lust.

He groaned at his own weakness. Then again, when she propped a foot on his lap and her leg dropped to the side, exposing the pink perfection of her flesh to his gaze.

"Problem?" She sounded angry. But he'd gotten used to that. He watched as she slid a hand between her legs and touched what he'd tasted and wanted to have so badly. She slipped a finger into herself then rubbed her clit, fast, with purpose. He swallowed hard as she used her other hand to pinch one of her nipples, arched her back and kept stroking, the rhythm perfect, sexy and mind-blowing.

He ran a hand up the leg draped across his, kept watching

as her hips bucked and she cried out, the heady aroma of her arousal wrapping around him like a blanket. She calmed, stilled, and he grabbed her hand to pull her up, sucking into his mouth the fingers she'd used to rub herself to orgasm. She put her other hand against his face, never breaking eye contact. In one smooth movement, she straddled him, staying up on her knees, the heat of her pussy igniting yet more fire up and down his spine.

He looked up at her. "I won't do this, Evelyn. Not if you don't really want it."

She smiled, reached down to position his cock then lowered herself onto him, one glorious, exquisite inch at a time. "Jesus," he groaned as she enveloped his cock. His ears kept buzzing, blocking all sound. His vision dimmed until all he saw or felt or smelled or knew was Evelyn.

"Now, isn't this much nicer?" She sighed, raising up to release him until just the tip of his cock still remained. Words escaped him as his body responded but his brain shut down. He grabbed one of her luscious breasts, sucked and tugged at her nipple, and shoved up hard, needing to be inside her to feel the perfection of her all at once.

"Yes, it is," he muttered as he moved to the other breast. "Very."

Her hum of satisfaction as she ground down onto him, taking his entire length inside her, nearly blew his head off, but that was nothing compared to the soft release as she rose again, making him whimper out loud with need. "I thought so."

He gripped her hips, looked up into her eyes. "I wanted this from the first second I laid eyes on you." His voice caught as she slid down again, his pubic bone pressed against her clit. "Shit, woman, you are enough to make a man... Oh...God...yes."

She rose and sat again. Faster, holding onto his shoulders. Her flesh grew hot under his hands and he watched, fascinated, as her fair skin flushed red, while her entire body pulsed with a strong spasm of energy, grabbing his cock so tightly he gasped.

"Austin," she whispered, eyes closed and head dropped back, the long line of her neck exposed and luscious.

The sound of his name escaping her lips drove him crazy. But he maintained his control, clutching her hips, as she dropped down onto him, using him to bring on her own shuddering, beautiful climax. Her breasts bounced in front of his eyes, and he sensed his own orgasm gathering strength at the base of his spine, roaring up and making him grunt with the effort to hold back.

He wanted to remember everything about this moment. The way the moonlight split the blinds behind her and lit her hair and one side of her face as her body gave a pulse and shudder, surprising him then making him rear up and hold her close, press his face to her breasts, sweat slickening their skin.

Her final convulsive spasms sent him right over the edge, groaning along with her as his cock stiffened and released. His hips kept moving, his mouth seeking hers as she leaned down to meet him. This most intimate connection of lips made his brain spin. And he knew, then, that his life as he knew it before was over.

She shivered as his skin pebbled in the aftermath of the monster orgasm. His eyes burned and his brain fuzzed, but he was damned if was going to let go of her. Finally, she rose, released his cock, and collapsed onto the couch with a moan of satisfaction.

"A fine tool and a man who knows how to use it. Lucky me."

He sat back, trying to calm his breathing. The moment of truth had arrived. And he dreaded it. She clambered off the couch, stumbled her way into the kitchen, the curvy beauty of her waist and hips making him breathless again. He put a hand over his eyes.

Now what, Fitzgerald? Gonna march in there and tell her to move in with you? You know that won't fly. As much as you want it to.

Evelyn clutched the edge of the sink after gulping down a glass of water, her body humming with energy. Damn, but the man was amazing. She had to get him out of there. Out of her life. She had no business fucking around with — and skirting dangerously close to getting attached to — Austin Bloody Fitzgerald.

No matter what he claimed about his ex-girlfriend, it would never work between them. It was up to her to make the next moments their last. That or risk heartbreak she couldn't endure.

She looked up and watched him as he wrapped the condom in a paper towel and tossed it into the garbage bin. Squealing when he grabbed her hips and pressed his still half-mast erection against her ass. "Cut it out. You aren't that young." She jerked out of his reach. "How old are you anyway?"

He turned her around, pulling her close. "You make me this way, Benedict. So blame yourself. And I'll be thirty-six next month. Let's plan a party. But first, we feast." He tugged on his trousers, then picked up his beer from the table.

"Great. A cradle robber too," she said, drinking him in with her gaze. This man, standing here in her tiny apartment, post-mind-blowing sex. She must be dreaming. "I'm only twenty-four."

He flipped on her television, grinning when the sports network flashed to life. "Nice. I like 'em young and fresh. And that?" He pointed to the TV screen. "Now I'm really in love."

"Yeah, I have that effect a lot. I like beer and sports and sex." She shivered, her teeth rattling with nerves and cold. He grabbed his abandoned dress shirt and draped it across her shoulders. She stuck her arms into it, reveling in its soft caress against her skin and the hint of his subtle cologne. She shoved down the nasty comment about spoiled boys letting their custom-made tuxedo shirts get girl cooties, ducked into her room to grab fresh underwear then joined him on the couch.

The resolve she'd talked herself into to make him leave faded when he tugged her against him. His voice rumbled through her. "And smoking hot, don't forget." She shut her eyes, feeling his lips against her hair. "So fresh…and mine." She pulled away and glared at him. "I mean, in as much as someone as independent and fabulous as you can be, that is. Jesus, Benedict, prickly much? Just let me have this, will ya? And pass that tikka masala before I starve to death."

Unwilling to think, just wanting to go with the moment, she passed him the food and settled in beside him, their thighs touching, the air between them warm and comfortable. That night she slept in his arms and her dreams were of Austin… and of Ross, the mysterious, sexy, German brewer.

Chapter Nine

"I still think you're crazy for doing this now." Evelyn fluffed her hair then pulled it up into a severe bun and glared at herself in the mirror over her tiny bathroom sink. Frowning, she bushed the concealer powder over her face, deciding her makeup was too tacky. Her pulse was racing and her ears rang and she was as pissed off as she'd ever been. But, yet, at the same time, a tiny part of her was hopeful this wouldn't be a disaster.

"I'm crazy, yes. But not for doing this." Austin leaned in the doorway behind her, picture perfect in dark trousers, a stark white shirt with heavy cufflinks, and a fancy red tie with tiny geometric patterns. "You look amazing. But not quite perfect." He stepped behind her and tugged her hair out of its up-do, letting it spill around her shoulders. "Now. It's perfect."

She stuck her tongue out at him in the mirror.

"I can think of something you could do with that, young lady," he said, flipping her around and kissing her, forcing the potential horror of this night out of her mind for a few seconds.

She molded against him, letting herself enjoy it for a bit longer than she'd planned. Gasping, she pushed him off her, noting the way he had to fiddle with his zipper to make himself comfortable. The reality of what she was about to do washed over her like an ice bath, making her stumble and put her hands over her mouth. "I can't," she said, her voice small.

Austin smiled and re-straightened his tie. "You can. We can. We are together on this, Evelyn. And trust me, it's merely a formality. To get my mother off my back."

"Right. Okay. So…I'm putting myself through this fucking torture so you don't have mommy trouble. Great." She stomped into the kitchen, downed two glasses of water then turned to glare at him as he calmly stuck his arms into the dark suit jacket sleeves. "I hate you," she declared, before squeezing her eyes shut.

When he wrapped his arms around her, the newly familiar warmth of his chest against hers made her sigh, and cling to him for a few minutes, willing herself not to cry. "I'd hate me, too, if I didn't think I was so fucking awesome," he whispered, finally, peeling her off him and kissing her on the tip of her nose.

"Yeah. Whatever. Let's get this over with." She grabbed her purse and let Austin drape a light pashmina shawl over her shoulders.

"It'll be fine. A great meal, that much is guaranteed." She glanced at him and was not reassured by the preoccupied expression on his face.

"I'm sorry. I'm making this all about me." She put her hand alongside his freshly shaven jaw. He covered it with his palm, smiled at her, and opened her apartment door. The fact that he hadn't contradicted her over that dug at her a little. But she buried that childish anxiety under the much, much bigger one—the one that had nearly smothered her ever since he'd told her they were invited to dinner "at the club" with his parents.

They drove the fifteen miles between her tiny world and his much bigger one in complete silence. Austin clenched and unclenched his jaw. Not a good sign, she knew. Trying hard not to be so self-absorbed, she put her hand on his thigh at one point, only to withdraw it when he flinched but didn't favor her with a patented, Austin-sweet, green-eyed glance.

Sighing, she sunk deeper into the leather seat, arms crossed, focusing on the concept of 'how bad can it be?' They were only human beings, not giant ogres, ready to devour her with one giant chomp.

What's the worst that could happen, really?

But she'd feel a hell of a lot better if Austin would talk to her, fill the air with nonsense words, soothe away the terror racing up and down her spine.

You're already too damn dependent on him. She slowly chewed off her lipstick and stared out of the window. *You are a grown-ass woman. You have a great job. You pay your bills. So what if you didn't grow up on the hoity-toity side of town, swimming and playing tennis with Muffy and the gang at the club? How dare they even think badly of her?*

Thus worked up, she got out of the car, ignoring Austin's proffered hand and stood staring at him for a few minutes in the glow of the lights under the fancy valet station.

He didn't say anything, merely met her gaze with his, hands in his suit pockets.

"Mr. Fitzgerald?"

She blinked, as if emerging from a daydream and saw a young kid standing by Austin's elbow, ready to take his car keys so he wouldn't have to be bothered driving the damn thing all the hell the way across the fucking street to park it. As if reading her mind, Austin dropped the keys into the kid's hand then spun on his heel, heading for the front doors, currently being held open for them by a couple of other teenagers, both of them smiling, bowing, scraping, whatever else the employees of this obnoxious place did for its members.

Stop being a bitch, Evelyn. This is Austin, not his parents. And you're making him a nervous wreck.

She slid her hand into the crook of his arm, relieved when he grabbed it and pulled her even closer as they stood for a few minutes in the large, marble-floored foyer.

"I love you," he said, loud enough for the couple nearest them to turn and stare for a few seconds before resuming their conversation.

"I know," she said, her knees shaking despite herself. "Can we...um, get a drink first? Maybe?"

"Great idea." He pulled her away from what looked like the entrance to a fancy restaurant. They ducked into an open door and she found herself in a regular bar, half-empty but for a few guys and some women in khakis and polo shirts. "The golfers' bar. A lot less stuffy." He indicated a plain-Jane bar stool and she slid onto it, hoping she hadn't run her pantyhose but afraid she had.

"Two bourbons," he said to the bartender. "Pappy. Neat."

"Uh, so, you come in here and suddenly I don't get to choose my own drink?" she asked, trying not to let her actual pique sneak into her voice.

"Yep," he said, his gaze somewhere over her head. "That's exactly how it works." He smiled, and gave light waves and nods to a few people before training his gaze on her. "Drink your drink Evelyn, okay? It's a fucking fifty dollar pour."

"Oh, well then, I see." Keeping her voice light, realizing that she was not helping things one bit, she smiled at the bartender and knocked back her 'fifty-dollar pour,' then put the glass down on the table. "Make it an even Benjamin."

The bartender glanced at Austin who nodded, before he poured another few inches of the amber liquid into her heavy rocks glass. When Austin put a hand on her shoulder, she felt herself relax. She sipped the second one, really tasting it this time, embarrassed at her childish display before.

"Relax, baby," he said, his lips near her ear. "It'll be fine."

She nodded and put her glass down softly this time, leaning her cheek into his hand. "Fine. Let's get it over with already."

He nodded and they walked out of the bar. "Don't you have to sign something with a tiny pencil, like at a resort hotel?" she whispered, grateful for the alcohol coating her nerve endings.

"It's not like that here," he said, distractedly nodding and smiling at various other well-dressed people who passed them as they made their way back to the restaurant. To her surprise, he stopped and turned to her, gripping her upper arms and staring so hard at her she squirmed. "Listen,

Evelyn, I… I can't promise that it won't be God-awful. So, I'm sorry in advance. They're—well, she—my mother is very, um…"

"There you are," a soft, fading away, rich-sounding woman's voice made him let go of her arms and turn around, blocking her view of the woman who'd spoken. Evelyn waited, trying not to freak out and run away, as he greeted his mother and his father. She tapped his arm and cleared her throat when he seemed to get frozen in place while his parents spoke briefly to someone else passing by.

Austin stepped aside and placed a proprietary hand in the small of her back. "Mother, Dad, this is Evelyn. Evelyn Benedict."

Evelyn stuck out her hand and smiled, wishing she'd remembered to re-apply her lipstick and feeling the woman's very subtle but very present eye-crawl up and down her expensively dressed body. The simple gray dress hugged her curves, highlighting them in a way she hadn't been completely comfortable with, though Austin had assured her it was classy, but sexy at the same time.

At that moment, she felt, in a word, slutty. Especially when Maxwell Fitzgerald shot his son a look of such obvious masculine approval it made her want to puke. Instead, she took a deep breath and fixed her gaze on Austin's mother. "I'm very glad to meet you, Mrs. —"

"Please, my dear, call me Virginia." The painfully thin, tall, not attractive but compelling woman kept hold of her right hand and patted it as she spoke. "And the pleasure is all mine. Really, Austin," she said, while keeping Evelyn's right hand in a death grip. "Keeping this lovely creature a secret. Shame on you."

Austin's shoulders lost a bit of their tension and he smiled at his mother wanly, tugging Evelyn out of her grasp. "Right, well, then. Let's eat." He guided Evelyn quickly ahead of him, letting his parents follow behind.

"Don't be so pushy," she said out of the corner of her mouth. "I think we were really bonding there for a minute over how shameful you are." She felt giddy, drunker than she should. When he pulled out a heavy chair for her, she tried to peck his cheek but he drew away. Virginia Fitzgerald raised one gray, carefully groomed eyebrow, then shot her husband a significant look. Evelyn's mood deflated ever so slightly as she slid into her seat, feeling her face heat up and praying she hadn't blown it with a little un-WASPY PDA.

They ordered drinks from the hovering waiter—two more expensive bourbons for them, a gin and slice of lime for Virginia, an old-fashioned for Max. When the drinks arrived, Austin dropped the soft linen napkin into her lap as she was taking a sip. Deciding not to react—he was only trying to help her after all—she sipped and smiled and let their conversation float around her for a few more minutes.

Austin fell silent as his father ordered a bottle of wine Evelyn knew retailed for seventy-five dollars. She could imagine what the country club mark-up might be. As she stared down at the menu in front of—one devoid of prices just like she'd read about in a book once—she felt the tears pressing against the backs of her eyes. This was not her world. She was a stranger, unwelcome here.

As if sensing her looming panic, Austin took her hand under the table and squeezed it. She shook her head, unwilling to meet his eyes lest she burst into tears or gouge his out with her fork for making her face this reality of her stupid, useless life.

"So, Evelyn dear," Virginia said, after putting her second clear alcohol drink down on the table and they'd placed their dinner orders. "Do tell me where you went to school. Austin has hardly told me a thing about you or your people."

In the impolite pulse beat of time that followed, Austin gave her hand another squeeze. She blinked slowly and swallowed.

"Mother, I did tell you and your selective memory is speaking for you again," Austin said, his voice tight with a sort of anger she'd never heard before. "Or maybe it's the gin." He knocked back his fourth pour of bourbon.

"Son," Max said in a low voice.

"It's all right, Maxwell," she said patting his hand which rested on the table next to his sugary bourbon drink. "I'm sorry. I meant…tell me about where you grew up."

Austin heaved a teenager-worthy sigh, confusing her for a second. But she set her jaw and focused on Virginia before she spoke. "I grew up in Grand Rapids, Virginia. The Garfield Park area. I'm pretty certain you've heard of it."

The woman's bony fingers flew to her throat. Her eyes — the same color as Austin's if a tad faded — widened. "Well, I'm sure I…" She seemed honestly flustered for a split second, Evelyn felt sorry for her. She glanced at Austin.

He smiled at her and mouthed, *"I love you."*

"I guess I've never really met anyone from there. Definitely never here, with Austin." She sipped and eyed Evelyn for a few seconds. "The silly boy was forever bringing a different girl here for us to meet. I mean, until Valerie, of course." Virginia sighed and looked wistfully at her son. "Poor girl."

"Mother," he said, his voice low like a dog's warning growl. Max drained his drink and raised a hand for the waiter. Evelyn's pulse went *whoosh-whoosh* in her ears, a warning sign of an impending, booze-enabled rager. She took a deep breath, not willing to be baited by this fucking skeletal excuse for a woman.

"Oh, I'll bet you did know someone from there. Your housekeeper, perhaps? A gardener or two?" She sipped some water and gave Austin's hand a squeeze.

"Possibly, possibly," Virginia admitted, smiling up at the waiter who'd brought their salads. A welcome lull in the conversation ensued as they chewed, swallowed, sipped, dabbed their lips with napkins and repeated it a few times.

"Well then. Where did you spend your summers, Elaine?" Virginia finished her gin and set the glass down.

"It's *Evelyn* and I told you already, Mother. She worked every summer so she could have money for college. Not everyone in the world, much less in Grand Rapids, got to spend the months of June through August in Charlevoix. Jesus."

"Language, son," Max muttered.

"No, no, I've got this." Evelyn pulled her hand free of Austin's and propped her elbows on the table, meeting Virginia Fitzgerald's evil expression with a serene one. "I worked at the hamburger joint at the corner of Fifth and Ballard most mornings, a dry-cleaners a few other mornings, and at a bar every night."

"A...bar..."

"Mother."

Evelyn held up her hand and didn't break the stare-down she was currently engaged in with Austin's mother. "Yes. I washed dishes until I was eighteen then I got a fake ID so I could wait tables. You should have seen my 'uniform'." She hooked her fingers around the word and winked at Max. "Skirt up to my chin, practically. I made great...tips."

Virginia blinked.

Score one for the barmaid, Evelyn thought, ready to leap up into the waiter's arms to thank him for showing up with their food.

The plates were all served at once—once again proving that some of the shit she used to read and scoff at as pure fantasy was, indeed, fact. Max and Austin had filets, Virginia a chicken breast with a side of brown rice—a dinner as dried-up as she was. When she'd ordered the scallops in pasta with capers and an unpronounceable olive oil, it had sounded delicious. But now, it sat there on the plate, like so much shit on toast. When she picked up her fork she couldn't bring herself to spear one of the fat, glistening shellfish.

Austin's leg pressed against hers but her vision was going wonky from anxiety. After gulping down half the water in her glass to buy herself some time, she picked up her fork again. No one else was bothering with conversation at the moment. When she sensed the woman's gaze on her, she met Virginia's ice-cold glare, thinking *Okay bitch, bring it.*

"You know, dear, if you wanted low calorie seafood, those are not the right choice." She put a miniscule bite of rice between her lips and chewed slowly.

"Oh, you know, I don't really count calories. Too boring. There's too much great food out there, after all."

"Well, that much is apparent," Virginia said.

"Oh for Christ's sake," Austin said, throwing his napkin onto the table, his steak only half-consumed. Evelyn put her hand on his arm, picked up her fork again, speared a juicy scallop and put it in her mouth.

"This really is delicious," she said. "Thanks so much for inviting me, Max." It was, most likely but it tasted like sawdust to her. She cleared the whole plate, stopping short of taking a third piece of the delicious bread in the wire basket between them. When the waiter arrived with his retinue to remove the plates, Virginia's was exactly half-eaten. She sipped the wine, observing Evelyn with a contemplative, dare she think, mildly admiring way.

She'd carried on a conversation with Austin and his father, purposefully ignoring the angry woman sitting across from her. By the time the dessert cart was rolled over, she felt almost okay, since Virginia had kept her mouth shut the rest of the meal.

"Let's split a crème brulee," Austin said, draping his arm around her shoulders.

"Really, Austin," his mother interrupted. "Let the girl order for herself." Evelyn opened her mouth to make what she hoped was a funny, just-us-girls comment before Virginia let her final verbal arrow fly. "Might I suggest the fruit plate, Evelyn?"

Max closed his eyes and knocked back the rest of his wine. Austin rose and held out a hand. Evelyn took it and stood next to him. "Mother, Dad, this was…about what I expected. And that's not good, just for the record. Come on, Evelyn," he said, handing her the pashmina off the back of her chair. "We're leaving."

Trying to stay silent, even though she knew bottling up

the massive head of rage steam she'd been building for the last hour and a half did not bode well for the rest of their evening, she tucked her hand into his elbow. "Thanks for dinner," she said. "I'd go for that one, Virginia." She pointed at a decadent-looking chocolate cake. "I hear the sugar might be good for your soul."

Max smiled at her, then said, "You've said enough for one night, Virginia," to his wife, before Austin steered her out of the busy restaurant and into the blessedly cool night air.

They drove to her place in the same sort of silence as before. She kept her fingers knotted together so tightly they hurt. The wild race of her thoughts made her breathless. She was, truly, a pariah. She would never, ever fit in with him and his 'people'.

With a sigh, she leaned her head against the window, allowing a single, hot tear to slide down her cheek.

Stupid Evelyn. Letting yourself think you could make this work — poor little rich boy Austin and his Porsche and his Lake Michigan summer house and his mother fucking country club.

She startled when he covered her entwined fingers with one, warm palm. They were at her apartment and she had barely registered the trip. When he turned off the engine and started to climb out, she put a firm hand on his leg. "No. Don't bother." She got out and started for the front door of her shabby, shitty building.

She sensed him walking a few steps behind her and she was thankful for it, but not at the same time. This was never going to work and it was up to her to end it. She turned to face him outside her door, the words, "I'm sorry, Austin. But we should just end this now," on her lips.

But the sight of him — her man as the words formed in her brain — made her hesitate. The long, lean lankiness of his, the huge green eyes, thick brown hair, patrician, too-perfect features — they belonged to her fucking man. She took two handfuls of the stiff front of his white dress shirt and dragged him to her, meeting him eye-to-eye in her sky-high heels. "You..." she began. She could smell his subtle cologne and that sent her spinning back to their first hours together, in her car, selling his damn beer.

He waited, not saying a word, not moving. She slanted her lips over his, shoved her tongue into his mouth and demanded everything she could of him without speaking. He met her halfway, pressing her against the door, shoving his thigh between her legs, pinning her hands up over her head.

She broke the kiss with an audible sound somewhere between a moan and a grunt of frustration. Her head ached. Her eyes burned. Her chest felt empty and full at the same time. So empty...and only one thing would fill her right now, drive out the painful sense of non-belonging and of wanting to have made a good impression so badly it infuriated her she hadn't—no matter the reason.

Yanking her hands out of his, she gripped his shirt again, tightly. "I want you to take me inside and fuck me so hard I forget this entire evening. You up for that?"

Please say yes. Please don't leave me.

He reached behind her, opened the door, picked her up and carried her inside by way of an answer. He made good on her demand, and then some. But the action was angry, brutal, and raw. When she'd woken up to an empty bed, an impotent rage had filled her again. She stomped into the kitchen, wrapping her ratty robe around her naked body. Pulling up short when she spotted him making coffee, or watching it brew, or something, his head hanging low between his shoulders. When he met her eyes, she had her first inkling of the depths of his frustration with his family and the loss of his twin brother.

She hesitated, the angry words drying up in her throat.

Go to him, her inner nice person urged. *Be there for him.*

She waited for a split second. Long enough for him to brush past her. "I'm going home," he muttered. She grabbed his arm. "Don't, Evelyn. I'm not in the mood. I can't reassure you every fucking second that you're beautiful and loved and perfect."

"I know. I'm sorry." She kept pulling him until he had her wrapped up tightly and she had her arms around his waist. They stood for a long time, as the coffee maker burbled and burped up the morning's caffeinated magic. "I'm sorry. I love you, Austin. I swear it."

He tilted her chin up so she had to look at him. His expression was serious, but a smile played around his full lips. She exhaled in relief. "I promise to never make you go within a mile of them ever again."

"Damn straight on that," she agreed, opening her robe and loving it when his smile got even wider. "Never again, mister."

"Never again, madam." She took his hand and led him back to her bedroom and, this time, they made love, and when they were done, her anger had faded.

Chapter Ten

Three months later

Evelyn shut her eyes as the restaurant closed in around her.

This was not happening. There was no way this could be happening. Not to her.

Clenching her fists around the linen napkin in her lap, she forced herself to look at the gleaming platinum and emerald ring resting in a velvet box next to her empty dessert plate. Austin stayed silent, sipping his beer, letting her absorb in that maddening, patient way of his.

"No." She kept her voice low. "Again. My answer hasn't changed since the last time."

"Reconsider," he insisted, casual and unworried.

"No." She stared at him while her heart tore into a million pieces. "It would never work."

He grinned at her and leaned forward, elbows on the table. "Listen, I already know you're an emotional cripple and sometimes a high-maintenance pain in the ass, but I'm willing to overlook all that."

"Fuck you." She smiled back at him, unable to stop herself.

He grabbed both her hands, making all her every nerve endings sing with delight. "Later, I promise. I love you, Evelyn. Marry me, God damn it."

She pulled away, unwilling to admit anything, not now, when all she wanted in the entire world was to say the one word he wanted to hear. But something held her back.

He held on to her fingers. "Look at me." She did, willing the tears back. "I want to take care of you. To have babies with you. To grow old with you. To fuck and fight, then fuck again. I need you. I want to take care of you. Why can't you accept that?"

"Take me home." She jerked her hands away, stood and walked out. He placed her wrap around her bare shoulders against a sudden extreme chill. "You're such a sap." She slumped into his side. He whistled and a limo pulled up. She rolled her eyes.

"Shut up, Benedict, and get in before I smack you and get arrested for it."

She sighed and climbed in. His single-minded focus on this...this...thing made her crazy in love all over again. She swallowed hard. "No, Austin. God, are you deaf?"

"Tell me you don't love me. Look me in the eyes and say it." He turned her so she had no choice.

The tears betrayed her. She brushed them away. He brought her knuckles to his lips. "I can't live without you and I won't be anywhere else but with you."

"Your parents."

"Can go fuck themselves."

"You are persistent. I'll give you that."

"You have no idea." He kissed her in that way he had that made her completely unglued. She wrapped her arms around his neck and pulled him on top of her in the wide back seat.

"Oooo, slutty, I knew you'd like the limo." He grinned and tugged her dress aside to get at her nipple. She gave in to his mouth, ran her palm along the bulge in his trousers, and finally acknowledged it.

"All right, I do love you." She heard it escape her lips but still could not believe she was there in that moment. "When I told you that I was flattered but that it was too soon, I meant it. And that was, um, a week ago? The second time you put that ring in front of me?"

His amazing green eyes were full of so much emotion it made her head ache. "I know."

"Where are we going, anyway?" He'd returned his

attention to her other painfully erect nipple. "Oh, crap, Austin, seriously. How long do we have in this car?"

"About thirty minutes."

"Perfect." She crawled out from underneath him and unzipped his trousers, releasing his beautiful, gleaming cock into the cool air. "Sit back, Fitzgerald. I'm gonna give you the ride of your life."

With one last significant look, she went down on her knees, sucking his long shaft into her mouth. He groaned, threaded his fingers in her hair and angled his hips, going deep toward the back of her throat. She relaxed, let him do it, loving the sound he made so much it terrified her.

"Oh, baby, I've been wanting to fuck your mouth all night." He'd figured out how much she loved seriously dirty talk and used it with that rough, naturally sexy voice to perfection.

She cupped a palm beneath his balls, relishing the hard, hot contraction of them in her palm. She licked around the edge of the head, lapping at the slit at the top, making him moan and thrust his hips faster. She slid her finger down, caressing the soft skin between his balls and ass.

Arching down over him, she sucked his cock into her mouth once more, letting it bump against the back of her throat before relaxing and taking him all the way.

"Holy shit, Benedict. Do it. You know what I want."

She released him, stared into his eyes, and slid her finger into her mouth. He watched her, eyes narrowed, breathing shallow then groaned in earnest when she slid her slick finger around the edge of his ass, stopping just short of insertion. "Tell me what you want, Austin," she insisted in a whisper.

"Bring that mouth back down, baby. I need to fuck it while you stick that sweet finger in my ass." He clutched his shaft, groaning while she teased the tight, puckered hole. She pressed her finger in nice and slow, using the angle she'd discovered he craved, before lowering her mouth over his dick. She went deep with her finger, just the way he liked it, all the while sucking, releasing to lick, then swallowing him all the way once more.

"Holy shit, baby, I'm gonna— Oh, God!" His ass clenched around her finger and his whole body arched and contracted. Hot liquid shot down her throat.

After a few seconds, she pulled her finger out slowly and released his cock with a quick lick to the still-swollen head. He stared up, breathing hard. "Jesus, Mary and Joseph." He sucked in a deep breath.

"Nope." She wiped her lips with the back of her hand. "Just me." She dropped into the seat beside him. "But I still won't marry you." She wondered why she kept saying that when she knew damn good and well that part of her wanted it more than anything.

But she couldn't. Not yet.

She grabbed tissues and pulled a small bottle of anti-bacterial gel from her purse, using them to clean her hands. She'd figured out pretty quickly how much he enjoyed that move. The thought of that made her shiver.

He zipped himself up, then tugged her close and kissed her, his eyes hooded and body relaxed. "It's okay. I'm persistent, remember? I'll ask again."

After about ten more minutes, the car stopped and he hopped out first, extending his hand to help her. They emerged in front of a charming bed and breakfast on the shore of a small private lake. He draped his arm around her shoulder as they walked to the front door. "I'll ask again," he reminded her.

She pushed him away. "I heard you the first time, dammit. Now let's get inside. I think you owe me." She smacked his ass and bounded up the steps, unwilling to let him see the longing in her eyes, hoping he would ask again so one day she could say yes.

* * * *

Austin sat, sipping coffee and watching the sun rise. He'd

slipped out from under the soft sheets and Evelyn's warm embrace, smiling as she mumbled and flopped over onto her other side. After a freezing five-mile run along trail around the lake, he'd come back, gotten coffee from the smiling B & B owner and sat, watching Evelyn sleep for a few minutes. After deciding to let her rest, he took his coffee to the adjoining room with a giant floor-to-ceiling window.

To say that life as Evelyn Benedict's boyfriend was tumultuous constituted an understatement in the extreme. Her mood swings were wide and at times breathtaking. She lived and worked with a passion matched only by her enthusiasm for sex.

And she expected a lot of the people around her, so when someone disappointed her at work, or in his case, at home, there was hell to pay. But he loved it. Absolutely fucking reveled in it, using his own much calmer nature to cool her, to temper some of her more egregious outbursts of anger and frustration.

Of course, 'home' was a misnomer. She refused to move in with him, keeping that shitty apartment like a badge of honor, staying over at his condo on the weekends but insisting on sleeping in her own bed during the week.

So he stayed with her, mostly. And since he'd never been a guy who gave much thought to his surroundings as long as his basic needs were met, he didn't care. Because she met every single one of his needs — emotional and mental with her constant questions and challenges about brewing, his company, and how to make it better. And her physicality — her near constant need for skin-to-skin contact — matched his in a perfect and sometimes scary way.

As for the sex, he'd never met a woman more inclined to experiment. One many levels, she reminded him of Ross — and not just the way she threw herself into sex, enjoying every moment, every touch, every caress as if it might be her last. She was also somewhat alarmingly like him in other ways — guarding herself, second-guessing anything that might hint at actual emotion, willing to let others commit before she would. Ready to retract into her hard, tough-girl shell, emotionless shell at the slightest provocation.

Maddening. But he was so deeply in love with her, he felt prepared to meet it, head on.

Most days.

"Austin?" Her voice behind him made him stand and stretch, his cock already tingling in anticipation. "Where did you go? Jesus, what time is it? Get your ass back here."

He grinned. "Think you can just boss me like that, woman?" He leaned on the door frame, drinking her in with his eyes. "Because you can't."

"I'm not bossing, dear. Just suggesting." She let the sheet fall aside, revealing her completely naked body. His smile widened when she bent one knee and reached down to touch herself. "You know, only suggesting that you get your sweet self over here and help a girl out."

He grinned, yanked off his shirt and shorts, and dove into the warm nest of sheets and Evelyn. The frustration at her most recent rejection was already forgotten in the amazing smell of her skin and the lovely sound of her moans as he did what she suggested, for an hour or two.

Later, when they lay tangled in damp sheets, catching their breath, their fingers clasped together between them, Evelyn sighed. "So, tell me something," she said. Austin forced himself up to full consciousness as best he could.

"Hmm," he said, turning to face her, taking in the flushed, well-fucked look on her face with more than a little self-satisfaction.

"How is it...I mean, with two, um, guys and a girl?"

Austin hesitated, then put her knuckles to his lips, buying himself some time.

She pulled her fingers free of his, sat up and wrapped the sheet around herself. One thing about his Evelyn, he mused, watching her. He would never accuse her of being indirect. About anything.

"Don't baby me, Austin. I mean it. I want to know."

"I have no doubt that you want to know, my love." He

propped himself on one elbow and ordered his thoughts.

"Don't think about it, damn you. Just...tell me." She swept her hair up off her neck, making his mouth water at the sight of her flushed skin. Making him want to grab her, hold her down, lick the sweat droplets and lose himself in her all over again. "Yo, earth to lover boy," she demanded, snapping her fingers in front of his face. "Spill it. What's it like? I mean do you... Would you... Oh hell, never mind." She turned and started to climb out of bed before he reached out and grabbed her arm.

"Hang on a second. I don't mind telling you. I guess I didn't expect you to want to know. Most...women...aren't that into it."

She let him pull her back into the warm bed and curled into him so he was pressed up against her back, his lips on her bare, delicious shoulder. "Stop it," she whispered. "Tell me what it's like to have sex with a woman with another guy in on the act."

He sighed and held onto her. "It's...pretty amazing," he admitted. "I mean, I can't speak for the women I've... We've...well, you know what I mean."

With a grunt of frustration, Evelyn turned and faced him, taking his face between her hands. "Are you bisexual, Austin? Because if you are, I want you to know I'm okay with it."

He chuckled and shook his head. "No, I'm not. Unless being comfortable watching my friend have sex with a woman right in front of me, or fucking her ass while he does the same to her pussy makes me bi, of course. Because I really do enjoy doing that."

Admitting this felt like a giant weight lifting off his chest—the last barrier to complete honesty with her was gone. Something about this made his dick hard. Or maybe it was the way one of her legs was draped over his hip, and the way her beautiful, lush breasts were barely covered by the soft white sheet right in front of him. Or perhaps it was the rich, raw, smell of her, of them, and of their recent activity in this small bedroom.

He shifted, pulling her closer, but she held back, not taking her gaze from his face. "You really enjoy it, eh?"

"Yes, Evelyn, I do. Feel this? That's how much I enjoy it. And I'd swear after the last hour or two it would take me a day to recover." He took her hand and put it on the erection tenting the sheet over his hips. Her slow, sexy smile made him shiver. "God help me, woman, I love you so much..." He kissed her hard, owning her, frustration with her melting away into a puddle of lust.

She broke the kiss, but kept up her hand work. "Tell me more, Austin," she whispered, leaning close to nip his earlobe. "I want to hear about it—how you do it. How you and Ross pleasure a woman together."

Austin froze for a split second, pondering the implication of this specific request. But the sheet covering her breasts drew away, distracting him. He reached out and held the pleasant heaviness of one in his palm. "You want to know how we do it, huh?" He grazed her nipple with his thumb, making her shudder and his dick even harder. She nodded, her blue eyes sparkling and bright, the now-familiar turned-on Evelyn sensations enveloping him.

"Like this," he whispered, pulling away and flipping her over so fast she squealed. When he yanked her hips up off the bed, he had a flash image, a memory he supposed, of Ross lying beneath her, his massive cock poised and ready, his broad chest slicked with sweat. Leaning over her to grab a tube of lube, he kissed the knobs of Evelyn's spine, one by one, making her shiver and sigh and press her ass back against him. "Ross can't really be here," he said, as he covered his aching dick with the lubrication, then used some to slide a finger gently into her ass. "He's too big. You know what I mean?"

In all the many times they'd fucked, made love, had sex, gotten off together, Austin didn't think he'd ever been this turned on. He honestly believed that he might simply come all over her back, right now, even after coming inside her so hard forty-five minutes ago he almost passed out.

"Yeah, I know," she whispered, looking over her shoulder at him. "Tell me more, baby." She wiggled her hips and spread her thighs wider, as he continued to prep her with a lubed finger.

"Okay," he said, easing slowly, carefully inside her tightest hole. "Oh Je-sus," he moaned, closing his eyes. He'd forgotten how good this felt.

"So," she gasped as he got all the way and held there, trying not to blow within seconds. "Ross is under me, doing what?"

"Oh, right now, he's sucking your nipples, hard, biting them, the way you want. The way you're begging him to. And he's teasing that sweet, sweet clit with one fingertip, making you moan." Austin gritted his teeth as she shivered. The pain-pleasure of fucking a woman in the ass had been among his forgotten memories but he was getting over that, fast.

"Why isn't he fucking me too?" she asked. "I want you both inside me."

Austin pulled back, needing the friction but not wanting to hurt her. "Because, your body can't hold us both, baby." He leaned over her back and cupped one full breast, tweaking her ultra-sensitive nipple and biting down on her shoulder to distract himself.

"Hmm," she said, arching her back. "So, how does this work, then?"

"Oh fuck, baby, I'm gonna..." He let go of her and gripped her hips for dear life, grinding deep and sensing the orgasm rushing at him like a freight train.

"Talk to me, Austin," she demanded. "Tell me what Ross is doing to me right now."

"He's... He's... We're taking turns inside you," Austin managed, making himself think. "I'm in like this, deep in your sweet ass, and he's fingering your clit, making you come hard. Then..." He swallowed and made himself do it. "Then I pull out of you, like this." He groaned, low and loud at the sensation. Evelyn gasped. "I'm sorry, baby. It hurts?"

"I...yeah, but...go on..." She was breathing heavily and so turned on he believed he could taste in the air between them. "So, you're out, and he's in...my pussy, right?"

"Yeah," Austin exhaled and spoke at once, his vision clearing ever so slightly as he imagined it, imagined Ross doing exactly that to his woman, to his Evelyn. Would he, could he, take it? "He's inside your pussy now, Evelyn. Can you feel him?" He reached down for a glass dildo he'd packed for them, but they'd not bothered with yet. "Here," he said, his voice hoarse. "Put this inside your pussy and pretend it's him."

Evelyn's hands were shaking but she took it from him and slid it into her. She groaned and arched her back, exposing the glistening pink opening he wanted so very much right now.

"That's it," he said, leaning back on his heels so he could watch the clear glass rod going in and out of her. "Now," he said, unable to wait another minute. "Pull it out. I need in and I'm gonna come so hard...you'd better be ready."

"I'm so ready," she gasped, dropping down to her elbows. "Oh God Austin, yes!" After coating his dick once more with lube to avoid hurting her, he eased in and came even harder than he'd thought he would, seeing stars within a few seconds.

He shook all over as his hips kept jerking forward and he leaned his head back, moaning with pleasure and pain, and the sudden, sure realization that something else might be on their horizon. When he eased himself out she whimpered, and dropped over onto her side.

"Oh God, honey, I am so sorry." He gathered her close, kissing her flushed cheeks over and over. "I didn't want to hurt you."

She was shivering so he grabbed the sheet and wrapped them both up in it, their flesh pressed together. But she pulled back, her honey-blonde hair nearly obscuring her almost manic blue gaze. "God, Austin, I need to…" He smiled, reached down and stroked her plump, eager clit until she came in a burst of energy and a small gush of fluid on his hand. "Oh…my God," she said into his chest. "I… That was…"

"Shh," he said, kissing her hair. "It's all right."

"Holy hell, I know it's all right," she said, biting his nipple so hard he yelped. "I mean…you know. Pretending and all." She wouldn't look at him. And as Austin drifted off, the inner argument arose in his mind again.

Could he share this woman? Would he be capable of sharing anything about her with Ross Hoffman? Did he trust the man not to fall for her? For that matter, did he trust Evelyn? They were so…fucking…alike…

"I love you, Austin," she said, on the edges of his sleepiness. "So much."

He smiled and let himself drift, figuring he'd leave all those unanswerable questions for another day.

* * * *

"By the way," he mentioned as he drove back to the Grand Rapids the following morning. "I want to interview you."

She tucked her sunglasses up on her head and stared at him. "Why? You a beer blogger now? God help me."

"No. For a job."

This was step one of his new plan. If she kept insisting on not marrying him then he wanted her to work with him. Together they could make Fitzgerald the number-one brewery in the state, hell, in the region, and he knew it.

"I already have a job." Her voice was even, but he sensed tension behind it. He put a hand on her thigh, pleased at the way she relaxed under his touch.

"Yes, but you hate it. You said yourself you wanted to interview across town with Ryan's outfit." He glanced at her, knowing his mention of a rival, larger distributor would rev her up.

"Oh, shut up about that already. I told them no, remember?" She slumped in her seat.

He grabbed her hand and kissed it, threading his fingers through hers. "Okay then. I want you to work for me. No, scratch that. With me. As marketing director."

"You don't even have a marketing plan, Austin. Why do you need a director? Your sales guys are good, mostly. We've discussed this."

"I want you to create the plan with me. Hire better sales guys. Fire the ones who are lame. Be the boss. You can do it, and I need it."

He could feel her eyes burning holes in him even though he kept his own gaze trained on the freeway. He let her stay quiet for about five miles, then released her hand. "You have to interview, though. I've posted the job and have two or three pretty impressive résumés already."

She smacked his leg. "Asshole."

"Yeah. So you'd better study and be ready to impress me. I hear I'm hard to please." He looked at her, happy to see the wheels turning in her head. "Call my secretary. She'll set the appointment."

She stayed silent the rest of the way home. And even though Austin knew he should ask, that they really ought to talk about that last little interlude—the pretend Ross, fucking her while he lost control inside her ass—he stayed silent, unwilling to cross that particular rickety bridge just yet.

Chapter Eleven

Evelyn stared at herself in the mirror the following Friday morning. Her color was high, her hair perfect, her body crammed into yet another too-expensive suit—this one funded by Austin's black American Express card, along with her new sunglasses, her computer tablet and her handbag.

The fact of all that, of all she'd allowed him to do for her, froze her like a deer in the proverbial headlights as the reality of her new life slammed up against her psyche.

She had an important interview today.

With Austin Fitzgerald, owner of the fastest growing brewery in the Midwest, her boyfriend—the man whose parents despised her and without whose voice and touch she would likely die most days.

She ran shaking hands down the skirt, admiring the way her hourglass shape gave her a sort of Marilyn Monroe-like stature. Marveling at her luck, at the amazing position she found herself in—a size twelve working girl from the wrong side of Grand Rapids, with the hottest bachelor in the state madly in love with her.

Stubborn bastard, always asking her to marry him, and now, this craziness. An interview—all formal and stuffy and plain old weird.

She sat, her feet seemingly frozen and unmovable. She had several appointments before making her noon meeting with Austin in his office, a place she'd actually never seen before.

He claimed it had a panoramic view of the brewing floor, just like he wanted it. Professed no need to have her near his parents again, just as she demanded. Claimed he loved her, wanted her forever.

What was her ever-loving problem? If this were a novel, she'd call herself too stupid to live, without a doubt.

She'd honestly believed he'd get in her panties a few times and that would be it. He'd consider the challenge risen to and be on his merry way. But he'd stuck. Gotten her expensive gifts. Taken her on romantic B & B vacations and even threatened a trip to Germany in the fall for Oktoberfest, for 'research', he claimed.

It made her insane. But every day the thought of not having him around, of not seeing his sexy text messages or flat-out raunchy emails, of not knowing he waited for her nightly made her slightly ill. Plus…that other option…the one that included Ross, the man he considered his friend, and whom she was starting to get mildly obsessed about, in a purely sexual way.

Her phone buzzed with a text. She glanced down to make sure it was him.

Good morning, glory. I look forward to our meeting today.

She smiled in spite of the vise that seemed to grip her chest, and shot back,

Well, I have a busy morning. I'll try not to be too late and mess up your afternoon golf game.

Yes, good plan, he wrote back nearly immediately. *Wouldn't want to upset your future boss.*

Keep calling yourself that, Fitzgerald, and see if I even show up.

She grinned and shook her head at his next message.

I realize I am a sexual harassment lawsuit waiting to happen with you but it's a risk I'm willing to take. If you are.

She bit her lip, wondering for the millionth time what had possessed her to get in this deep with him.

Tell you what – maybe I'll let you harass me, as long as you promise to do it the way I like it.

His response did its usual tap dance on her libido.

Oh, I know how you like it, baby. See you at noon.

Her morning passed in a blur of nervous energy and when she found herself standing sweaty-palmed in front of his secretary's desk, she was pissed off that she felt so uptight. The woman looked her up and down, then pointed to a chair. "I'll tell Mr. Fitzgerald you're here."

Evelyn sat, taking in the various awards for brews and packaging and whatnot. Tasteful photos of Lake Michigan, lighthouses, farmland and of downtown Grand Rapids graced the walls. She jumped when the massive wood door opened and Austin strode out clutching a stack of papers dotted with colorful charts. His green eyes snapped with anger when he slammed the papers on his assistant's desk. The woman nodded toward Evelyn.

The smile he shot her made her fillings melt, she'd swear it. He'd truly turned her into some kind of drooling Pavlovian dog whenever he so much as looked at her. But she stood, tossed her hair back, and held out a hand. "Mr. Fitzgerald, thanks for agreeing to meet with me."

"Of course, Ms. Benedict. Please. Come in." The hand in the small of her back seemed to burn through her clothes. "Oh, and Mrs. Richardson, you can take the rest of the afternoon off. Enjoy your Friday!"

Evelyn took in the huge room. Two walls were floor-to-ceiling books, trophies, medals, and other awards. Plans for what looked like an expansion were spread out on an antique drafting table alongside an industrial-looking steel desk in front of a glass wall.

His laptop sat open on it, with a printer, a cup of coffee,

and three small framed photos. She blushed when she realized that one featured the two of them at a recent beer and art festival.

The other was of Austin and a tall, broad-shouldered man with long blond hair tied back with a strip of leather, and a lightly bearded jaw. She picked it up and stared at the man she'd never met but who, based on her admittedly dogged questioning of Austin, intrigued her on a lot of levels. His light blue eyes were sparkly and his body firm and strong-looking underneath the goofy lederhosen he and Austin were wearing at some Bavarian festival. Her scalp tingled as she studied him, recalling Austin's words – *He's too big, if you know what I mean* – when they'd engaged in their pretend threesome. She put her fingertip to the photograph, biting her lip, lost in entirely inappropriate thoughts. Finally, she put it down and swallowed her urge to ask more about him, to ask what she really wanted to—would Austin let her have that moment, the full attention of both men, just once in her life?

This one was of Austin in a graduation gown, his arm around the shoulders of another young man—one who resembled him, but at the same time, didn't. Brock, the twin brother, whose backstory she'd coaxed out of Austin a little at a time. She studied it, seeking answers to the one thing that had the power to bring her man near to tears every time he allowed her to dig a little deeper. Both Austin and Brock were grinning in a similar fashion—the Fitzgerald grin, she'd come to refer to it—but Brock was slightly shorter and fairer of hair and eyes than Austin. And his grin had seemed strained, even then.

She put the picture down and gazed out over the expanse of the busy brewery floor, focused on the breathtaking hustle and bustle below. The huge stainless steel fermenters, large brew house, and what looked like twenty people walking to and fro, laughing, carrying out their duties. Music breached the window barrier. The Clash. She smiled.

"So."

She turned at the sound of his voice. He sat, fingers tented together in front of his lips. Her heart leapt at the sight of him. He was clad in dark denim and a slightly wrinkly, button-down white shirt. "Why don't you have a seat, Ms. Benedict. Tell me what you would bring to the marketing effort here at Fitzgerald?"

She slid into a soft leather chair opposite him and crossed her legs. He wanted to play this little game, no problem.

She'd come loaded with pertinent questions, a few facts about his recent sales slump, and ideas for a new line of lagers that would cost a shit ton to add to his lineup but could be a whole new niche for the company. Sliding her hand down her neck as she spoke, she gave her background — everything he already knew.

Satisfied with the way his eyes darkened, she trailed her fingers down to the tops of her breasts, exposed just enough in the V of the silky camisole under her suit jacket. She uncrossed her legs and let him get a good look at how bare they were, then re-crossed them, sat up, and glared at him.

"The truth now, Fitzgerald. You tell me why I should leave a job that is about to make me sales manager of the largest beer and wine distributor in the state to come here so you can ogle me every day."

He started and straightened, the moony, horny look draining from his face. She sat back and crossed her arms, pleased at the way he squirmed in his seat from what she knew damn good and well was a giant hard-on. "Well?"

"Jesus, Evelyn, do you really think I'm doing this so I can ogle you?" He got up and walked over to the large window. "You've got such an annoying inferiority complex. Can't you just accept that you're awesome at what you do? You're the perfect person for this job."

She watched his jaw clench and felt her heart go along for the ride.

Dear God, she loved him. Despite all her attempts not to do that very thing.

"Well then, you're going to have to make a few commitments." She stayed seated, fighting the urge to go to him, hold him, let him do whatever he wanted, including dragging out that damn engagement ring again.

He turned, one eyebrow raised in question. "Like?"

"Like not being such a Scrooge with the budget. You told me yourself you didn't want to spend money on point-of-sale stuff or on simple things like decent T-shirts and giveaway trinkets and trash. That has to stop." She held up a hand to keep him from interrupting. "Oh, and you need to let me be in charge of that lazy sales director. He has potential, but you're letting him get away half-assed, which is why your sales fell this quarter. He won't like me. I promise you that. But we will slap this thing into high gear, and he'll get his holiday bonus. Which he *will* like."

Austin grinned and stuck his hands into his pockets, looking like the adorable man she adored so very much.

"And one last thing."

He nodded but stayed quiet.

"I get to come in this room anytime I want and do this." She rose slowly and took the five steps between them, slipping out of her jacket and into his arms.

"Well, I'm not sure about the budget thing but this last request..." He laughed as she struggled out of his arms. "I'm kidding, Benedict, Jesus. You know I'm gonna turn this whole shit-pile of marketing over to you, gladly, and you will have carte blanche to do whatever it is you need to do."

She smiled, molded herself against his long, lean body and kissed him, loving the smell and taste of him. The way he knew all her buttons to push and which levers to pull to calm her down when needed.

He parted her lips with his tongue, maneuvering her back until her ass connected with the drafting table. Reaching up under her skirt, he broke from her lips and whispered, "My only requirement, Ms. Benedict" —he teased her clit with the pad of his thumb, while sliding some combination of fingers into her — "is that you always come to work like this." She gripped his shoulder as he pressed in deep, kissing her with an intensity she loved.

"Austin," she whispered as he pulled his fingers out of her and slid them into his mouth. "I want you, right here."

"Oh trust me, that's on this meeting's agenda." He grinned, unzipped his jeans, and span her around, yanking up her skirt in one quick motion. She spread her legs and arched her back. "And I plan on doing it to your specifications. A lot." He slid into her in one long, smooth stroke, grabbing on to her hair, forcing a moan from her lips.

"Look," he said, turning her head so she could see them, clearly outlined in the mirror-like surface of one window. She shoved her hips back and her legs farther apart. The perfection of his body inside hers was something she still marveled at and swore not to take for granted. "Reach down and touch your clit. Pretend it's my tongue. Pretend it's Ross' tongue. And then watch while I fuck you."

She touched the firm nub of flesh and rubbed as he did just that, shoving her up against the table she was propped up on with her other hand. Watching them in the window and crying out as she came in a rush of emotion, loving the warm sensation of his release deep inside her. Tears threatened as they always did, but for the first time in their months together, she let them flow, needing that release almost as much as the one he'd given her seconds before.

Austin collapsed over her back, holding her close, then slipped out of her and turned her around. "Don't cry, my Evelyn. Please don't ever cry. I can't stand knowing you're unhappy about anything."

She shook her head, helped him zip up, and adjusted her skirt. "I cry all the damn time. Don't flatter yourself." But he tilted up her chin, made her look at him. "I love you," she whispered. "The jury is out on how well we will actually work together, but I'm willing to give it a shot."

He smiled, brushing her lips with his calloused thumb. "Okay. Now, I'm going to ask you one more thing."

She sucked in a breath, realizing this was the moment. If he asked, she'd say yes. She knew it.

"Move in with me." He kissed her nose, her cheeks, her lips. "Let's do a dry run with the marriage thing."

"Oh, um, well." Her face flushed. Living with him hadn't entered her mind, at least not unless they were married. But the relief that washed through her told her all she needed. "Sure." She smiled and shrugged. "But I don't clean. Or cook."

"You think I don't already know that? I wouldn't eat anything you cooked anyway. I cook. We split the cleaning and what we don't do the housekeeper does, including the laundry because I am not doing that."

"God, you are such a spoiled brat." But her chest had loosened and the moment seemed perfect. This was good. They would make it work. "But what about your—?"

"Nope." He put a finger over her lips. "I don't care what they think. I won't stop being their son, but I won't subject you to them. Even if you do finally succumb to my obvious charms and marry me."

She sighed and wrapped her arms around his waist. Her mind spun a million miles an hour already at the giant task of organizing the chaos that was the marketing effort for the brewery. He kissed her hair and held her close. "Relax, my Evelyn. It's Friday. We'll deal with work in a few days. For now, it's time to go home. With me."

* * * *

When she woke with a start in the middle of that night, her body was sore in all the right places. Once she realized she was in Austin's bed, not hers, she sighed and stretched, then rolled out, needing to pee. That business accomplished, she splashed water on her face and stared at herself in the large mirror over the granite countertop in Austin's master suite bathroom. It took her a few seconds to acknowledge the distinct lack of anxiety over staying here, over the general sumptuousness of his living space and her self-described 'invasion' of it. Relief coated her nerves, making her smile at her reflection.

Yes, she thought. An easy enough word to say.

What's my problem with it?

Yes, she thought again.

"Yes," she whispered to herself, before she turned to the dark bedroom and padded over to the large bed. The large, comfortable bed in her large, comfortable life where her man loved her and she had no reason to worry about anything.

She hesitated a few seconds, content to listen to Austin breathe, to the whirr of the ceiling fan, the light hiss of rain hitting the window.

"Yes," she whispered again as she lifted the covers and slid underneath, curling herself around Austin's warm back. "Yes," she said, kissing his shoulder. "Yes," she repeated, as she ran her hand across his bare chest.

He stirred and mumbled something. Evelyn smiled, loving how in tune she was already to his little tics and nuances. Loving him so much at that moment she wanted to weep. Instead, she reached lower, repeating the one, easy word between kissing his shoulder and the nape of his neck. She stroked his cock to full hardness even as he remained half asleep.

"Yes," she said, when he rolled to his back and she climbed on top, taking him inside her with a sigh from her and a low moan from him. As she rocked against him, taking her own pleasure and watching his dark-stubbled face, tears did fall, alarming her but also reaffirming the word.

The one word—the yes.

She moved her hips faster, leaning over him and letting her hair curtain their faces. She kissed him, shoving her tongue between his lips, needing that connection almost as badly as any other.

Austin matched her downward movements with upward thrusts of his own, finding their familiar rhythm. He broke the kiss and watched her as the orgasm made her shudder from head to toe as her body pulsed with a sort of energy only Austin could provide.

As her body calmed, she lay on his chest, hating the tears but knowing them for what they were. He stroked her hair a few seconds, then lifted her chin so she met his eyes in the dark.

"Nice way to wake me in the middle of the night, dear, thanks."

She sniffled and nodded, but the anxiety remained at bay. This was her place. She could let go now, be with him, fully, side by side at work and at home.

This home. *Their* home.

She sensed his cock inside her, still hard, and she smiled down at him, lifting up on her hands so he could get at her breasts. He cupped their heavy, firm curves, lapped at their tender, rock-hard tips. She sighed as her hips moved again in a primal way, reacting to his touch, as if there were a little string connecting her breasts to her pussy and Austin knew exactly how to give it the perfect tug.

Evelyn arched her back, tilting her hips and exposing her ass as she gave into a now-familiar fantasy — one she'd not found the courage to express to Austin, even though he'd indulged her fantasy at the B & B. In her imagination, Ross' strong hands were on her hips, his lips were on her nipples, his broad, chest was below her, and her fingers were tangled in his long, blond hair while Austin was poised behind her.

She glanced in the mirror, taking in the sexy view — her back arched, her ass ready to receive him. "Oh...God," she moaned as her fantasy took her there, let her have both men, let both men have her — let Ross pleasure her, too.

As if sensing something new, Austin released her swollen nipples and dropped his head back. She glanced down at him, her body on the ragged edge of a monster climax thanks to the imagined sensations swirling through her head.

"I want on top," Austin growled as he hooked one of

her legs with his and rolled them, the king-size of his bed allowing for it. She sighed and wrapped her legs around his hips, taking him ever deeper. "Evelyn, look at me," he said, his voice low, his breathing fast.

She opened her eyes and put her hands on either side of his face as he pounded into her. "Fill me," she commanded, even as the orgasm she'd fantasized herself into gripped her and she cried out with him as he came inside her.

"Damn." He sighed, once he'd opened his eyes again. She glanced down where their bodies were joined together. She felt her face flush with a combination of embarrassment and a sliver of illicit anticipation at the memory of the fantasy — one she'd entertained more and more lately. But first things first.

Keeping her legs locked around his waist, she looked into Austin's eyes and said, "Yes."

"Okay," he responded as he flopped onto the bed beside her, one arm over his eyes. "So you'll take the job, then."

She propped up on her elbow and ran her fingertips across her man's smooth, mostly hairless, firm chest. "Yes, that too."

Austin blinked at the ceiling, then turned his head and stared at her. She smiled and touched his lips. "Yes," she said for the millionth time, mainly because it felt so damn good to say it. "Yes, I will marry you. Where's that damn ring?"

Austin rolled to his bedside table. He handed her the ring box in silence. She opened it and took the beautiful piece of custom-made jewelry from its velvet bed. Without a second's hesitation, she slid it onto her left ring finger then held it up, allowing herself to admire it for the first time since he'd been after her to wear it.

"Jesus, finally," he said, his voice slow and sleepy-sounding. He held out his arm and she snuggled into his side, her head in the crook of his shoulder and chest. Her left hand draped over his chest. Moonlight split the blinds and hit the emerald, making it shimmer. "I love you," he said, kissing her hair and heaving a deep, I'm-about-to-go-to-sleep sigh.

"I love you too," she said, staring at the ring and wondering just what she'd gotten herself into, on all fronts, with Austin Fitzgerald.

Chapter Twelve

One month later

"Austin, honey?"

When he looked up from the computer screen on his desk, all his senses seemed to open at once, bombarding him with noises, sights and odors. He'd spent the last half hour crunching final numbers for a massive report Evelyn had requested for a 'special project' and he'd likely been faded out for half of that time, ever since he'd seen the first, tell-tale flashes of light around the perimeter of his vision.

They'd been putting in extra-long days lately, mostly thanks to his new marketing director. She'd been pushing him not only to jump start sales by kicking his sales director in the ass but was also exploring expanding their distribution into both Florida and New York—to markets she claimed were 'ripe' for their more 'tame products.'

And now, this damn special project thing that required the full history of his sales, plus all the investments he'd made in the tap room attached to the brewery. Not that he couldn't put his hands on it, but she wanted it in a very specific reporting style, which he'd apparently done wrong the first time, leading to this, another seven p.m. moment in his office after way too many of them in a row.

"Babe?" Evelyn put a hand on his shoulder but even her touch hurt at that moment. "What's wrong?"

"Migraine," he muttered, shocked, since he hadn't had one in almost fifteen years.

She leaned over, studying the miles of spreadsheets he'd been crunching as he leaned back in his chair, eyes closed, willing the looming brain-cruncher of a headache away.

"No, babe, I need it this way." He felt her push his chair aside and opened one eye to see her tapping away at the keyboard, altering the structure of the spreadsheets yet again. Her look, when he caught it, was one of tight, barely concealed impatience mixed with frustration.

"You know, if you'd just tell me what this was for…"

"I told you already. It's a surprise." Her voice was tight with stress, which ramped up his anxiety, which in turn, made his headache worse.

"Ugh. Jesus. I gotta go home." He rose, stumbling a little when his equilibrium wouldn't do its job. Without saying anything to him, Evelyn merely slipped into the chair he'd vacated, her attention still fixed on the damn computer screen.

He signed and leaned back against the long work table where he had the entire history of his brewery spread out in a series of thick, three-ring binders, blueprints, and, of course, more spreadsheets. Evelyn had promised to work wonders, but to piss a lot of people off in the process. So far, she'd delivered. Half the time he wanted to strangle her — after yet another disgruntled Fitzgerald employee had come running to him, complaining that she was a ball-buster, a know-it-all, too demanding.

All things he'd known her for, which was why he'd hired her in the first place. As he watched her tapping away on his keyboard, a rush of exhaustion hit him, making him more than a little weak in the knees. He leaned over and kissed the top of her head. She shot him a quick, wan smile. If he were working around the clock, she'd given new meaning to the phrase.

"Let's go home. We can talk, or do more about this, there. I need to get out of here."

I need to get laid.

He took in the long line of her neck, exposed by the messy bun she had her hair yanked into. They'd done more arguing than he liked but he'd sort of anticipated that, as she established her territory around her at the brewery. But by God, it was almost eight p.m. on a Friday, and he needed his woman, not this somewhat deranged-looking, hyper-focused, out-to-prove-something harpy.

Ignoring the alarming way his vision wobbled since taking his eyes off the numbers on the screen, he touched her arm. When she didn't respond, he put his other hand on her shoulder, and slid the other down her arm and around to cup her left breast under its layers of blouse, camisole and bra. It felt great and he knew this was the right thing. They needed their physical connection to re-establish their own relationship equilibrium.

Grinning, he pressed his lips to her neck, tasting her lotion and the slight, malty tang that was inevitable, working in a large brewery. She continued ignoring him, the tip of her tongue caught between her teeth as she worked away on the god damned spreadsheet. "Evelyn," he whispered, nipping her earlobe around the diamond drop jewelry he'd given her the week before. "Baby..." He sucked in a full breath of her, of her skin below her ear, still cupping one breast, his position awkward and unsustainable over the back of the desk chair.

She shook him off like so much rain on a raincoat. "Not now, Austin. If I could just get this...I'm almost..." She never even glanced at him. Trying hard not to yell at her, he stood back up, grabbed his phone and keys and walked out of his office, his brain on fire with need, pain and frustration.

When he got home, he downed two pain killers and two powerful sinus pills, praying this old remedy would work and he could avoid the prescription pills he used to have to take in high school. As he leaned on the counter, counting backward from a thousand to calm his racing pulse and quell his rising fury at Evelyn's single-minded focus on his business—and not on him—the doorbell to his condo rang, making him flinch when the noise settled deep in his aching skull.

Without checking to see who it was, he opened the

heavy wooden door and found himself face to face with his mother. She was dressed to go out – little black cocktail dress, high heels, gray hair swept back and held in place with a familiar, decorated hairpin. Austin dragged a hand down his face and turned away from her, stumbling as he made his way toward his large leather recliner.

"Austin." Her voice was sharp with worry. He felt her hand on his arm as he found the chair and flopped into it, hand over his eyes. "My dear. Whatever is wrong?"

He sighed, unable to find words for this odd, after hours meeting with one of the many women in his life whom he adored but who had seemingly gone out of her way to making him miserable.

God, don't be such a whiner.

"I'll make you some tea," she said. "Do you have honey?"

He watched, bleary-eyed, as she took control of his small but well-appointed kitchen and let himself drift, coming back to consciousness when she reappeared with a steaming cup of tea and a tray of some kind of food.

"There, now," she said, smiling at him in such a genuine way, he felt his inner small boy, eager for his mother's undivided attention, rise and grip his chest. "Here." She handed him the tea cup. He sniffed it – honey, a touch of lavender, an undertone of mild tea leaves. He hadn't even realized he'd owned a tea that smelled like this – like heaven. He sipped and she observed him in silence.

"So," she said, taking a small slice of fruit off the tray and holding it in her hand. It was what she did, he now recalled, to appear as if she were eating. "What's all this I hear about major life changes for you? You can't be bothered to tell your own parents that you're engaged to be married?" Her tone was mild, neutral. A trap, and he knew it well.

He put the cup on the table between them and leaned back. The headache was fading, slowly, but was putting up a fight as it went. Going from the frying pan of Evelyn into the direct flame of Virginia was not how he'd imagined this unbelievably stressful day might end.

"Yes, Mother. But based on your one and only meeting with her, Evelyn has asked me not to involve you or Dad. And I respect her wishes."

"Hmm." She nibbled a corner of the apple slice. He grabbed one off the plate, chewed and swallowed it, which seemed to shove the pain back into its cage even further so he inhaled the rest of them along with the grapes and some kind of a cracker he also didn't know had been in his pantry. "Seems to be going well so far," she said, eyeing him as he devoured the snack. "You're here, in real pain, starving for dinner and she's..." Virginia waved her fingers and rolled her eyes ever so slightly — an expression he recalled from his boyhood that used to drive his father mad with fury, at least until got his first drink into him.

Austin closed his eyes, refusing her bait. Maybe, if he pretended to sleep, she'd just leave him alone.

But where the hell was Evelyn? He figured she'd be pretty much right behind him. But it was pushing nine o'clock now and his phone hadn't even buzzed with any communication from her. A hand touched his knee.

"Why don't you get a shower? I'll find some real food for you."

"Mother, I don't need you to — "

"Don't be silly. I'm happy to help." He opened one eye and studied her, wary of this, yet somehow grateful.

"You're going out," he said, stretching, then standing slowly, relieved when the pain didn't re-emerge. "You look too nice to be here babying me."

"Oh, I'll go later. My son needs me. That's more important right now." He eyed her, shocked, even more wary but too damn tired to process or fight it. "Shower," she said, pointing to the rear of the condo. "Do you have a preference for takeout?"

"Anything but Chinese," he said, making his slow way down the hall, realizing he should grab his phone and warn Evelyn of their unexpected dinner guest while at the same time thinking it would serve her fucking right, showing up at whatever hour still dressed for work and finding him sharing takeout with Virginia.

The shower helped and when he emerged, pink-skinned and dressed in a pair of jeans and a soft sweatshirt, he found his mother sitting on the couch, legs primly crossed, flipping through a magazine. A small glass of clear liquid with a slice of lime sat on a coaster on the coffee table. He blinked, still amazed that she could conjure all these things. They barely kept the kitchen stocked with much more than the basics — coffee, orange juice, bread, some fruit. And at that moment, as he was pondering the odd sparseness of the past month, even with Evelyn officially moved in, wearing his engagement ring, working alongside him, the door opened. The distinct and alarming lack of sex since they tended to fall into bed, side by side around midnight and drop immediately into sleep.

"Austin, baby, I'm so sorr—" She froze. The strap of her expensive briefcase slipped off her shoulder, sending it to the floor with a soft thump. Austin watched her swallow, then put her purse on the foyer table, then her keys, then her phone. She was buying herself time not to explode in anger and he knew it. But hell, he had every right to be mad, too. So let her pop off, and see how that went with the present company included.

Oh, Jesus H. Christ. Fitzgerald, you did not mean that.

Maybe I did.

He watched, fingers tucked into the jeans pockets, his skin tingly from the shower, his brain still somewhat echoey from the migraine. As he and Virginia watched, the doorbell rang behind her, so Evelyn turned, accepted the bags of food and walked into the kitchen without a word to either of them. Virginia met his gaze with a 'oh, dear, dear, what's wrong now' sort of expression that made him clench his jaw.

He followed Evelyn and watched her as she pulled out the various dishes and placed them on the counter, then got out two plates and some flatware. Finally, she turned to face him. Austin felt immediately guilty at the lines of exhaustion on her face. *Damn it, she was working this hard for your sorry ass. For the betterment of your floundering sales and market position. Cut her some slack.* He was reaching for her, pulling her close so they could just stand in each other's arms for a minute or two when his mother appeared.

"Well, then, thank you, Evelyn, for putting out some dishes for dinner."

"I'm sorry but I wasn't aware we were hosting you for dinner, Virginia," she retorted, the distinct edge in her voice making Austin's nerve endings fire.

"Oh, I just stopped over to see how he…how you both were doing." Her gaze dropped to Evelyn's left hand. "To congratulate you, on the impending wedding."

Evelyn shot him a hard look then trained her gaze back on Virginia. "Thank you. And thanks for stopping by. A call first, next time, perhaps? By this time of night, we're usually, well, a bit indisposed, if you know what I mean."

Virginia's face flushed red. Austin suppressed a groan of consternation and a smile of amusement. She stood firm, facing his mother, her shoulders set, her face neutral.

Good girl. Don't let her get to you.

"Yes, well, anyway," his mother turned to him. "When can we begin planning?"

"Planning what?" He honestly couldn't process the question. Evelyn handed him a plate piled high with chicken shish, rice with almonds and hummus. His mouth watered when the delicious odors hit his brain.

"I'm assuming she means the wedding, dear." Her emphasis on the endearment made him snap his attention from the sustenance to the conversation.

"No need, Mother. We'll handle it." He took the plate and shrugged at Evelyn, mouthing the word "sorry" to her. The flatness of her expression did not bode well and he knew it. But fuck it, he was borderline passing out exhausted and this little tête-à-tête was the opposite of helpful.

He set his jaw and turned to Virginia who was, in turn,

staring holes into his fiancée.

"Well, then, actually I'm here for another reason, if you must know."

"Oh, you mean you actually *aren't* here to congratulate me. No big surprise. Excuse me." Evelyn shoved her way past them both on her foot-stomping way to the back bedroom. Austin sighed and put his plate on the high granite eating counter.

"Okay, Mother, I'll bite. Why *are* you here?"

Virginia dragged her flaming gaze away from Evelyn's retreat and squared her shoulders. "It's your father. He's... Well, he's sick. I mean, not cancer or anything." She waved a hand dismissively as if anything less really wasn't worth speaking about. "It's his blood pressure."

"There's medication for that," Austin said, acknowledging the dread building in his chest and throat.

"Yes, he's on some. But for some reason...well, he spent the night in the hospital last night and — "

"God damn it, Mother," Austin spat out, as he dumped his untouched plate into the sink already piled high with dirty dishes. "Why didn't you call me? I'd have been there."

"Well, dear, your...girlfriend has made it clear that you don't want any part of us and so..." She gazed wistfully out of the window.

"You know that's not the case."

She arched one carefully manicured eyebrow at him.

He sighed and plowed on. "I mean, not if it's a medical emergency. You're the one who's made it clear she's not welcome. She's just responding to your petty, stuck-up bullshit."

"No need to curse, dear." Virginia managed to seem shocked, appalled and triumphant all at once. Austin's vision got red around the edges, and the lurking headache crept forward out its cage.

"You know what? Fuck you, Mother. Where is Dad now? I'll go see him." He started back to the living, room, his mind roiling with all the various consequences of this little news bombshell. There was no one Maxwell Fitzgerald trusted with his super successful business. No one but Austin, of course. When he turned around, a million questions on his lips, he saw something he'd not seen since Brock's last disappearing act—tears standing in Virginia's faded green eyes.

"I don't understand you, son. I really don't. You had a perfectly lovely young woman to marry—someone who understood us, what it means to have a family legacy, how to nurture it and grow it and protect it. And you just dump her for that...that..."

Evelyn reappeared, dressed in jeans and a soft blue sweater that hugged her breasts, emphasizing them in a way that Austin loved. His head seemed to expand out from his temples, throbbing with this new stressful reality.

"Where is Max now, Virginia? At home?" Her voice was soft, non-confrontational and non-committal. Austin grabbed her hand and yanked her to him, wrapping one arm around her so they could face his mother as a team, a bonded pair, whether she liked it or not.

She leaned into him a split second, then pulled away to start packing up the food. "Tell you what," she said, looking up at Austin. "You go on over with your mother. I'll come behind you with this so we can eat and visit with him."

Austin smiled at her gratefully. Head whirring and aching, he tossed the keys to his car on the counter. "Let's go, Mother."

"Really, dear, you don't have to—"

"Come over to your house?" Evelyn had everything packed back up and was putting it in canvas bags with the Fitzgerald Brewing logo on them. "I'm sure you'd rather I not. But, to be clear, I do care about Max and want to see with my own eyes how he's doing. You can do whatever you like to pretend I'm not there. But I am...here. And I'm engaged to marry your son and you will *not* come between us no matter how hard you try." Both Austin and Virginia gaped at her a few seconds. He was shocked that she'd managed these words in such a calm, matter-of-fact tone. And he was damn proud of her, too.

"Mother?" He held out a hand to indicate that she should precede him out to the living room and to the front door. With a little sniff and patented chin-raise, she did that, not favoring either of them with another word.

Limp, reamed out emotionally and physically, he stared across the kitchen at Evelyn for a few seconds. "I... I love you," he choked out.

She pulled her hair up and into a high ponytail. "I know, Austin."

"We have to talk...more."

She glanced up at him, her blue eyes soft and inviting, making him wish they could just stay here, eat, fuck, talk... anything but what they were about to do. "It's all okay, Austin. Now go on, take your mother home before I toss her off the balcony." She crossed her arms and cocked one hip in a jokey way. Austin ran a hand down his face, nodded and turned to follow his mother to the condo's front door.

* * * *

Later, as she drove them home, she said out of the clear blue sky, "I don't want to plan the wedding for next year. It's too much right now. I have... We have a lot to get done first."

"Okay," he said, figuring it for more Fitzgerald-family avoidance. But something about the way she said it—as if assuming he'd be all right with whatever she said about this important aspect of their lives—dug into his psyche like a burr.

"And, frankly, I can do without a big fancy wedding. I mean, if that's all right with you."

They were parked under the building now, still sitting in the car and staring at the concrete wall in front of them. "I have to wonder," he said, knowing he should keep his stupid, tired, borderline sick mouth shut but unable to do that, "if you even give a shit what is all right with me."

She turned to face him, her blue eyes alight in a way that would make him horny — were he not so bone-deep exhausted. "What in the hell is that supposed to mean?"

"You are great at the job, Evelyn. You're doing exactly what you'd promised you'd do. You are making my job harder, but I know in the long run it's all for the good of the company."

She kept staring at him, breathing heavy, nostrils flared, cheeks flushed. "And...your point is what?"

"I don't know... I mean, shit." He pressed the heels of his hands into his eye sockets. "You're not..."

"I'm not being a sweet, soft-spoken, ladylike employee."

"No. I mean. Yes. I mean... You're taking this whole I-don't-care-what-anyone-thinks-of-me thing too far. You don't have to be such a fucking...ball buster all the time. You're, I don't know, out of balance, or something."

"Out of balance," she repeated softly, as if testing the words in her mouth.

"Evelyn, honey, I'm so tired I am seeing double and if I don't get into a dark, quiet room soon you're gonna have to take me to urgent care for a migraine."

She opened her mouth, then closed it. But she didn't move from behind the steering wheel. "You want me to cave to her, don't you?"

"Cave...to who?" He put a hand on the door handle, praying for escape before he made it worse.

"You want me to get along with your mother."

"I don't give a flying fuck what you do about her. You know that."

"But it would make your life easier, wouldn't it? If I just took her random, rude bullshit and absorbed it like a sponge, smiled, and passed the mother fucking teapot, right?"

"Well, yeah. But—"

"Great. Okay. Well, thanks for the honesty." She got out of the car and headed for the elevator without him.

Chapter Thirteen

Denver, Colorado
One month later

If Austin had to shake one more hand, listen to one more drunk tell him how awesome his beers were, or get one more slap on the back, he would scream. Not that he'd be heard over the nearly five thousand people crammed into the Denver Convention Center.

Participation at the American Beer Festival was a necessary evil in his book. An expensive one at that. After shipping out beers in cold trucks, paying the exorbitant booth fees and for the necessary staff to fly out and stay in a half-decent hotel, crafting a unique and eye-catching display, and buying endless rounds and dinners after the festival doors shut each day, it blew the marketing budget every year. And at that moment, a total whopper of a headache was lurking and muttering behind his eyes, which didn't help matters.

He knew he sounded crabby to everyone around him, which was so unlike his usual easy-going personality that people were starting to talk. He knew this thanks to his ever-diligent secretary who, while she respected Evelyn for being a hardworking female in a male-dominated industry, didn't really care for her as a person.

Pretending to study his booth display, he sought out the one set of blue eyes that would calm him. She was working her magic on the other side of their massive end-cap booth, laughing, drinking and schmoozing as only she could. As if sensing his gaze, she glanced up and met it. But instead of winking and smiling as she normally would, she looked away, refocusing on her task, unwilling to give him what he so desperately wanted.

He'd apologized for the stupid comments about his mother. She'd accepted. They'd kissed and made up, more than once. But something in her had changed. He knew her well enough to acknowledge it but once she'd finally spilled it that she wanted to enter them into the Brewing Associations Annual Mid-Sized Brewery of the Year contest, hence all the need for specific reports and numbers and crap, they'd poured themselves into it, leaving everything else, including physical intimacy, behind them for a solid month.

The annual award came with a ton of free publicity, and bragging rights she would use like mad for years, he knew. It was important. And they could do it. He gave her a ton of credit for trying and figured he owed it to her to give it everything he had, too.

He ground his teeth and forced the image of her body out of his head. He hadn't seen it in a while, at least three, possibly four weeks.

Pressing fingers against his burning eyes, he turned, pasted a smile on his face, and resumed the torture that constituted a national beer event. After another hour, convinced everyone in the building was too drunk to matter anymore, he declared himself done for the day.

He recalled that Evelyn had glided over to him about twenty minutes earlier, brushed her lips against his, and mumbled something about catching a drink with Rene and Kim, two female owners of west coast breweries. He'd gripped her arm, needing to talk to her, to get her alone and away from this madness, so they could talk about something other than that fucking award, and sales reports and the god damned brewery.

"Damn it, Evelyn, you can't do this."

"Do what? Have drinks with my friends?" She'd glared at his hand then looked around, not meeting his eyes. Austin had tried not to shake her like a rag doll. She could be the most frustrating woman on the planet. And he loved her so much it made his teeth ache. She was operating under the biggest shoulder chip he'd ever encountered and the more he got to know about her, the bigger and more uncompromising that damn thing got.

Defeated, he'd let her go, had met her flat stare with one of his own.

"Fine, pretend you don't know what I mean. Have fun." He'd turned away, his chest so tight he could barely draw a breath. Her scent had invaded his nose, had let him know she remained at his shoulder. But he'd had nothing to say, nothing that would do any good anyway.

Even if she'd wanted to speak, she wouldn't, and he knew it. One other thing he'd learned about his roommate and lover of the past few months was that she could be the most emotionally unavailable human being he'd ever encountered. She could slam a wall down between them so fast and hard he could hear it, could feel the breeze it made as it passed him.

Admittedly they were stressed for a lot of reasons. The application they'd made for Mid-Size Brewery of the Year had taken a lot out of them both. The past month and a half had been a blur of time spent collecting the necessary data to fill out the reams of reports required to even apply for such an award. It had left them both exhausted and cranky. Which had added to the cooling between them.

Of course, the hard fact of his father's declining health hadn't helped. The three words 'congenital heart failure' had haunted his nights for the past month. More than one morning had found him wide awake, sitting in his recliner still clutching a cup of tea. The fact of the matter was, if Max Fitzgerald died, he, Austin, would be handed reins of the food supply empire. Something he'd never wanted, and had made clear, but somehow, both of his parents remained deaf to this for the past years—even after observing the success of the business he did love and nurture, biding their time, as if figuring that he'd get over his silly brewery obsession, leave it and return to the Fitzgerald fold where he belonged.

"That girl, can't she run the beer thing?" his mother had asked him the week before over lunch at the club, something he'd been doing once a week by way of placating her.

"She's a woman, and yeah, I guess she could. But what about Grant, or Ken?" He named the two men closer to his father's age who were his number two and three in charge — one of logistics and the other of the money. "Why not name one of them as interim president and get him trained up?"

But she'd waved it off, in that way she always had, discounting his brewery as a lark, a silly hobby, that he'd toss aside the second he was handed the Fitzgerald company to run. That had been four days ago. He'd come home from work that evening to find her on the couch, wrapped in a robe, sipping tea and reading sales reports after spending the previous three days meeting potential distribution partners in New York.

Something about seeing here there, hair up, face scrubbed clean of makeup, comfortable and happy in his — in their — space had driven him to drop to the floor in front of her and lay his head in her lap. "They're not going to stop until I leave the brewery and take over for my dad," he said, gripping her legs as she ran her fingers through his hair.

"Shh, don't talk about it."

He'd raised his head from her lap, furious and shocked that she'd say such a thing. "I mean it, Austin," she'd insisted, putting her finger to his lips.

"Good god, you are unbelievable." He'd gotten up and headed for the shower.

"No, I'm not. We have enough to worry about at this moment, right now. Okay? Let's cross that bridge should it arise. Max looked great the last time we saw him. I have to believe that —"

He'd whirled on her, grabbing her wrists and backing her against the wall outside the bathroom. She'd frowned at him, squirmed to get away, which had lit a match to his neglected libido. He'd glared at her for a split second before slamming his lips over hers, shoving his tongue inside her mouth and grinding his erection against her stomach.

"Austin, stop," she'd said. He thought. It didn't really matter at that point. He'd brought her to a loud, wet orgasm on his fingers before he shoved her down on the bed, yanked off his belt and trousers and rammed into her. He came fast and hard with a loud cry of half-satisfaction, half-frustration and without a damn thought in his head to anything but the tightness of her pussy and his need to get laid. He hadn't even kissed her after he pulled out and got up to make his way to the shower. And when he'd come back into the bedroom, embarrassed with relief that he'd knocked some of his edge off, it was empty.

He'd heard her in the kitchen, pulling out last night's takeout to warm for dinner, so he made his way there, taking a few minutes to observe her. She'd prepped them both plates, heated his in the microwave first and handed it over. Her hair had been tousled, her color high. But her eyes had been flat and expressionless.

"I want to set a date," he'd said. "For our wedding." Something about the unknown, the extreme instability of everything around him, thanks to his father's illness, made him need an anchor. Something that he could count on.

"I'm not ready. Come on, let's read through the last application draft."

"Fuck you and your fucking application. I never wanted that award. I want you. I want us. I *need* us, Evelyn. Badly."

"I'm right here. I'm not going anywhere." She'd started to walk past him with her plate but he held out an arm like a traffic cop, halting her and taking the plate from her hands. "What? You wanna rough fuck again? Fine." She'd yanked open her robe and turned around. "Make it fast though, doll. I have fucking work to do. Work for your god-damned company."

He'd glared at her ass and actually considered it for a half second. But for the way her eyes had shone with tears when she glanced over her shoulder at him. "Stop it," he'd said, pulling her up and tying the robe's belt around her waist. "Just stop it."

"Stop what, Austin? Stop being me? Stop working so hard? Stop letting your mother say whatever she damn well pleases to me?"

"Stop avoiding my question."

She'd blinked fast. He'd taken her in his arms and pressed his lips to her forehead. "Let's go to the courthouse tomorrow. I want to be your husband. I want you to be my wife. I want to be together."

"I'm not ready," she'd said into his chest, her hands twisted into the back of his T-shirt. "I'm afraid."

He'd tilted her chin up and kissed her cheeks, tasting salt and hating himself for being such a shit head. "You have no reason to be afraid of anything."

"That's how much you know," she'd said, sniffling and moving away from him, clutching her elbows in her palms. "I can't talk about this right now."

With a sigh, he'd picked up his plate. A truce would have to do tonight, he'd figured. Later, in bed, he'd held her close, feeling safe and happy for a few minutes anyway.

"I'm sorry," she'd whispered. "I'm a pain in the ass."

"Truer words never spoken. But you're *my* pain in the ass, right?"

"Of course," she'd said, snuggling closer to him.

"You're less PiTA and more emotionally unavailable, I'd say."

She'd stiffened. He'd run a hand down her arm and smiled, hoping keep her calm. "Just don't shut me out, Evelyn. Even when you think have to. That's one thing I can't take any more of, all right?"

She'd nodded, and within a few minutes, her breathing had evened out, leaving him awake and staring into the darkness.

And now, four days later — four days spent in a flurry of

activity on the trip out west—he watched her walk away from him. Then he grabbed a sample glass, filling it to the brim with the nearest pitcher of beer on his table. After slamming the rich chocolate stout, he poured another, then another, until his shoulders and jaw unclenched and he relaxed just enough to avoid putting his fist through a wall. He stood back and let volunteers and staff run their mouths as the last of the festival attendees filed past.

"Austin?"

He frowned, trying to place the voice amongst the noise and the beer sloshing around in his system. When Ross Hoffman's tall form glided into view, Austin had the oddest feeling—relief and dread, all rolled up into a shiver that ran down his spine. With a wide smile, Ross strode around the back of the elaborate display Evelyn's marketing team had designed and pulled his friend into a fierce hug. Austin's throat tightened, but he willed himself calm. This wasn't the place or the time to have a breakdown. "I didn't think I'd see you here. Last I heard you'd gone back to Munich."

The tall, handsome German shrugged, running a palm over his lightly bearded face. "Got a new job. With Jefferson." He named one of the most famous craft breweries in the nation, if not the world.

Austin whistled. "Nice. Good thing you never took me up on my offer to come to Michigan. I had no idea you were that expensive." Repressing the urge to be pissed off that Ross had taken that job without even talking to him, he slapped his friend on the back. Finally, someone he could talk to.

"Let's get the fuck out of here. I'm exhausted and need a real drink."

"Perfect. Where's your woman?" Ross looked over Austin's shoulder. He'd never met Evelyn and Austin had not sent him pictures, just kept to the bare facts of her existence, their engagement, her position at the brewery. The reasons why he'd done that he kept buried and hidden even from himself. The memory of that morning in the B &

B when they'd pretended Ross was there, in bed with them, had never faded far from his consciousness. He'd gotten distracted, between the brewery of the year application and his father's illness. Because that was behind him now. The whole threesome thing was in his past and should stay that way. He couldn't even think about sharing Evelyn... or could he?

"With some friends, someplace." Austin waved a hand, not willing to get into it. Not until he had a seat, a double scotch and a quiet moment. He smiled, nodded to a few fellow brewery owners and escaped the building, the cool Denver air caressing his face.

* * * *

Ross Hoffman had been seeking his old friend Austin Fitzgerald since he'd hit the festival floor that day. The recent offer to work for Jefferson as brew master had been somewhat of a surprise and he wasn't sure he even wanted the damn job.

The founder and owner of said brewery, Brad Jefferson, had a rep as a class-A prick. He'd come after Ross with laser-focused determination to get the famous Munich-based brewing instructor attached to his operation. It was strange, really. But Ross had relented, having nothing more to keep him tied to his home country ever since his latest personal disaster had rained fire down on his head.

He'd wanted to talk over the opportunity with Austin, get his perspective on the bizarre scenario of working for one of the most difficult prima donnas in the craft brewing world. But Ross knew his friend had a crazy-busy life. With a family who did nothing but loudly disapprove of his choices, no matter what they were, the poor guy probably only got a few hours of sleep each night.

He'd considered Austin's offer to come to Michigan and work for him a few months prior, but he'd been caught up in his own personal drama, unwilling to subject his old friend to it. Even if he'd written more than one email asking Austin if the offer still stood, and erased them each, one by one. His feelings about Austin were a complex mix of loyalty, warm friendship, mild competition and a healthy dose of jealousy. He'd had so much handed to him, and now, he ran his own successful brewery and was engaged to the woman of his dreams — at least according to the updates he'd absorbed through brief emails and the occasional text message.

Besides, Ross knew his own failings when it came to asking for help or opening himself up for advice. So, he'd avoided it, and let the opportunities to reach out to his friend pass. But now here they were, walking side by side down the busy Denver streets toward a favorite restaurant of his.

He glanced over at Austin as they waited for a light to change so they could cross. Ross had been chasing pussy all over Europe with an enthusiasm born of boredom after Austin had left Germany. He'd spent the last eight months falling so hard for a woman who'd been the polar opposite of everything he'd once claimed he wanted in a life partner that he'd not seen the end coming. When he'd gotten dumped on his ever-loving ass, he knew it had probably served him right. But it still stung. And now, he realized how much he'd missed his friend, on many levels. "What's up? Brewery okay?"

Austin smiled at him, sending a thrill of fresh jealousy to Ross' brain. "Yeah, great actually. Evelyn's given the whole thing the marketing kick in the butt it needed. She's worked miracles."

They stayed silent until seated at a booth in the back of the busy restaurant and each held a double scotch on the rocks. Ross stared hard at his friend. There was something seriously wrong, but he figured Austin would spill it. The man wore his heart on his sleeve ninety-nine percent of the time — and Ross would admit to missing that touch of emotion he never allowed himself to experience, at least in public.

"What's wrong?" he asked after their touched their glasses together.

"Oh, I don't know," his friend said, running a hand down his face. "I mean, I do know. It's dad. He's sick—it's his heart. He's on a ton of meds and lost a bunch of weight. They're really giving me the full court press to come back and take over for him." He knocked back his drink fast, and waved at the server for another round.

"I'm sorry. That's shitty."

"Yeah."

"But you're good with...ah...Evelyn, is it?"

"Yeah."

Austin looked down at the table, then back up at Ross, his gaze intense. Ross leaned back, wondering if he wanted to hear what was coming next. "I can't...she won't...we...oh, fuck." He downed the second scotch and slammed the glass down on the pockmarked wooden table so hard people nearby glanced at them. Ross touched the hand Austin had clenched around the glass.

"Relax. I've never seen you this unglued unless it was over a batch of ruined wort."

Austin barked out a harsh laugh. Ross sat back, frowning.

"We've been living together over a month and work together every day. My parents make no bones about hating her, and since I broke up with Valerie, my mother has taken every opportunity to nag me about taking over for my dad instead of my 'little beer project with that girl.'" He ran a hand down his face.

Ross leaned forward. "So? You've never let your mother bug you before. Why care now?"

"Evelyn is... She's... Well, she's shut down on me or something. I don't know. We've been under a lot of stress, mainly for this stupid event. It's making me nuts. I mean, I know this thing with my folks is taking its toll. Plus, she won't commit to a wedding date, even though she finally agreed to get engaged."

Ross frowned. "Why screw up a great relationship over a legal document?"

Austin slumped back in his seat. Ross was startled to see that intense look in his eyes again, bordering on desperation.

"I don't know. I mean, I'm settling for this living-together thing. But until we actually get married, I have to keep enduring my parents' bullshit — my mom's blatant criticism and Dad's passive-aggressive version of it."

Ross signaled the waitress as he spoke, not taking his eyes from Austin's. "So, let me see if I get this. You want to marry her so your parents will leave you alone. Wow. Romantic much?"

Austin glared at him.

Ross held up a hand. "Don't get me wrong. I'm not the most romantic guy on the planet either. You were the first one to call me emotionally constipated, if I'm not mistaken. That hurt." He put the hand to his heart, relieved when his friend's frown turned to a bemused smile. "But maybe she senses you're pushing matrimony for the wrong reasons." He raised an eyebrow. "Maybe she's got her back up over it now."

"Yeah." Austin ran his fingers through his hair. "One of the many things I love about her — and you will too, once you meet her — is her single-minded, headstrong stubbornness. Tinged with a smart-ass, hot-as-shit attitude. But when it's turned against you — "

Ross looked over Austin's shoulder and immediately laid eyes on the most beautiful female he'd ever seen.

Tall, elegant and curvy, not hard and angular like so many women these days. Clad in dark jeans and a light sweater, Ray-Bans pushed up over her golden-blonde hair, deep blue gaze moving around the room, obviously seeking someone, she oozed sexy. Ross had a hard time not staring openly at her. She spoke with a few people, her face breaking into a grin and revealing twin dimples that he ached to taste. He shook his head and refocused on his friend.

"Oh hell, Hoffman, I hate it when you're right." Austin

leaned over the table and Ross had the odd, almost déjà vu sensation of being caught in a significant moment. One of those split seconds between the before and the after that he would never forget, when he'd recall it, and shake his head at himself for being so blind, or naïve, or both.

He swallowed hard. They sat in silence for another few seconds as Ross allowed himself another surreptitious perusal of the goddess now seated at the bar, one foot propped on the rail, her long, wavy blonde hair tumbling halfway down her back. He took a breath and resisted the urge to lick his lips. His cock, which had experienced a lovely workout just last night with one of the groupies Brad Jefferson kept around, leapt to painful attention. He let his gaze wander down the woman's frame, imagining how her sumptuous curves would feel under his practiced hands.

"Yo, dude. Did you hear me?"

The woman turned as if sensing his laser focus. Her blue eyes widened at his stare.

"Um, huh? Sorry. I was…" He tore his gaze from her, shrugged and grinned into his nearly empty glass. "Let's eat something before we get too drunk to sit here."

"All right. Evelyn should be here by now. Although, I'll warn you, we aren't exactly talking beyond the basics." Austin's eyes darkened. "She's shut down on me. Pretty classic Hoffman-style, actually. You two would be quite the pair." He stood and motioned to someone. To Ross' utter surprise and slight horror, the amazing woman he'd been ogling appeared at his friend's elbow.

"Evelyn." Austin stood and put his arm around her waist. "This is my good friend, Ross."

Chapter Fourteen

Thirty minutes earlier

Evelyn frowned at her friend, frustration coursing through her, deafening her with its buzz.

Rene Matthews, spouse and business partner owner of one of the most successful breweries in Kentucky grinned and sipped her martini. "Listen, hon, your man is nothing if not totally open with you, right?"

She nodded and toyed with the olive in her drink, wishing she hadn't agreed to come out for drinks with these two. While they were the sorts of friends every woman should have — fun, funny and honest — she wasn't sure she could handle a dose of them right now.

She sighed and propped her chin in her hand. Austin was that — honest, open, loving and supportive. He calmed her in ways she never thought she could be. Could coax a laugh out of her in the most stressful of situations. And nearly had her trained to orgasm with a glance from his deep green eyes, a certain lift of one dark eyebrow.

"It's his dad. He's sick. Dying. It's just a matter of time now."

"Oh no," Kim said, waving down the cute waiter for another round.

"I'm sorry to hear that," Rene said, eyeballing her closely. "Where does that leave the family business?"

"That's just it. They expect him to drop the brewery like some kind silly hobby and come back to run the 'real business'." She hooked her fingers around the words, feeling petty and stupid. And pissed off at the missing twin brother. Brock should be here taking over for their father, not forcing Austin to make this horrible choice.

"Why aren't y'all married yet?" Rene asked. "I mean, you know, if you don't mind me asking."

Evelyn rolled her eyes, but was grateful for the opportunity to talk about it with a couple of objective outsiders.

What was her major malfunction? Why, even after she'd agreed to wear his damn ring, was she still holding back, refusing to commit to anything beyond an engagement to the richest, hottest, most eligible bachelor in the Midwest?

"I don't know, honestly." She sighed and stared at her fresh drink. "There's…a lot to consider, you know?"

"No, not really," Kim said. "Austin Fitzgerald is hot, rich, driven and madly in love with you, my stubborn friend. Get over yourself."

"You're right, I know you're right."

"Damn, skippy," she said, holding up her glass. The other two women clinked theirs and sipped. The alcohol tasted medicinal to Evelyn and she could barely swallow past her closed-up throat.

A nagging small voice of doubt kept her up at night. Watching him sleep, running a hand across his hair, down his back, choking back tears, she'd remind herself that this was very likely still some sort of perverse rich-boy nose-thumb at his parents. And until he acknowledged that, she would not add Fitzgerald to her name. His parents hated her ever-loving guts. The very few times she'd been forced to be around them had proven that.

The new, ongoing stress about Max clouded everything lately, leaving her more than a little panicky most days at the thought of what they'd do if and when he did pass away, leaving that huge company without a family member to lead it. She knew damn good and well his parents were pressuring him to take over. She also knew that he would likely have to do it. What she didn't know is what that meant for the brewery, and for her.

For the past couple of weeks, she'd toyed with reaching

out to Ross Hoffman herself. To ask him to come and help Austin sort through the brewery issues so he could focus on finding a new president for his father's sprawling food supply business. She'd even gone so far as to pull up his Skype contact on Austin's laptop, only to spend a solid fifteen minutes staring at the small photo and reliving that super-hot moment when Austin had let her pretend they were all three together, in bed, connected in the most intimate way possible.

So, now she had guilt. Guilt over the increasing power of her fantasies regarding Austin's friend and one-time partner in female conquest, the tall, hot German brewer. Guilt over her need to have him, for some reason. To add him to their mix at the brewery—and maybe somewhere else. And that couldn't be right, could it? That was the stuff of fringe romance novels. Threesomes didn't work in real life, did they? How could two men—one of whom she knew for a fact was a walking alpha dog and another whose reputation for being one level above that preceded him—possibly agree to share…her?

But yet…she couldn't seem to let go of it. Between the tiny tingle of desire to experience it, and her own ongoing uncertainty about Austin's parents, she knew she was shutting down. She hated it and wished she knew how she might break down the wall she'd been building.

Aggravation and stress had made her so single-minded for the last few weeks, she'd alienated him and she knew it. They'd stopped talking about anything unrelated to the brewery. If she would open her stupid mouth and just tell the man how she felt, it would likely go a long way. But something held her back. She had no name for it other than fear.

Fear—no, more like abject, gut-wrenching terror—of losing him.

"Honey," Rene interrupted her inner musings about Ross, and the sort of three-way sex she'd never experienced but wanted to now, for some reason. "That man is head over heels for you. Don't ruin it by being so bloody stubborn."

"No shit." Kim tossed back the dregs of her last drink. "Screw his parents. He doesn't care what they think. A guy like that will only take no for an answer so many times before he gives up."

"I know, I know." Evelyn took a breath and blew it out. "You're right. I do love him and I've been such a raging bitch lately. I don't deserve him."

"Yeah, well, none of our men really deserve us." Rene had signaled for the check.

"You guys are on the verge of something huge with your brewery, hon." Kim had patted her shoulder. "Don't ruin it by borrowing trouble that isn't there. You aren't marrying his parents. You're marrying him. Or would be, if you'd get over yourself long enough to see reason."

"And besides," Rene said, her eyebrows raised over her glass, "from what I hear, Ross Hoffman is looking to make a move."

Evelyn blinked fast, wondering if these women knew what she did about Austin and Ross' playboy history together. "What does that have to do with the price of tea in China?" She rose, legs a little wobbly, and shouldered her purse.

"I'm sure I don't know," Rene said, barely concealing a smirk.

"Oh, stop being obtuse," Kim demanded, leaning forward with something a hair shy of a leer. "I hear Austin and Ross make a killer BOGO."

"A…what?" But she knew, of course. What shocked her was that other people did, too.

"Don't be a bitch." Rene smacked Kim on the arm. "Seriously, hon, get your ass out of here. Marry Austin. Hire Hoffman as brewmaster. Enjoy…life."

She felt a sudden and immediate urge to be back in Austin's arms. To reunite, to apologize and make amends. She owed him big-time. The desire for his embrace and his lips had nearly choked her. "I should go. Austin is…" The two women had exchanged a knowing look.

"Seriously. Go, go." Rene had waved her off. "I've got this. See you tomorrow at the awards."

"Oh, and, Evelyn?" Kim said with a wide grin. "Do tell us how it works out with…them."

"I'm sure I don't know what you're talking about," she said, her face hot with imagination and anticipation. Kim elbowed Rene in the side and the two women waved at her, a knowing glint in their eyes.

By the time she'd exchanged texts with him, desperation to see him had made her breathless. Sinking back into the pedi-cab seat, she'd white-knuckled her fingers, the sparkle from her engagement emerald hitting her eyes, accusatory somehow. She loved him so much and needed to prove it. Tonight.

The restaurant where he'd said he'd be was packed, so she'd sat at the bar, ordered a beer and sent him a text, frowning when it didn't go through. Too many people clogging up the network, no doubt. She'd sipped and tried to compose her words. Because she had to tell him everything. She wanted no secrets between them, no matter how illicit and fantasy-driven. She had to confess her ongoing dreams about the mysterious Ross before she agreed to set a wedding date.

When her scalp tingled with a 'someone's watching' sensation, she glanced over and caught the eye of the tallest, handsomest Viking of a man she'd ever seen. His thick, dark-blond hair was tied back with a strip of dark leather. A light red, neatly trimmed beard covered his square jaw. He smiled straight at her, as he carried on a conversation with someone across from him, someone just out of her line of vision.

She turned back to the bar, her head humming with likely too much booze and the image of the guy ogling her – the guy she now recognized as the tall, handsome stud who'd been driving her darkest, most erotic dreams. Her hands twisted together in her lap. She fiddled with the strap of her purse, with her sunglasses, the tasteful drop earrings Austin had given her a few weeks ago.

This was her own damn fault. She'd asked Austin what it meant, how it felt, how it *worked*, for Christ's sake. How they'd fuck her, together, between them. Her scalp tingled and she chanced another peek over her shoulder.

The man who'd been her husband's close friend and confidant, his partner in female conquests, and the now populated her most fevered fantasies, was sitting across a busy bar, in Denver, fucking, Colorado. That was him, in all his tall, blond, bearded, tempting glory. He was staring at her, his cornflower blue eyes sparkling with a kind of mischief and more than a touch of flirtation. She turned away fast, so fast her hair whapped her in the face, making her eyes sting. Or at least something made her eyes sting.

Dear God. What was she going to do now? Where in the hell was Austin?

Her phone dinged and she stood, looking for the one face she needed to see more than anything. When she spotted him, her knees got wobbly, mainly because he was standing at the table where Ross still sat, one elbow on the table, smirking at her.

Keeping her eyes on Austin, she made her way over and wrapped her arms around his waist, pressing her face to his chest. When she turned to meet the man who'd been staring at her earlier, reality hit. This handsome hunk of perfection who slowly rose to his feet, smiling at her, blue eyes twinkling was, indeed, none other than Ross Hoffman, legitimate brew master and one of the most attractive men she'd seen in a long time. His was a subtle, slow-moving handsomeness — one that made her blink when confronted by it. Different from Austin's overt, model-like attractiveness. In tandem, standing shoulder to shoulder, the two men were like dark and light, yin and yang. Between them, they emitted a sort of energy that made the sparse hairs on her arms stand up.

Evelyn felt herself blush all the way up from her heels

to her scalp as the intimate details of her most recent wet dream featuring him, and Austin, and her together filled her consciousness.

"Pleased to meet you." She held out a hand, eager, yet shivering slightly when he touched her.

"The pleasure is entirely mine," he said, taking her hand and grazing her knuckles with his lips, keeping his gaze on hers the entire time. The slight sibilance of his German accent made her swallow hard as he held on to her hand a beat longer than was probably necessary. She couldn't stop staring at him — the amazing span of his shoulders, the length of his legs, the way his Adam's apple was moving as if he, too, were swallowing against a dry mouth.

Austin stayed silent, giving them time to size each other up, take each other all the way in. When Ross finally let go of her hand, it dropped to her side, her arm floppy and awkward. Austin touched her hair, tucking a stray lock of it behind her ear, letting his fingertips play along the hanging earring — a soft, gentle gesture that might has well been a stroke to her achingly hard nipple, or her plump, eager clit. She sensed her legs giving way, while both men gazed at her, their intentions as clear as if she were watching a porn loop of the three of them on continuous, alarming replay.

She looked from one to the other, heart pounding in her ears. They stood in a strange tableau, the threesome-ness of it making her dizzy, and so unbelievably horny she could barely catch her breath. Finally, needing something familiar to get her through the moment, she grabbed Austin's arm. "Honey, I... I need to talk to you." She glanced over at Ross. He was still smiling, but he'd backed away a bit, to give them room. "Alone," she whispered.

Was this how it would be? This odd dance of space, of each man attempting to show he could do it — could share her attention in some way that might suit them both? They were both so compelling, intriguing — so very alpha — she sensed herself slipping into a warm, wonderful place inside her head.

Austin put his arm around her and pressed his lips to her cheek.

"Hang on a second. I'm gonna hit the head. You guys talk amongst yourselves." He leaned in closer, kissed her neck right below her ear, making her shiver all over. "Get to know him, my love. You won't be disappointed." She drew back staring at him, her pulse racing. His calm, boyish, beloved smile relaxed her. "See where it takes you," he said, for her ears only.

She watched him walk away, then turned to face the other man, struck all over again by the unreal beauty of him. When he actually reddened under her scrutiny, she smiled and took a seat across from him, forcing herself to be calm and see where this might take her.

The minute he'd sensed the obvious chemistry between the two people he loved, Austin had known what he had to do. The longer he'd sat with Ross, the more he'd realized how much he'd missed their connection — their odd mix of competition and companionship, of friendship and rivalry for the affection of the women around them. It was nuts, but he'd felt he had a moment to capture, and needed some time to gather his thoughts and figure out a couple of things. One, if he could handle it and two, if he could convince her to try it.

Because, at that moment, right there in an overcrowded bar in Denver, nothing seemed more perfect in his universe than to be with them both.

He stared at his reflection in the mirror, splashed water on his face, and made a decision. How he'd gone from frustrated and furious and convinced he should tell her to move the hell out if she wouldn't commit, to horny and contemplating a threesome escaped him. But before he chickened out, he sent a quick text to Ross.

Make an excuse and meet me in the back hallway.

Then he sat on the bench outside the men's room, his

heart pounding, his stomach in knots.

The sight of his tall, handsome friend relaxed him immediately. He kept his voice low.

"Let's all go back to our suite. We can eat and talk there. In private."

Ross sat, staring straight ahead. "What exactly do you want to talk about?"

"I think you know."

Ross turned to look at him, disbelief in his deep blue eyes. "You are certifiably insane."

"What? You don't find her attractive?"

"If you were not my very good friend, you would surely gut me for what I'm thinking about her right now."

Austin smiled. Maybe this could be the answer. He was fine with it at least on the surface. It would be good for her. It would bring her happiness and that was one thing he'd do most anything to bring her right now. It would also bring his friend back and who knew, maybe he could even convince Ross to join him at the brewery.

Nothing had ever seemed more right. His innate need to fix, to make things better, to calm the fever of her recent frustration combined with his sheer happiness at seeing his old friend again. Which perhaps made him exactly as insane as Ross suggested. Austin sucked in a breath and plunged ahead.

"Good. Hold that thought. Go ahead, I'll be right over." He watched Ross walk away, gathered his composure, and joined them, smiling at the sight of the two people he cared about eyeing each other in a way that felt utterly and completely...

Perfect.

He shoved down the small voice of protest, the part of him that demanded sole possession of her. He was sharing her body, perhaps a bit of her heart, but he would manage it. He had to. She wanted it. He'd known as much from the first time they'd engaged in that hot fantasy. He trusted her and how she felt about him. Having Ross in their mutual presence made that clear, in a way even he couldn't explain to himself. He sat quickly, planting a long, lingering kiss on her lips. She broke away and glanced at Ross, pulling her hair into a ponytail, her face flushed.

"So," he said, leaning forward toward Ross while keeping his hand on her thigh. "You two get to know much about each other yet?"

"Not nearly enough," Ross said, finishing his drink and flashing his patented smirk. Austin ignored him and focused on Evelyn.

"Tell me something about him," he said, running his finger along her jaw line.

"Um, let's see"—she picked up her beer and feigned deep thought—"he thinks he is God's gift to women."

"Ha, darling, this is a fact, not a mere thought," Ross said, laughter in his voice.

"And...," she went on, also ignoring the nearly un-ignorable man across the table from them. "He's considering working for that super jerk, Brad Jefferson."

"I heard that," Austin said, leaning on his elbow, his attention fully on her. She smiled at him. "What should we advise him about that?"

"We aren't advising him on shit," she declared, flipping her ponytail over her shoulder and giving Ross a quick, flirty glance. "He's a big boy, I think. He can make his own decisions about where to work."

"Agreed," Austin said, tracing the outline of her full lips with his fingertip. "How do we feel about trying to pay him more to work for us?"

"I don't think we can afford him, my love," she said, sipping her beer and trailing her fingers down her neck, a sure sign she was good and horny. Exactly the way he wanted her.

"Oh, we might could work something out," he said, licking his lips as he watched her touch the tops of her breasts, before sliding her fingers into her hair, pulling out her ponytail slowly.

At that moment, he glanced over at Ross. The man's jaw was hanging open like a teenager's. This gave him a moment's pause. Ross did not impress easily and seeing him this gobsmacked over his fiancée caused a slight tickle of worry, a minor red flag to wave in his brain.

"She's right," Ross said, his voice neutral. "You can't afford me."

"Let's go," he whispered in her ear. "I can't take another minute of these damn crowds."

"Okay, but what about…uh…your friend over there? The tall blond with the Viking beard with his mouth hanging open?" She gave him a significant look.

"Oh, he's invited. We have a lot of catching up to do."

Her eyes took on a hard edge again. He had a brief moment of panic but cupped her neck, bringing her face near his.

"I'm only proposing a nice, quiet dinner between friends. In our suite. Away from the maddening throng." He brushed his lips over hers. "I love you. Relax. See where it takes you," he repeated the odd phrase. She pulled back, her face red, clutching his thigh. He held her gaze. When she glanced across the table at Ross, Austin could practically see the sparks crackling between them.

He hesitated, recalculating the possible costs if this thing went pear-shaped.

She sucked in a breath. "Okay. Let's go."

Austin smiled, threw some money down on the table, and took her hand.

Chapter Fifteen

The warm water caressed Evelyn's skin as the lilac and vanilla infused steam soothed her rattled nerves. She smiled and sank deeper in the massive tub, holding her breath as her hair billowed out above her. She emerged to the sound of loud, masculine laughter from the next room. Ross' deep, accented voice, then Austin's own raspy reply made her tingly all over.

Weird.

But yet, somehow, exactly right.

"Honey?" she called out. Austin poked his head around the corner. The relief she felt on seeing his grin made her grateful all over again for him. "Can I get some of whatever you guys are drinking?"

She sank back below the water again, but when she sat back up she found the man who stood holding a large bottle of rare Imperial stout was not Austin, but Ross. Clad in only his jeans. She tried not to stare.

He was physical perfection writ large, with wide shoulders tapered to a narrow waist. A light dusting of yellowish red hair covered his muscular upper chest. His legs were impossibly long. And that face—it was as if chiseled from granite, with high cheekbones, large bright blue eyes and topped with a shock of shoulder-length thick blond hair. She curled her fingers into fists under the water against the urge to plunge them into it or to touch the light beard on his jaw and slipped back beneath the bubbles.

When she reemerged, his smile had grown. He held up the bottle.

"Austin said you were thirsty. And I need a shower. Do

you mind?" His slight accent only added to his appeal.

"So, do I have to get out for that bottle or are you going to bring it here?" Her face heated up at her boldness. This had to be the strangest day of her life, but it was beginning to take on a tinge of reality, of a sort of flirty, yet comfortable level of appropriateness between the three of them that she'd only dreamed might be possible. Ross walked over and knelt, trailing a long, elegant finger through the water.

She took the bottle from him and drank, letting the rich, roasty essence and alcohol burn set fire to her already zinging nerve endings. He stayed put, staring at her. A bit of the dark brew dripped down her neck. He touched it and when he placed his fingertip near her lips, she licked it off, shivering as she attempted to keep her painfully hard nipples hidden by sliding farther down into the water.

Oh my sweet God. Could this actually be happening? Did she want it to happen? Would it lead anywhere good?

She needed Austin, wanted his voice, his hands, and his reassuring presence.

"You are very beautiful. My friend is a lucky man," Ross said before he stood and stepped out of his jeans. She averted her gaze at first, then took another deep draft of the rare brew and allowed herself a good look at all of him. The muscles of his thighs and ass were as sculpted as the ones in his chest. She watched him lean into the slate-tiled space to gauge the water temperature. When he slipped underneath the spray and turned to face her, she had to bite back a gasp. His cock was just as impressive as Austin had led her to believe, matching the large, over-the-top rest of him. And it was ready for action.

She slid back under the water to keep from embarrassing herself. She'd never been averse to trying new things, sexually speaking. She'd even spent a few weeks visiting BDSM clubs when she'd dated Trent and had enjoyed its forbidden eroticism. Her own rampant fantasy life in the past weeks, during the drought of actual sex with Austin, had led to exactly this moment. It was no time to chicken out.

Something tapped her on the top of the head, so she rose into the now even steamier room. Austin knelt behind her, his hands on her shoulders — he'd put the bottle on the floor next to the tub.

"Thanks." She let him work through her tension. Tears stung her eyes for some odd reason. "I so don't deserve you."

"Huh. Funny how you're the last one to figure that out."

She sighed and lay against the tub's tall back once again. He made his way down her front to each breast, cupping them, flicking a thumb over her nipples. When he tilted her face back and up, his beautiful, lovely mouth worked its familiar magic. She had missed him so much and had no one to blame but herself for the iceberg between them. She broke away, needing to tell him.

"Seriously, Austin. You were right."

He cocked an eyebrow at her. "Hang on, need to get my recording device. This is an historic Gettysburg Address-style moment."

"Shut up and listen."

He resumed working her shoulders and neck, adding his lips to the mix, forcing the warmth from her face straight down between her legs. When she looked up at Ross' tall form still encased in the shower, shampoo coursing down his body, it made her whole body zing in response as internal heat rose from somewhere around the middle of her back, spreading outward and making her lick her lips.

"Really, Austin, you're right. I'm being a stubborn, irrational bitch. I'm going to try to be better." She grabbed his hand. "Let's set a date. For a wedding."

His mouth tickled her ear. "Okay, but first I need to ask you something else. About someone, actually." His fingers took hold of both nipples, making her arch up at the same moment the steam cleared enough for her to get a nice long look at Ross, who stared straight at them through the steamy glass wall. "I love you, Evelyn. I will always love you." Austin's lips found her neck again, making her shiver.

He interspersed his commentary with nibbles and light suction along her shoulders. "I want you to be happy."

She sat up, sloshing water over the side of the tub. Austin moved around beside her so he could look her in the eyes.

"I am happy. You make me happy. I just, I don't know, lost it for a while, but I'm good. Honestly."

He smiled and she relaxed back again, allowing the realization of what he was about to suggest burn a hole in her libido. She wanted him to say it—to ask her if she wanted it.

He leaned forward, tilting her chin up so she was looking straight at Ross on the other side of the glass barrier. She glanced over to find Austin staring at Ross, as well, a knowing smile playing around his lips. "Why don't we see where this takes us?" He ran a finger down her cheek. "Something tells me I'm not the only one of us to consider this option. I know you, Evelyn, and I know what you want." He took her hand and pressed it between her legs, making her gasp and close her eyes. "I want you to be happy and I think I know how to do that." He bit down on her shoulder. She gasped and opened her eyes, taking in the vision of Ross, hand on his giant cock, propping himself against the glass with his other, his gaze right on hers.

She reached back and pulled Austin around to her side, covered his mouth with hers, and slipped her fingers into his coarse hair, loving everything about the man who'd changed her whole life, in spite of her own stubborn resistance. He broke the kiss, smiling at her, soothing her in the way only he had. "I love you, Evelyn." He held out his hand. She put hers in it and rose, the water sluicing off her body, aware of both sets of male eyes on her.

Chapter Sixteen

Exhaustion stole over Ross as he stood under the scalding hot stream of water. The endless rounds of negotiations with Jefferson after a whirlwind trip from Europe, and now the long, late hours necessary for a huge beer fest had taken their toll. He'd been operating on about four hours of sleep for the last couple of nights. The water beat against his skin. He kept his head lowered, trying to ignore the pulsing in his cock that had refused to soften ever since he'd touched Evelyn's cheek. Only to catch that drip of beer, of course.

He'd admit to a bit of jealousy over the fact that Austin would fall so hard for a woman. They'd been well matched in the pussy-chasing, non-committing thing at one time. He'd also admit to avoiding communication with Austin for the past few years, unable to admit even to himself how much he missed Austin's company.

But now he fully understood. And Evelyn Benedict's magnificence left him speechless. He rinsed the shampoo from his hair and turned his face up to accept the deluge. Focusing on why Austin had brought him here—to talk, he'd claimed. Which had been why Ross had sought the man out in the first place, anyway. To talk.

He was able to make out Austin pulling Evelyn from the big tub and helping her out onto the warmed marble floor. As he watched, mesmerized by the sheer perfection of the woman's hourglass figure, Austin began to gently dry her skin. Ross gulped as Austin dropped the towel, met his eyes through the shower's steam, then picked Evelyn up and set her on the granite vanity top.

Shocked, but perhaps not completely surprised, Ross kept

watching the way he knew he was meant to as Austin laid a kiss on her that made Ross want to do the same thing so badly his dick sprang back to attention. He grunted and had to prop both hands on the glass wall to keep from toppling over. Austin kissed his way down the long, porcelain line of Evelyn's neck as she leaned back, lips open. He kissed her shoulders, her collarbone, then cupped one full breast in one hand while using his other one between her legs.

The shower water muffled all sounds, but Ross could definitely detect his own breathing getting short as his pulse raced and his skin tingled all over. Evelyn's body arched back which forced her hips forward, close to Austin, who had leaned into to suck one of her firm, large nipples into his mouth.

She had her fingers coiled in his dark hair and her hips were thrusting now, moving fast against Austin's hand. Her red-toenailed feet wound around Austin's bare legs, tugging him closer. Ross had to swipe at the glass again with one hand as he gripped his cock with the other, mesmerized, fascinated, and hornier than he'd been in a damn long time, watching the show right outside his shower.

He could see Austin's biceps and triceps flex as he fingered his woman to an orgasm that broke well through the sound of the water still beating on his back. Ross groaned and moved his hand faster at the sight of the woman's beautifully flushed face, haloed by curling wisps of her golden blonde hair. She was still moving, still moaning as Ross watched, unable to rip his gaze from her.

In the meantime, Austin had divested himself of his shorts. The familiar contours of the other man's ass made Ross smile with familiarity. He and Austin had a firm hold on their own heterosexuality but had double-teamed enough women in their day that Ross felt he knew Austin's musculature almost as well as his own.

At that moment, Austin turned and caught his eye, making Ross stumble back, afraid of what the man might do next. He wasn't ready. He wasn't worthy to share Evelyn and he was starting to feel uneasy about this whole thing, because one thing he wanted to do right then was to grab her, toss her over his shoulder, throw her down on the bed, and take his own damn turn.

"*No*," he mouthed, letting go of his cock and watching as the steam cut off his view of the two of them. As he leaned back against the shower tile, shaking all over, he reminded himself of the many times a girl had requested this — that one of them fuck her while the other one watched. It was no big deal.

And yet, somehow, all of a sudden, it was.

He reached out to swipe at the steam, unable to stop himself. Evelyn was on her feet again and was kissing Austin with the sort of passion that gave Ross a fresh jolt of jealousy. With a glance back at Ross, Austin pulled away from Evelyn and said something to her that Ross couldn't hear. He reached up and wiped what looked to be a tear off her face, kissed her gently then turned her around.

Evelyn gripped the edge of the vanity top and arched her back, exposing her ass while Austin leaned over her and cupped both her breasts, still nibbling her neck. With a gulp, Ross took a step forward and watched as his oldest friend and confidant, and the woman he'd spent a solid fifteen minutes entertaining the sort of fantasies about that would make a sailor blush, moved in a sinuous, erotic rhythm. Their flesh looked sweaty and slippery as they fucked, not four feet from Ross' amazed eyes.

He could see Austin's dick sliding in and out of her body, watched as the man gripped her hips and started pounding into her, groaning loud enough so Ross heard it clearly over the sound of the shower. Evelyn's full breasts jiggled with every hard thrust. She threw her head back at one point and Austin grabbed onto her hair, pulling hard and making her cry out. But she didn't stop meeting his every thrust forward with her own back into him. Her plump, luscious lips were parted, her eyes closed, and when they came with a cry, Ross joined them with a shudder, one hand propped on the glass, the other now coated in his own fluid. He let go of himself and kept watching as Austin pulled Evelyn up, kissing her neck and shoulders again as their bodies stayed connected, still moving in a primal way.

"I love you, so much," Austin said, loud enough for Ross to hear it. Ross opened eyes he hadn't realized he'd closed and met his friend's deep green gaze. Evelyn moved forward, releasing Austin's cock which was still hard and gleaming. Ross swallowed hard, trying to deny his own urge, his base need to leap out of here and take her to yet another depth of sensuality, but with him this time, while Austin watched.

"No," he said out loud, then turned to face the shower, letting the heat and noise of it fill his senses once more, hoping to drown out the new drumbeat of need in his chest. Damn Austin and his show-off ways. What the fuck was he thinking?

When Ross turned around to face the bathroom again, Evelyn was gone, but Austin was there, a towel around his waist, staring holes into him. With a sigh, he turned off the water and opened the door. Austin handed him a towel, never taking his eyes off Ross'.

"I don't know what you're playing at here, but..."

Austin held up a hand to stop him, slipped off his towel and ducked into the shower behind Ross.

"I'm not going to do this."

"I know," Austin said with a smile as he turned the water back on full blast. "Just go talk to her. Get to know her. I need a shower. We'll eat something after."

Ross nodded, his throat closed up at the thought of being around Evelyn without Austin watching.

"It's all right, Hoffman," Austin insisted before he shut the glass door. "I trust you. And I want the two of you to get to know each other. That's all."

Ross nodded slowly, dried his hair a few seconds with the towel then wrapped it around his waist. His heart was thudding so loud it almost hurt. And, of course, his dick was not cooperating either. It remained rigid, practically quivering in anticipation.

"No," Ross repeated for the third time, staring down at the stupid bulge in the towel until it finally subsided.

Chapter Seventeen

Stop it. You told him to do it. Do not be that woman. One who says yes when she means no.

Evelyn's heart pounded and her mouth was all dried out. A dark shroud of reality had stolen over her as she'd crept out of the bathroom after putting on that blatant show for Ross. And now, if she were a hundred percent honest with herself, she still felt it.

Threesomes, she thought for the zillionth time, were best left to fantasy. It was simply too strange, too unnatural. These were serious alpha males, she reminded herself as she brushed her wet hair, her thighs still quivering from exertion and post-orgasmic excitement. She put the brush down and stared at herself in the mirror over the hotel's desk. Her face was flushed red, her pupils dilated, the tops of her shoulders covered in a sheen of sweat. She trailed her fingers down her neck to her tops of her breasts, visible above the towel she'd wrapped around herself, admitting that she did, indeed, want more.

She wanted Ross.

God, she was sick. A pervert of the highest order.

But, yeah. She wanted them both.

The sound of a male throat clearing behind her made her drop the hairbrush. It clunked the side of the glass someone had been drinking out of and had set too near the edge. The glass toppled in slow motion, landing on her big toe and sloshing a couple of ounces of dark beer onto the hotel rug. She stared down at it, then up into the mirror, meeting the very blue eyes she'd been wishing she could see. But even as she admitted to an overt horny thrill of excitement, she clenched her jaw against it. She and Ross stared at each other, using the mirror as a buffer for a few seconds.

"I should go." Ross' German-inflected voice hit her ear, making her shiver. He blinked. She turned to face him when a sharp rap and a "Room service" call hit her ears. Ross grabbed his jeans and ducked back into the bathroom, leaving her to deal with the rolling tray of food and drink, the check and the slight 'have a nice evening' smirk from the waiter.

She picked up a piece of toast—they'd all been craving breakfast food and this hotel served it twenty-four-seven for an outrageous amount of money. But it tasted like warm, buttered cardboard so she put it back down and crossed her arms, cupping her opposite elbows in her palms. Ross emerged, redressed, his hair pulled back in that leather tie once more. She stared outright at his statuesque perfection—the high cheekbones, the soft, reddish curls of his beard.

She sensed herself backing away from him, in a movement that felt more like self-protection than anything. Her legs made contact with a chair and she dropped into it.

"Nice meeting you, Evelyn."

Ross caressed her name with his lips and tongue in a way that made her shivery with her own inability to take this to the next level. One she knew she wanted, but was somehow now unable to fulfill.

He walked over to her and crouched down so he was at her eye level. She sucked in a breath against the raw, visceral need that rushed through her then—a need to reach for him, to pull him close and into their circle.

But no. That's not fair to Austin. Or is it? Wasn't this kind of his idea in the first place?

She found herself recalling some of the wilder moments Austin had told her about—the just shy-of-orgy situations he and this tall, gorgeous, hunk of Nordic perfection got into together.

But she resisted it. Ross touched her lips with his rough

fingertip and smiled.

She smiled back. "Sorry," she said, her voice croaky. "I'm just not...um..."

"Shh," he said, leaning toward her, filling her vision and world with his magnificence before pecking her cheek and standing. "I understand. Thanks for..." He made a gesture in the direction of the bathroom where she and Austin had fucked, knowing full well he'd been watching. Evelyn bit her lip and nodded, then stood and ran for Austin who'd emerged from the bathroom, rubbing his hair. She buried her face in Austin's chest, mortified, horrified at her wild, careening fantasies, wishing Ross would just go. But willing him to stay.

Austin held her close against his bare skin. She could tell from the vibrations in his chest he was talking, but she shut her ears to it, sickened by her own lame behavior and needing more space to process this. Whatever the hell 'this' was.

She must have slept, because the room was dark when she next opened her eyes. Austin lay next to her, awake, his green eyes shimmering with emotion. She put her hand alongside his cheek. "I'm sorry, honey."

He took her hand and put it to his lips. "It's all right. I love you, you know that, right? No matter what...I love you."

"Yes, I know that." She swallowed hard. "But tell me more about Ross."

Chapter Eighteen

By the time they made it to the convention hall the next afternoon, the place had filled with craft beer fans, eager to see the long-awaited awards for each category. After the Brewers Association president announced the last of the one hundred-plus awards for individual brews, the crowd would be prepped for the Big Ones — Small, Mid-Sized and Large Brewery of the Year.

They'd entered Fitzgerald in the mid-sized category although it was a bit of a stretch. Evelyn and Austin had gathered the year-over-year sales data, plugged in all the necessary media coverage and growth strategies and had sent the thing off without a thought to collecting an award — or so they both claimed.

Evelyn smiled as she watched Austin greet fans and media gathered near the brewer's entrance to the hall. When she caught sight of Ross, her skin tingled.

In the last twenty-four hours, her life had flipped totally sideways, upside down, and inside out. In spite of Austin's insistence that this was about what she wanted, she now knew in her heart he'd be happier if they were all together. It would complete him, somehow. It was up to her to make that happen. She held the key to their happiness in her trembling, uncertain hands.

"You are the most beautiful woman in here," Ross whispered as the steep escalator took them to the upper floor, where the other brewery VIPs gathered, milled around, drank beer and chatted, everyone pretending not to be as nervous as they all were.

"Flatterer," she whispered back. Austin turned and

smiled down at them both before stepping off the top step. He turned at the last minute, wrapped his arm around her waist, and tugged her close.

"I love you." Austin grinned, nuzzling her neck.

"Cut that shit out, you damn lovebirds."

Evelyn laughed as Greg Zeller put his arms around them both. As owner of Michigan's largest and most successful brewery, Zeller always made a big show of being worried about Fitzgerald, after his initial dismissal of them as a one-off.

Evelyn shot him a fake angry glare. "What? It's the secret of our brewing success. You should try it." She smacked Austin's ass and moved away but not before she heard Zeller laugh and shout to her retreating back.

"With you? Name the day, my darling."

She flipped him off on her way back through the growing throng, catching sight of Ross as he accepted a beer from his new boss, the infamous Brad Jefferson. He raised his glass to her.

She frowned, and made her way in a different direction, her face burning at her own rudeness.

After nearly an hour of schmoozing and random, forgettable discussions, Evelyn's head was pounding. She slumped against the wall behind the podium where the awards would be announced and closed her eyes.

"Hey, there you are."

She opened her eyes and saw Ross with a water bottle. Austin was on her other side, smiling his beautiful smile. She focused on him and sipped.

She hated to admit how comforted she felt by this — by the laser-beam attention of both of these men. Surely she didn't deserve this. And she could possibly serve as a catalyst for something bad — what if they got jealous of each other and the time they spent with her…pleasing her…fucking her?

Oh God in heaven, Evelyn Benedict, snap the hell out of it. That is not ever going to happen.

Panic surged through her, making the meager breakfast

she'd managed to choke down threaten to make another appearance. "I gotta sit, boys." The dynamic of this — of two strong men attentive to her every need — made her dizzy with the possibility and the potential responsibility.

She leaned into Austin's ear as they walked down the wide aisles between the hundreds of beer booths. The place was still empty but that would change, quickly, the second the doors opened to welcome the day's beer expo visitors. "Thank you." He shot her that killer grin, the one she'd seen the first time in a back hallway of a beer store, that damn smile that had melted her soul on the spot.

He knew what she was talking about, no need to explain. He gave her a squeeze.

"Anything for you." His normally rough voice sounded hoarser than usual. She glanced up at him, as the eager public flowed around them. Her heart pounded. She needed him to understand, now.

"No, Austin. Thank you. For everything. I—" She looked down. The teeming, raucous crowd faded. She looked up and cradled his face between her shaking hands. "I want to be with you. Forever. I'm sorry I've been so prickly and unreasonable. You really are the best thing that ever happened to me." His tense face softened and he gathered her in his arms, kissing her with a fierce passion that turned her knees to jelly. She sensed the room filling up, heard the wolf whistles and cat calls but didn't care. When she broke away, he brushed the tears off her face.

"We're nothing if we aren't together," he said, sending her heart into palpitations.

"Oh my God, I'm gonna be ill." Zeller strode by and yanked Evelyn away, pulling her laughing and only half protesting to sit by him. She looked back and saw them, her men, standing together. The dark and the light, the long, lean beauty of Austin side by side with the strong, broad, rugged handsome of Ross. Their shoulders touched and they moved apart. Ross had to sit with his new employer, she knew. She broke from Zeller's drunken grasp and found two seats, accepted a beer from someone next to her and settled in for the awards.

Austin's head pounded in a wholly unwelcome and familiar way. He plucked a couple of pain pills from his pocket and dry swallowed them, unwilling to admit that he would just as soon be lying in a completely dark and silent room as sitting here, but it had to be done. This was his moment. He felt it. After accepting two awards for beers, one for their black lager and another for an experimental old ale, he sat, staring straight ahead, willing the pain away, Evelyn's hand clutched in his.

"You all right?"

He shook his head.

"No. I'm not gonna make the tap take-over after party, Evelyn. I'm sorry."

"Well, not to make it worse but—" She jerked her chin, making him turn. His father stood at the back, looking about as out of place as a human could look, staring straight at him. Max Fitzgerald waved and gave them a jaunty thumbs-up.

"Holy shit." He closed his eyes.

"It's okay." She rubbed his thigh.

He felt the room narrow a little more.

"Honey?"

His gut churned. There were two more awards, one for Distributor of the Year, one for the Pro-Am competition, before the brewery awards were announced. He winced and put a hand on Evelyn's leg. "I may not make the tap takeover." They'd contracted with a local famous beer bar to replace ten of their tap handles with Fitzgerald's brews. It would be a gigantic party for the public, featuring their best-selling products. "It's a bad one." He'd been getting migraine-level headaches off and on for years, but usually a few hours of sleep did the trick. This one had a crappy sense of timing, however.

She kissed his cheek. "It's okay. We'll get through this,

then get you back to the hotel." Worry etched her face.

"I'm sorry," he whispered. The skin on the back of his neck prickled. Which meant that his father was staring at him, at them, at her. The man hadn't spared a civil word for him since…well, since he'd paid him off for his initial investment then turned around and started living with Evelyn.

He'd decided that, until they acknowledged how happy he was with Evelyn and with his brewery, his parents could sit in their godforsaken too-big house and rot. Their own stupid close-mindedness has cost them one son already. But the tickling reminders that he no longer had his parents to fall back on did not help ease the vise currently crushing his temples.

He'd planned to break that news to Evelyn once they returned to Michigan. Not that he was worried about her reaction—he knew she'd welcome independence from the elder Fitzgeralds' overwhelming disapproval. And he'd had the sense to wait until the year his trust fund released completely to him so he could at least maintain his mortgage, groceries, and the basics of living.

The addition of the Ross wrinkle had not been something he'd anticipated, however. And the necessary machinations of the night before—the unbelievably hot hook-up Evelyn had encouraged him to have while Ross watched, then her seeming inability to go any further with it—combined with the ongoing, run-of-the-mill stress he was under— no wonder his body was rebelling by ushering in what promised to be a real whopper of a brain squeeze.

"Here we go." Ross' accent tickled his ear. He smiled at the sight of the other man, who'd thrown off his new boss and come to sit beside them for this last part of the awards. He tightened his grip on Evelyn's hand. They were a long shot at best, an impossibility at worst.

The Small Brewery of the Year accepted their award, had pictures snapped, then all eyes turned to the man at the podium. He launched into a brief history of the mid-size brewery winner and Austin's headache clamped down, making it hard to hear. Evelyn gasped at one point, then wrapped her arms around his neck. His eyes popped open before he realized he'd closed them when he heard, "Fitzgerald Brewing Company, Grand Rapids, Michigan."

They'd done it. He and Evelyn had truly made this happen.

He grinned, and without thinking, tugged Ross to his feet along with Evelyn.

"*Nein.*" The tall, handsome German shook his head. "Go with Evelyn. Congratulations, my friend. You deserve it."

Evelyn pulled him out into the aisle, and they made their way down, accepted the trophy, and had photos taken, making lights dance around in the corners of his vision. He could barely hear and his heart pounded in his ears as he smiled, accepted kudos, and tried to find Ross in the crowd. Finally, he appeared and put his arms around him and Evelyn as they smiled for more pictures.

Austin sensed his vision narrowing from the outside in. Ross' grip tightened around him. "Get me out of here," he whispered.

He barely remembered the cab ride back to the hotel but could hear the whispered conversation between them. Evelyn wanted to go to the ER. Ross advised water and sleep. "He used to get this way in Germany. It will fade. He'll be fine." Evelyn's hand touched his face and he leaned into it.

"I love you," he mumbled as they half carried him to the elevator and down the hall to their suite. Evelyn's lips were against his ear. He had a panic moment and grabbed her hand. "I'm sorry, honey. I...oh, dear Christ, it hurts." He lay back. "Turn off the lights when you go." He was asleep before the lights faded.

Chapter Nineteen

Ross leaned his head against the cool taxi window. This day had been such a whirlwind, so incredibly intense, almost more than he could handle. He sucked in a breath and had to sit on his hands to keep from pulling Evelyn close. He watched as she rolled her head around, trying to relax for about two seconds before her phone rang. Frowning, she answered it.

"Hey. Everything set?"

Ross continued to study the Denver metroscape, trying to come to terms with the depth of his feelings for the woman next to him and his own desire to have her, while keeping Austin as his friend. When tension crept into her voice, Ross started paying attention.

"What do you mean the kegs are 'bad'? What the fuck is that about?" Unable to stop himself, he put a hand on her leg. She glared at him. "Listen, I'm about three minutes away. Tell the manager to turn them off, all of them. I won't serve them if...what? No, God damn it! Put Kyle on the line."

When the taxi pulled up at the beer bar where Fitzgerald was supposed to be featuring their brews, she jumped out and ran through the crowd. Ross paid and followed her, attempting not to be rude to the many people who waylaid him with congratulations on his new job. Out of the corner of his eye, he noted two five-tap vans with the bar's logo emblazoned on the side parked toward the back of the lot.

By the time he joined her in the huge, smelly basement where ten Fitzgerald kegs were lined up and tapped, she was ripping the bar manager a new asshole, her voice rising every second. Ross touched her shoulder and she flinched but stopped yelling and took a breath. He jumped in before she got enough air in her lungs to resume the reaming session.

"Unhook them all, now," he said. The manager made a feeble protest. "What part of 'now' don't you get?" Ross used his very best intimidating stare, one he knew damn good and well would melt the resolve of the strongest personality. "Your lines are filthy. I can see them from here."

He pointed to the plastic tubing that ran from the kegs up through a hole in the ceiling. What should be clean-flowing beer looked murky, cloudy and disgusting. "I don't know what your line-cleaning schedule is, but you obviously need to change it. In the meantime, Fitzgerald's will not tolerate you ruining their beer by sending it through these tubes full of shit. Unhook them." The man gestured and two waiters started unhooking the kegs. "Well done. Now, get the keys to those vans, pull them around front so we can hook the kegs up out there. You'll announce that the first round is on the house. You have fifteen minutes to make this happen or I call the health department."

He put a hand up to stop Evelyn from jumping in and kept his gazed fixed on the smarmy manager. Her anger roiled around the room and he knew he'd be dealing with that later, but for now, this potential disaster had to be averted and fast.

Within twenty minutes, the front parking lot and large patio were full of happy beer drinkers with fresh glasses of clean-flowing Fitzgerald brews in their hands. The owner of the bar had shown up and fallen all over himself apologizing to Evelyn. Ross watched, proud of her ability to handle the guy diplomatically. She dropped into a seat next to him and pushed her hair off her face.

"Nice save, Hoffman."

He sipped, not looking at her. "*Ja.*"

"But don't ever cut me off like that again or you'll pay

for it."

"*Ja.*" He kept watching the happy throng of drinkers. She poked his side. Her blue eyes sparkled with restrained humor. "I just did what Austin would have done."

"Well, maybe." She moved away from him a few inches. He reached out and pulled her back, keeping his arm around her, not giving a shit who saw them as he leaned into her ear.

"It's fixed. Just go with it, no?" No longer willing to resist the compulsion to make the first move, he bit her earlobe. When she shivered, a wave of pure lust washed over him, making his cock slam against the back of his zipper. He kept whispering. "I could fuck you right now, you know? And I think you'd like that, wouldn't you, Evelyn?" He tightened his grip on her shoulders, could smell her perfume as it became tinged with a hint of her own need.

She shuddered as he nuzzled her neck. The dark corner he'd found on purpose served him well as he trailed his hand down her shoulder and touched the top of her full breasts. "Mmm-hmm... Let's go back to the basement. I need to show you something." Ross' whole body was clenched tight with the urge to prove something to her, even as a tinge of disloyalty hovered, reminding him that he had not received permission from Austin for any of this.

"Evelyn?" A deep voice pierced his fuzzy brain and she leapt away from him as if burned. Confused and bone-deep horny, Ross attempted to process that a man who looked like a sixty-year-old version of Austin Fitzgerald stood in front of them, glass in hand.

"Mr. Fitzgerald." Evelyn shook his outstretched hand. The deep freeze between them was palpable. "What a surprise." The older version of Austin sipped his beer and appraised them.

"I see that." The man's voice was lighter than Austin's and his eyes were cold and calculating. But after about thirty seconds, he seemed to relax, or give up. He grabbed Evelyn's hand again. "Congratulations. You guys have really done it."

"Thanks." She kept her voice neutral, Ross noted. He stood beside her, held out his hand. "Oh, um, Maxwell Fitzgerald, this is Ross. Ross Hoffman."

"Ah, yes, Austin's friend from Germany."

"*Ja.*" He couldn't think of anything more to say. Max's negative energy oozed around them, poisoning what had turned into a great party. He found himself wanting to put an arm around her, to protect her from this asshole. But he didn't. The silence was awkward at best.

"Where's Austin?"

"He's not well. Had to rest back at the hotel."

Ross sensed her anxiety at this encounter as if it were a live thing he wanted to strangle, to banish from her forever.

"Ah. Headache?"

"Yes. A bad one."

"Yes, he had them as a teenager. But doctors never found any reason for them, and they stopped after a while."

"Oh, well. Anyway, that's where he is."

"Evelyn." Austin's father took a step toward her and Ross felt his entire body tense, ready to pounce, although he knew that was utterly irrational. She stood her ground.

"Yes?"

"I want you to know that I'm... We... I'm very proud of my son. Of what he's done."

"I'm sure he knows that, Mr. Fitzgerald."

The man seemed to collapse in on himself, grow older by fifteen years before his eyes. Ross grabbed a chair and helped him into it while Evelyn stood, watching.

"Please, please, my dear. Call me Max." He sighed. "No, he doesn't know it, and that's my fault."

Ross sat, and she sank into the chair next to him.

"You see, my wife, Austin's mother, she thinks, well, she poured so much of herself into the boys. They were her one reason for living it seemed. And now..." He shrugged, saying more in one gesture than in a thousand words.

"She did a fine job." Evelyn's words made Ross stare.

She put a hand on the Max's thin knuckles. "Truly, Mr...
um...Max. Austin is an incredible man, an amazing,
loving, giving human being. I know that doesn't happen by
accident." She sat back. "I just wish—" She stopped, shook
her head. "I wish I could have known Brock."

Maxwell Fitzgerald's eyes narrowed as he regarded her.
"You realize Austin has reduced our ownership share of
the brewery to one percent? He paid me back my initial
investment with interest, keeping us on the board because
we shared a last name. He told me that was the only reason."

Ross stared, but Max kept his eyes trained on Evelyn.

"I see you didn't know that."

"No, I didn't. But I'm sure he was going to tell me."

Ross frowned, shocked that Austin had given up the
parental safety net. He was pretty sure Fitzgerald operated
in the black but just barely, given the expansion plans
he'd seen. What had come over him? He smiled, watching
Evelyn relax and talk with Austin's father.

He'd never claimed anything resembling introspection,
but at that moment, with Evelyn, knowing that Austin had
taken a step to bring him into their relationship on purpose,
Ross experienced the sort of gut-deep happiness he'd not
felt...in his entire life.

Chapter Twenty

"Dear God, if I say one more word about these beers, I'm gonna puke, or kill somebody." Evelyn pulled her hair off her neck. The bar had been a sweltering oven in the unseasonably hot Denver fall. Her throat ached and her heart pounded. She kept checking her phone, hoping Austin had revived enough to contact her, but the screen stayed blank except for all the Facebook, Instagram and Twitter notices she kept getting about their win as Mid-Size Brewery of the Year.

Sighing, she stuck her phone in her pocket and leaned against Ross' back in a move that felt more natural than anything.

Without realizing it, she'd relied on him as she would Austin and he'd rallied, solving the immediate problem—albeit without much of Austin's diplomacy, but solving it, nonetheless. And the bombshell Max had dropped, about Austin cutting him off from brewery ownership and in the process cutting them off from his family and their financial safety net, had settled in her gut like a stone, making it hard to concentrate.

Surely, he knew what he was doing. She trusted Austin implicitly and figured he would have told her eventually.

They watched the party progress, standing close enough that she could lean into Ross' strong torso and take some of the pressure off her aching feet. Eight of the ten kegs were blown, and the last two were on their last few pours so the bar was beginning to empty.

She'd had at least two beers spilled on her as people hugged their congratulations—she felt sticky and smelly.

Exhaustion stole over her, combining with the incessant worry about Austin's health. As if sensing her distress, Ross put an arm around her and brought his lips near her ear.

"Let's get out of here."

She nodded, sensing her thighs tighten and her nipples harden against her will. Guilt washed through her, pouring ice-cold water on her libido.

"He texted me."

She looked at his phone's screen.

Hey. I'm lonely and sad and feeling sorry for myself. Can't get Evelyn's phone. Come back. Bring food.

She grinned, let herself relax for the first time in hours, and followed Ross out. "Let's walk. It's not far. I need the air," he said as he draped an arm around her and they made their way through the milling crowds on the Denver sidewalks. After they stopped in an all-night market for some cheese, fruit and bread, she tucked her arm through his and took a deep breath, pondering the interesting, odd new shape of her life. He stopped, tugged her into a darkened doorway, and held her close.

"You okay? Really? With this...?"

She put her head against his chest, listening to the beat of his heart. "I haven't sorted it out yet, to be honest." He tightened his grip and she sensed his lips against her hair. "But I like it so far. I just don't want there to be—I don't know—weirdness. I sort of freaked out on you guys last night and I don't know why. The last thing I need right now is a bunch of bullshit, alpha-male jealous crap."

"Evelyn, what you and Austin have, no one can change, take away or lessen in any way." He put a finger under her chin and tilted her face to his. His blue eyes gleamed in the dark and she gave in to the urge to touch the rough, short beard along his jaw before reaching back and releasing his long hair from its tie-back and burying her fingers in it. It felt soft, perfect and she mentally ticked off one of the items on her fantasy to-do list with Ross Hoffman, ever since she'd seen that photo of him and Austin together.

She sighed as he covered her mouth, his lips full and firm. Her body responded instantly and she had to pull away to keep from going any further in public.

"Dear God, woman, you are..." He released her and shoved his hands into his pockets. "Like I said." But she stopped him with a finger over his lips.

"I know, Ross. Let's see where it takes us, okay? But together, as three. We don't sneak around. This is not cheating. It's just... Oh hell, I have no idea what it is." She stopped, dizzy with the possibilities — good and bad. Ross took her arm and pulled her hand back into the crook of his elbow as they walked the last four blocks to the Marriott in comfortable silence.

After a long kiss-and-grope session in the elevator, Evelyn shoved him out into the hall, laughing at his sheepish expression.

He shrugged. "I can't keep my hands off you. Sorry."

She pointed toward their suite. "Go. I need a shower. Give him some food and company while I clean up." He sauntered down the hallway alongside her, whistling and swinging the bag of groceries.

"About damn time." Austin was perched on the bed, laptop on a pillow, sports on the television. His grin was genuine. Evelyn kissed him, long and deep. "Mmm, nice. But you reek, my love. Did you bathe in a keg or what?"

"Don't ask," she tossed over her shoulder before closing the bathroom door. Leaning a moment against it, she wrestled with a complex stew of relief, happiness, tension and a small twinge of stress. She knew damn well that these men would butt heads over her, but, damn her to hell and back, she wanted them. She wanted this.

While that amazed her, nothing felt more perfect. She sighed and turned on the shower full hot blast, and stripped out of her limp clothes. The erotic visions of the two men cradling her between them filled her head. She stayed a solid thirty minutes under the spray, relishing the sensation of being washed clean of every molecule of the day's craziness.

Emerging, pink-skinned and breathlessly horny, she wrapped a towel around herself, brushed her teeth and fluffed up her damp hair before opening the door.

"Hey, you, hot blonde chick. C'mere." Austin held out an arm, encouraging her to snuggle into his shoulder. She hesitated. Weird, inexplicable tears pressed against her eyes.

"I don't know, Austin." She looked away and watched steam roll out of the bathroom.

He went up on one elbow and touched her bare leg, making her skin pebble. "I heard you talked with my dad. I'm sorry you had to hear it that way. I was going to tell you, after…" She shrugged and willed the tears away. He sat and gathered her in his arms. "It's okay, baby. I'll make sure everything works out."

She broke from him and stood. "Austin, you don't have to make sure I'm okay. I'm a grown woman. I want to help. I'm here to help make your dream a reality. *Our* dream. *Our* brewery." She paced and he sat back, not rising to her bait, which made her even madder.

"God damn it, do you ever get mad? Seriously, you are such a nice guy. Smart, logical, responsible, Jesus!" Her ears rang, and she looked around for something to throw to relieve the pressure building up in her chest. Clenching and unclenching her fists, she sat, calming her breathing. "I don't care that you cut yourself off from your parents. I don't even care that your father was the one to tell me. Frankly, we had the most adult and rational discussion we've probably ever had because of it." Austin raised an eyebrow. "That's right, I talked with your father. Does that piss you off?" She glared at him.

"Should it?" He stood and pulled on his jeans. "What is this really about, Evelyn, hmm? I know I've thrown a lot at you this weekend, but—"

She shook her head and stood in front of him, the twin urges to punch him and throw herself into his arms making her dizzy.

"No. I can handle it. I want to handle it. But together, with you. You should have told me you were taking that step with your parents, Austin. We're partners, remember?"

He sighed and tugged her close and she wrapped her arms around his waist. "You're right. I'm sorry. I get this weird protective thing kicking in with you sometimes. Don't know why. You've never been anything but annoyingly independent."

She looked up at him. "I love you, Austin Fitzgerald. From the minute I laid eyes on you. God damn it. You dragged it out of me although I tried like hell to fight it. Now that I've opened up, you have to let me in, all the way."

He nodded, slanting his lips over hers. When she sighed and reached down to touch his hardening cock, he deepened the kiss, possessing her with his tongue, twining his fingers in her damp hair.

He broke from her lips and held her face in his hands. "And this wedding thing? I meant it when I said I won't pressure you anymore. I only want you to be happy."

"I know. We have a lot to do now — we gotta make the brewery really soar this year. I know the books, remember. And those loans…ugh." Stress poured into her brain, but he held her tightly. "But how do you feel about a May wedding? Next year?"

He sighed into her neck. "We will be fine. We know what we're doing. And a May wedding sounds perfect to me."

A set of arms encircled them both. Ross' deep, accented voice penetrated her ear, making her smile. "*Ja*. If there were two people who knew more between them, it would be a crime." He pressed his lips to Evelyn's cheek chastely, then let go. "I should get some sleep. My flight's early tomorrow."

Austin leaned back, faking anger, but Evelyn burst out laughing at him. She knew they were holding back, letting her set the pace on the upcoming, inevitable intimacy. And she loved them both all the more for it.

She took a deep breath. "Actually, I think I...um..." She stepped back from them clutching her elbows, unsure what to say or how to proceed. "Let's try a three-way?" or, "I want him in my ass, and you in my pussy?" or, better yet, "Make a sandwich out of me, boys!"

The utter ridiculousness of the whole thing embarrassed her to the point of nausea. She backed away from them. She dropped into a chair, her mind awash with images, her heart pounding, her throat closing up in something like fear. And her entire anatomy below her belly button on fire with need.

"It's all right, Evelyn," Austin said, moving toward her, holding her captive with his familiar gaze. "Relax. We don't have to do anything now."

She gnawed at her lower lip, her gaze flittering from Austin's to Ross' and back again. The recent memory of Ross' lips, his hands, his voice filled her brain. She pointed to him with a shaking finger. "He... I... We..."

Austin smiled and tugged her back up and into his arms. She pressed her face into his shoulder, feeling like the most clichéd, virginal ingénue in any book. God damn it, she'd let some guy bend her over a spanking bench in the middle of a BDSM club once, unable to even understand why the sting of his open palm had made her come so hard she'd screamed with the sheer joy of it. Surely she could handle this.

But this...this entailed something much deeper than a simple physical connection, a Tetris-worthy puzzle, a basic fitting together of three bodies. She felt something more for both of these men and that was simply too weird for her to handle.

"I know, I know," Austin soothed, holding her close. "He's pretty irresistible, I hear." She giggled. When she wrapped her shaking arms around his waist, she finally relaxed. "It's okay, honey. We don't have to do anything you don't want to do."

"But I do, want to I mean. I just don't know…how you'll feel after, you know? About him." She lifted her face to Austin's, needing to meet his gaze, to connect with him so he'd understand. "And how he'll feel about you. And how I'll feel about…myself."

Austin took her chin between two fingers and grinned at her. "I think I already know," he said, leaning in to brush her lips with his, making her quiver all over with renewed lust—lust that was quelling her inherent reluctance to take the next, physical step. "Let's just lie down a minute, what do you say? No pressure?"

She kept her gaze on Austin's, unwilling to peep over his shoulder at the man waiting for her—the other man she wanted, almost more than she wanted to take her next breath. Speechless with anticipation and a tiny tickle of fear, she nodded as Austin eased her onto the bed, keeping her relaxed with his kisses, his caresses. At one point he picked up her left hand and pressed his lips to the emerald he'd given her as a hard symbol of his love for her.

"She says the wedding's on for May, Hoffman," he said, not taking his eyes off hers. "Can you make it? I'll need a best man."

"You can count on me for that," Ross said, still keeping his distance. "Among other things." The low, accented cadence of his voice sent a powerful shock wave of desire through Evelyn. Tears stung her eyes, but she kept her gaze on Austin, needing him, requiring him to guide her though this…this thing, this madness, this utter perfection.

"I'm a little nervous," she admitted, her voice strange-sounding and croaky.

Austin smiled and slid his fingers into her hair, massaging her scalp. His touched his lips to her exposed neck, sucking and biting in a way that almost always sent her straight over the edge. "Mmm-hmm," she said, knowing he was trying to ease her stress and willing herself to give in to it. "That's nice." She hooked her leg over his hip, wanting him closer to her.

Everything around her faded. All she knew was this man, her man, his perfection and his ability to draw perfection from her. He cupped her breast, flicking a thumb across her peaking nipple before placing a line of kisses up her neck and ending with her lips, filling her mouth, her every nerve and molecule with his presence.

"May I join you?" The soft, accented voice startled her, but she tore her gaze from Austin's to meet Ross' bright blues. He stood, his hair a flaxen waterfall over his shoulders, his fair skin flushed. She took a deep breath and looked back at Austin, uneasy again.

When Austin nodded, Ross settled himself on her other side, up on an elbow. Nervousness flooded through her, but Austin's quiet words calmed. "Relax, my love. We won't do anything you aren't ready for." His lips grazed her collarbone. "But something tells me you are ready, hmmm, am I right, my dirty, dirty girl?" His voice had an edge to it that she chose to interpret as lustful. She shivered and shut her eyes then reopened them when a fingertip touched her cheek. She turned to face the man lying on her other side.

Ross.

He stared, as if studying her for a test, but when his lips touched hers, it felt more perfect than it should have, as perfect as kissing her own future husband. She gave in to the urge to wrap around him, to feel every inch of his large, strong body against hers. He lay back, pulling her on top of him, their lips never breaking contact.

His hands roamed her body, as if unsure what to touch first. He clutched at her ass, slid his palms up her back, then into her hair. She shifted, relishing the sensation of his extreme thickness against her. He moaned into her mouth, tore his lips away, twined fingers in her hair. She sat up and he cupped her breasts, running fingertips over her nipples as she stared down at him, unable to believe she was living out this extreme fantasy.

Austin moved behind her and gripped her waist. His

lips met her shoulder. He lifted the heavy fall of her hair and kissed the nape of her neck. "Do you want this, my Evelyn?" he asked. She flinched, her body prickling. When she ducked out of his reach, Ross let go of her breasts and stayed quiet.

"Little late to ask me now, isn't it?" She glared at him when he sat beside the two of them.

"I want you to be happy," Austin said. "I want you to have whatever it is you want." He glanced down at Ross. "And there is not a man in the world I'd trust more than this one to be with us."

A thrill of panic ran down her spine. This was nuts. She had no business letting him talk her into a…a…threesome. All of a sudden, she felt wrong, dirty, and slutty. And somehow….just right.

She put a hand over her eyes. Austin grabbed her arm, keeping her in place. She let the tears fall.

"And you? What do you want?" She glared down at Ross as anger nibbled away at the hard core of lust she'd been building for the last few hours. "Oh, spare me. You want to fuck me. I get it." She turned to look at Austin, ready to end this whole improbable scene. "I don't know what I want. There, I said it. Are you happy now?"

The words kept coming as she clambered off Ross' body and stood, naked and exposed, her legs shaking and her teeth chattering. Ross rose and sat next to Austin. She bit her lip and forced all the erotic images straight out of her head.

"You kept pushing me with the marriage thing, expecting me to fall at your feet grateful for the opportunity. But I got past that. I made my own decision about it and when I was ready I said yes." Betrayed by tears, she turned away, wiped a hand across her face, and grabbed a discarded towel to wrap herself in.

"Keep talking." Austin's voice was light, as if they were discussing the weather. She blinked fast, confused. "No, really. Please. This is first time you've ever had anything resembling a decent explanation for any of your endless delays committing to me."

Ross started to rise. "I should go," he muttered.

Austin put a hand on his leg. "No. Stay. I started this and I plan to end it one way or another."

The sound of his words sent a thrill of panic down Evelyn's spine. But he was right. She owed him an explanation after all their passion, hard work, mutual goals for the company at the very least. "I love you, Austin."

He tilted his head in that unnervingly patient way he had in the face of one of her angry, irrational breakdowns. "I would hope so. Finish the next sentence that begins with 'but'."

She took a shuddering breath. "But I... I'm now afraid to marry you, because I'm afraid of how I feel about...about him."

Ross cleared his throat and both Evelyn and Austin looked at him. He stood and pulled on a pair of boxer shorts. "This is completely not my business, but I will go on record as saying you"—he pointed at Austin—"need to be more in tune to what she actually needs from you. You don't have to marry her to prove something to your parents."

Evelyn blinked, realizing he'd put into words what she'd long thought but couldn't bring herself to accuse Austin of. She knew he loved her. But also knew his issues with his family went bone-marrow-deep.

Austin frowned and licked his lips. Ross turned to her, pointing a long finger, his blue eyes snapping with anger. "And you, you need to lighten the fuck up, too. You're both too damn intense for your own good, finding trouble where there isn't any." He flopped into a chair and put his feet up on a nearby table.

Evelyn glared at him. "You don't even know me." She allowed a bit of self-righteous indignation to tinge her words. "You aren't entitled to an opinion."

Ross' laugh was loud and musical. It allowed the rapidly increasing tension in the room to dissipate somewhat.

Austin walked over to him and put a hand on his shoulder. The two of them standing there together did a song and dance on her nerves.

She ran a hand up the pebbling skin of one arm.

"He's right," Austin said. "As much as I hate to admit it. I may very well be thumbing my nose at my parents. But I've been doing that my whole life. Me even opening the damn brewery was a gigantic 'up yours' to the Fitzgerald food empire. You know all of this, Evelyn. I'll admit the whole thing seemed pretty illicit and forbidden when I met you, but I will be damned to hell and back if you didn't make me fall in love with you, you fucking stubborn female."

Before she knew it, Austin was in her face. His lips covered hers and he did what he did best—kissing away her worries. He picked her up and tossed her back on the bed. "I don't want to live without you. Or work without you. Or sleep without you. Ever. Is that clear?"

She nodded, speechless and getting more breathless by the minute. Austin flopped onto the bed, propped himself on an elbow. His amazing, open face held no secrets. She sensed something give in her psyche then. A lightening or at least, a letting go of long-held assumptions about him poured over her heated brain. She put her hand to his rough face. "I do love you. So much."

He smiled. "But you haven't answered me." He took her hand and put it to his lips, making her shiver at the touch. "Is it clear?"

"Yes," she whispered. Because it finally was. He understood her now. Now they could get on with the business of being in love without the pressure to do what everyone else thought they should.

"Finally." Ross joined them on the other side of her. She felt blood flush through her from head to toe. He ran a finger up her leg, to her hip, along her side. "That was beautiful just then."

"I know." Austin kissed her, cupped a breast, thumbed her nipple, as Ross worked his way lower, making her

187

squirm. "She is amazing." He leaned back, his grin sexy, one eyebrow raised. "Where were we, hmm?"

She squealed when Ross pulled her up as he lay back, making her straddle his hips.

He rubbed her thighs and shifted, smiling at her gasp when she felt his impressive girth beneath her.

"Jesus, if I weren't so secure, I'd worry about you two being perfect for each other," Austin said as he knelt next to her and turned her face to meet his. "But you are mine, Evelyn. Forever. Mine." He slanted his mouth over hers, sweeping into her with his tongue, leaving her breathless. He released her slowly and she opened her eyes. "And don't ever forget it." He fell back on the bed. "Now, why don't you just relax and enjoy yourself?" He propped his arms behind his head. "It's my damn turn to watch."

Ross cleared his throat. "Glad I can oblige you both." They all laughed and Ross tugged her close again, his lips strong, different and yet still perfect, the rasp of his beard rough against her face. His tongue asserted its intention between her lips, making her heart pound. She felt Austin's hand on her ass, then her lower back. She shifted and pressed her needy clit against Ross' shaft.

Breaking the knee-melting kiss, she stared at down at Ross, the long yellow curtain of her hair shutting out everything but the two of them. He smiled and held out a hand. Austin put something in it. "Hang on one moment," he said as he opened the condom packet and rolled the thing down his dick. His blue gaze intent, he angled his hips down then thrust forward.

"Holy shit!" she cried out and closed her eyes at the exquisite pain and pleasure of the penetration.

"You okay, baby?" Austin's voice sounded rougher than normal. She nodded, taking it in, letting herself go, feeling herself give way, her flesh spreading to accommodate him. She sucked in a breath, realizing he wasn't even all the way in yet. Ross spoke softly, and to her. "You are so goddamned beautiful."

He shoved up higher, latching onto to her nipple. Her back arched at the sensation just as a lubricated finger rubbed against her tightest hole. She sensed Austin's hips against her backside, the tip of his cock replacing the finger. He slipped inside, slowly, making her exhale.

"Oh, dear God," she groaned, every fiber of her soul crying out for release, but unwilling for it to end.

"It's all right, my love." He caressed her hips. "Arch back against me, like I taught you. Think about that butt plug you love so much, and just relax." He draped over her back, kissing between her shoulder blades. She had never felt more loved than at that moment between the amazing men. Austin grabbed her hair, pulling back, bringing a bit of pain that she loved, and Ross latched on to her other nipple.

"Make room for me," Austin grunted, and Ross withdrew, still loving her breasts, cradling them and sucking, nuzzling their sensitive tips. Austin's grip tightened and her body gathered energy, her breathing got ragged, the edge of a precipice near. She pictured herself, ready to jump. Ready to take the incredible leap, pain or no, dangerous emotional territory be damned. And it did hurt, a little, but she wanted it. All of it.

"Take me, Austin." She spoke while staring into Ross' eyes. Austin pressed deep into her ass, owning her, marking and filling her. Ross sucked at her nipple, and he angled his hips to bring needed friction to her clit, the result a breathtaking climax that made her sob with its intensity.

Evelyn had never experienced so many sensations at once. Two sets of masculine hands caressed her. She closed her eyes and went airborne in her head, giving in to the touches, the lips and hands and bodies below and behind her. It hurt, but it was a good kind of pain, hard to explain but luckily all she had to do right then was just enjoy it.

Finally, after a few moments of shivering, shuddering release, she opened her eyes.

Ross stayed quiet, cradling her breasts as they bounced from Austin's efforts behind her. He reached up and brushed her tears away, his gaze soft. She sniffled as Austin sighed and withdrew slowly from her body, making her wince and yelp. "Shit, that hurt. But don't mind me. I'm a regular tear fountain."

Austin flopped down next to Ross. "Sorry. Needed that." He looked up at her, his handsome face open, content and happy. She refocused on Ross. Without a word, or taking his gaze from hers, he shifted his hips again, filling her so completely she experienced a quick flutter of pity for any woman not herself right at that moment. She smiled, her entire body buzzing with satisfaction and began rocking her hips, pressing her clit against him as she hummed with happiness. He shoved up high, making her gasp and sit up, propping herself on his thick chest.

"*Heilige Scheiße*," he muttered. His gaze bored straight into her soul. "I need to kiss you. Please, Evelyn, I need your lips."

She dropped over him and covered his mouth, her tongue darting in, giving him what he wanted. She lifted, then slid back down on his shaft, the delicious thickness of his cock bringing a newly familiar measure of pain to the pleasure coursing through her.

He held her close then sat, bringing her legs around to either side of his hips so they were rocking together. His fingers slid into her hair. Her vision brightened at the new angle. "Let me," he whispered. She nodded, speechless, as he set the pace and rhythm.

She gasped and clutched at his broad shoulders, saw Austin watching them, his eyes dark. He mouthed the words "I love you" to her just as Ross angled deep against her G-spot. Her body seemed to dissolve, then reform itself. The room dimmed around her as she cried out, clutching at him, wanting this one perfect moment to last forever.

Ross' breath warmed her neck. "Evelyn, that was amazing."

She loved the sound of her name on his lips, the way his accent drew out the syllables, made them beautiful. With a grunt, he flipped them over, his shoulders and large, hard body filling her universe. And that incredible shaft still pinning her, fucking her. She wrapped her legs and arms around him. "Make me come again," she gasped.

He sucked a nipple into his mouth, biting down, making her body move against his, their erotic dance taking on something of a purpose, a primal function. Their combined lust permeated everything, making her dizzy. "Oh dear Jesus, Ross." The orgasm rushed toward her again, blinding her like bright, oncoming headlights. His lips covered hers and his tongue invaded her mouth.

He tore his lips from hers at the last minute and groaned, hips thrusting, pounding into her, filling her with her completely. Finally, their breathing calmed and they stared at each other. Her heart constricted with something she didn't recognize. He pulled out and she winced. "Sorry." He dropped to the bed on her other side, chest still heaving. "I'm sort of…"

"Bloody huge, that's what. Damn." She glared at Austin when he burst out laughing. He rolled her up on her side to face him, cradling her face.

"My lovely, blunt girl." His lips were familiar against hers. "That was amazing, but you probably know that already. I love you," he whispered. "But I need a shower. Go on, rest with him."

She curled into the curve of Ross' body, forgoing her usual trip to the bathroom post-sex, too tired, too sated to move. His breathing evened out, warming her neck as the sounds of water and Austin's whistling made her smile. *Perfect.* She drifted off, cradled in her new lover's arms.

Chapter Twenty-One

Ross woke when a shaft of early morning sunlight hit him square in the eyes. He sighed, took a deep breath of the woman in his arms, and kissed her bare shoulder. She stirred and rolled onto her back away from him. He stared at her, his cock already standing at attention, his chest constricted by the memory of the night before.

He ran his finger down her face, neck and arm, smiling as the delicious pink buds of her nipples reacted, hardening, begging for his lips. But he waited, wanting to stroke every inch of her — from the soft curve of her hip, down her strong thigh, and back up.

"Hmmm…keep that up and I won't be responsible for what happens next." She rolled away from him, wrapping herself around Austin's still-sleeping form. "Ah, yes, just what I wanted."

Ross swallowed hard. He should go. Now.

"Don't go." Her voice, newly precious to him, pierced his soul.

Trying not to betray any unsteadiness in his voice, he cleared his throat and sat in a chair next to the bed. "All right. But it's my turn to watch, I think." He smiled and fisted his aching shaft. "Show me." He leveled his gaze at her. "Suck his cock, baby."

Austin put his arms behind his head. "Yeah, what he said. I took a shower for a reason." He raised an eyebrow.

"Great. Two bossy men." But she positioned herself between Austin's legs and lapped at him, slipping her tongue along the slit, running it around the edges of his swollen head.

Ross groaned, using his leaking cum to lubricate his own efforts, watching as she did exactly what he'd told her. Austin threaded his fingers in her hair and arched his back, thrusting into her mouth. The sounds she made as he fucked her throat brought a buzzing to Ross' ears. He tensed, ready for release.

But just when he thought Austin might blow, she released him and moved up his long body to his lips. The man rolled her over and pinned her beneath him. She wrapped both long legs around his waist. Their eyes never left each other's. Their lips moved, forming words Ross couldn't hear. The emotional connection they shared flared sharp and hot, a visceral thing Ross could almost see and smell and wanted to hold fast to himself.

"Harder." Her voice was raw with emotion. "Please, Austin, I feel you. I need you to... Oh God, yes!"

He leaned down to suck a nipple between his lips, altering the angle of his thrusts.

Every nerve ending Ross possessed burned. His brain shut off and his body took over. He dropped onto the bed beside Austin and watched her face, intent until he realized that Austin had slowed his movements.

"On your side, Evelyn. We both want to make you come," Austin said, his low voice hoarse.

It was a familiar scene to Ross. The nameless, naked girl between them, Austin in one orifice and Ross in the other, hands on her breasts, her hands on one of them. Her cries. Her moans.

But this was one hundred percent not that. He very well might love this woman and that was a recipe for disaster. Ross tried to disentangle himself, to escape before he ruined a friendship and potentially Austin and Evelyn's relationship. He knew himself too well and he knew Austin. This would never work in the real world.

But Evelyn arched her back and pressed her sweet ass against his erection and all logic flew from his head like so much smoke. He grabbed the lube on their bedside table and used it on one finger then pressed against her, then inside her, going slowly as Austin thrust into her pussy and sucked her nipples. The raw smell of her lust and body filled his brain, making him dizzy with need. As he angled his hips so he could penetrate her gorgeous ass, she gasped and froze.

"Whoa, hold up," she said, breathless. "I don't know how many women you could do this to, but I don't think this particular configuration is gonna work for me. Sorry."

Austin leaned back, his green eyes dark and his face flushed. Then he smiled, chuckled, then burst out laughing. Ross frowned as they shifted so Austin was standing and Evelyn was sprawled out on the bed like the world's most delicious smorgasbord. Austin snagged the lube from Ross' hand and nodded at her.

Ross propped on one elbow, confused and still somewhat dizzy. Evelyn took his hand and placed it between her legs. That focused him. He grinned and started kissing and nibbling his way down her smooth, soft skin, teasing both nipples until she was squealing and her hips pumped upwards, then to her stomach, then to her sex which was warm, pink and wet.

"You like this, I take it," he gasped as she threw her legs over his shoulder and dug her heels into his back. He grabbed her ass and tugged her forward so he could run his eager tongue around the edges of her labia, tasting her, drinking her in. She kept thrusting up and her fingers tangled in his hair, but he went slow, wanting to savor this, to remember it forever.

When he latched onto her clit and slid fingers inside her pussy, she groaned and the sound was like the sweetest music to his ears. Her hips thrust against him and he kept up his suction and massage of her G-spot until she came with a loud cry and full-body shudder, her thighs grasping either side of his head. When she flopped back, releasing him, he smiled and knelt between her legs, committing her body to memory.

"Man's got some skills." Evelyn sighed as she stretched and writhed under his gaze.

"So I hear," Austin said in that new, odd voice that gave Ross a tickle of worry. But when he met his gaze as he sat next to Evelyn he seemed fine.

"Damn," Evelyn said, gazing at Ross' erection. "That is truly…intimidating."

Ross reddened for a second until she yanked him down, spread her legs, covered her lips with his and took him inside with a quick shift of her hips. They groaned into each other's mouths and he started moving fast and hard and needy.

"Roll her over, Hoffman. We get to share this time, remember?" Austin demanded. A quick flash of frustration hit Ross' brain but he chose to ignore it. He rolled, bringing Evelyn with him then latched on to her nipple, making her sigh and tilt her hips so she could take her other man inside her.

Austin lubed and prepped her ass, then slid into her with a low moan of satisfaction.

"I'm gonna come again," Ross heard her whisper.

"So am I," Austin declared.

The dance ensued, Ross in her pussy, then sliding out with a loud sigh as Austin entered her ass, just as slowly, his loud moan of satisfaction making Ross' dick even harder. They moved in a perfect, choreographed rhythm, in and out, sharing her gorgeous body between them. Finally, Ross clutched Evelyn's hips, his entire body jerking with effort not to come.

Austin wrapped his arms around them both a moment before pulling out of Evelyn. "*Ach*, Evelyn, I need to come," he said. "And I forgot the condom," he said, gasping, near to bursting. She angled her hips down, giving him the most incredible, gripping angle. "Come inside me," she commanded. "It's all right, Ross. I… I…. I want it."

Barely able to breathe, he did as he'd been told, coming so hard he saw stars, heard music, and had the oddest sensation of perfection. When he opened his eyes, she was smiling down at him. She kissed his raw lips, then flopped down on the bed bedside him, chest still heaving with exertion.

Austin smiled at them both before dropping in on her other side. "Holy shit," Ross muttered, his brain already fuzzing over, pulling him into sleep.

"No shit." Evelyn rolled into his chest and he put an arm around her. Austin curled into her backside with a contented sigh.

"I'll ask it once more," Austin whispered, before touching his lips to Evelyn's shoulder. "*Das ist gut, ja?*"

Ross smiled. "*Das ist gut, ja.*"

Chapter Twenty-Two

Three months later

Evelyn put her book down on the empty chair next to her and sighed. As she wiggled her toes farther down in the sand, she relished the pleasant soreness between her legs

Austin had surprised her Christmas morning, waking her from a dead sleep with a smack on the ass and a stocking full of Ray-Bans, sunscreen, a couple of paperback books, and a plane ticket. She'd wanted to say no, but they'd been working so damn hard since returning from Denver, a ten-day beach getaway sounded like a slice of heaven.

So here she was, fresh-squeezed orange juice at her side and the amazing deep blue of the Mediterranean Sea a few feet from her cushy lounge chair. And her men — Ross had met them at the small airport with a huge shit-eating grin and a giant hug for them both.

A blush crept up her face at the memory of that first night. They hadn't seen each other in a while and the reunion had been, to say the least, one for the record books.

How she'd managed to find herself there — marketing director of a hugely successful brewery and engaged to its handsome owner and founder who was madly in love with her — when he wasn't yelling at her over spending too much money on point of sale, advertising, or upgrading packaging. Plus, double bonus — he was an incredibly talented and adventurous lover.

And, of course, triple bonus — he'd introduced her to Ross, pulling his friend into their emotional and physical circle with the sort of ease very few men would be able to achieve.

She sighed and got to her feet, having managed to beat the men outside, enjoying an hour or two of solitude before they joined her. Today they were going scuba diving — or at least Austin and Ross were. The thought of being underwater and breathing at the same time freaked her out, so she planned to take pictures and get some sun on the boat.

They had a couple of hours before their ride showed up, so she opened the French doors from the huge patio into the cool interior, stopping in the kitchen to put on coffee. Gazing out into the movie-set perfect lawn, she sipped more juice and decided to wake her men with a little surprise.

Slipping out of her bikini and padding down the long hallway to the luxurious bedroom, she tingled in anticipation of their lips and bodies all over her. Smiling, she opened the door slowly, already picturing them — Ross' long, strong blond god-like perfection likely sprawled on top of the covers on his back, one arm thrown over his eyes. Austin would be on his stomach, his dark head half under the pillow, one leg under, one on top of the silky duvet.

She frowned at the empty bed. The evidence of their kinky playtime the night before still littered the room. A couple of dildos, a tube of lubrication and a set of handcuffs all lay tumbled in a messy pile of silk that used to be her nightgown until Ross had ripped it off her in his haste to have his turn, as he liked to say. She picked up the shreds of one of the most expensive Victoria's Secret items she'd ever bought, her natural thriftiness making her irritated by the waste.

She walked to the closed bathroom door. Although bathroom was a bit of a misnomer — the room was more like a spa. A giant shower big enough for a family of six boasted side nozzles, and a huge showerhead in the ceiling.

The deep tub had tiny little jets along the bottom and was hands-down perfect for three. There was an extra side room, with a small fridge, flat-screen TV, and a huge leather-covered mattress on a wooden platform, where they'd ended up that first night, in a tangled-up trio of arms, legs, lips and tongues.

She opened the door and tiptoed in. There was a note on the vanity in Austin's handwriting.

Gone out for a run and some coffee. Will meet you guys at the diving boat. Behave. Or not. Your choice.

Evelyn dropped, seemingly boneless, into a chair, smiling at the sight of Ross in the shower, shampoo rolling down his perfect body. She trailed her fingers across her breasts, watching him prop his hands on the wall as the water sluiced across his shoulders and back.

Dear Lord, was there a woman on the planet luckier than her? She doubted it very much.

To her pleasant surprise, Ross turned around to face her, his hand wrapped around that giant dick, which was as hard as a rock. His blue eyes met hers, flipping a newly discovered erotic switch in her head. She dropped her fingers lower and started stroking herself as he did the same. She bit her lip, pinched her nipple, and watched his hand move up and down the extreme length of his dick. Shocked at her capacity for the ongoing orgasm-fest they'd been enjoying, her face flushed hot and her clit hardened under her finger. She moved faster, spreading her legs so he could see her.

He smiled and moved his own hand faster, which made her tingle all over. The orgasm caught her by surprise. She shivered and stretched on the huge leather chair in the over-the-top bathroom in this incredible paradise she found herself inhabiting.

"Oh, God." She sighed, staring at the Italian tile ceiling over the tub. "Yes." She closed her eyes.

"Now that is one of my favorite words." Her eyes flew open when a deep, raspy, familiar voice filled her ears. Ross stood in front of her, water droplets beaded up on his perfectly sculpted chest. "But not quite good enough."

She smiled, threaded her hands into Ross' thick golden hair and propped one foot on his shoulder as he zeroed in on her still-pulsing sex. His hands worked their way up and cupped her breasts, flicking at her nipples. "Agreed," she said. "Let's see if we can do a little better."

She sucked in a breath at the smell and feel of him, the musky unmistakable scent of him filling her senses as she tugged him up so he loomed over her. Her eyes prickled with tears.

"What's wrong, lovely Evelyn?" Ross kissed her cheeks, her nose, and her lips, deepening his kiss in a way that blocked everything from her consciousness.

"I think... I... Oh, please, yes," she sighed when he penetrated her, moving slowly, rolling his hips, pressing deep then retreating so he could do it all again. "Oh, Ross," she said as she angled her hips, and opened her mouth to his kiss once more.

"I'm not gonna last long," he gasped into her hair. "You had me pretty worked up just now, naughty *Liebling*."

She grinned and moved her hips faster, meeting his every thrust, loving this and him and... *No.* She couldn't love them both. She just loved this. All this glorious, amazing attention. Because it was short-lived. They'd part ways in a few days and he'd go back to his life in California, likely bedding his fair share of women.

Evelyn froze at that, literally stopped moving mid-thrust.

"Oh, shit," Ross grunted and closed his eyes as the orgasm made him groan and fill her body. "Oh...wow." He opened his eyes and stared down at her, then his brow furrowed. "What? Did I hurt you? I'm sorry. Sometimes I forget and go too fast."

She frowned at him, trying to make her voice work. "You... You have other girls, right? Out in California?"

His double-take was so comical she giggled, then winced when he pulled out of her. She lay, sprawled and sticky, and so jealous she would swear she could see green at the edges of her vision.

Ridiculous, Evelyn. The man owes you nothing. He's just a plaything. The three in your stupid, selfish threesome.

He ran a washcloth under warm water, squeezed it out, and pressed it between her legs. She let him, still unable to form coherent sentences and afraid to try lest she sound like a crazy person. He stroked and cleaned her gently, then pressed his lips to her belly. She held him close, biting back tears as best she could.

"You are my one and only," he whispered so softly she could barely hear him. "No other woman compares to you, my Evelyn."

She blinked. He'd never called her that. Only Austin called her that. She pulled him up so his face was level with hers and cradled his bearded cheeks between her hands. "I'm marrying Austin," she said, not sure why she was did so. "I mean…this is… I don't want it to get weird."

He opened his mouth at the same time as the bathroom door flew open, revealing Austin in his swim trunks, holding a cardboard cup of coffee. "What's going on in here, kids?" His voice had that strange, sharp edge to it. As if he wanted to sound nonchalant and blasé and not as jealous as he actually was. Evelyn's skin pebbled and her pulse raced at the sound of it.

Ross rose to his feet, still naked, the warm cloth dangling from one hand. "I have to leave," he said, his voice clogged with emotion. "I was just saying my goodbyes."

Austin's eyes narrowed as he glanced at Evelyn who didn't even bother to hide the fact that this sudden goodbye involved them having sex without him knowing about it. It was a rule, if an unspoken one. Evelyn always checked with Austin if she and Ross were going to engage in any foreplay or intercourse.

Until today, of course.

She sighed and got up, found her robe, and wrapped herself up in it. When she put her hand on Austin's arm, he flinched and glowered at her.

Great. This was exactly what she didn't want or need in

her life. *Time to give up this particular fantasy because the real world has officially come knocking at the door.* But he seemed to relax after a few seconds.

"Go? Why? We have this place for three more days." He put a proprietary arm around Evelyn's shoulders.

"Brad called," she said, making it up as she went along, realizing that Ross really should go if they were going to let go of this nonsense with everyone's egos, psyches, and emotions intact. "He needs Ross back. Some emergency."

"Ah," Austin said, squeezing her tighter. "I see."

"Yes, so," Ross said, brushing past them. He grabbed his suitcase and started tossing his stuff into it. His face was flushed, his eyes bright.

This, Evelyn thought, was bad. This had to stop now.

He zipped it up, put on his jeans and a T-shirt and shoes then met their gaze. Neither of them had moved and Evelyn could sense Austin's rapid heartbeat against her side.

"Well, thanks for the vacation, Austin," Ross said, holding his hand out.

Austin glared at it, then down at her. "So, this is it?" he asked.

She nodded. "It's best, I think. Don't you?" She pressed her lips to his cheek. "I love you, Austin. You know that. Don't make this awkward and risk your friendship over it."

Austin swallowed hard, shook his head as if to clear it, then dragged Ross forward into a huge group hug. It was warm and comforting and made her happy. But she knew it for what it was. Austin's way of saying, 'No more. She's mine. I want to keep you as a friend so this has to stop.'

Ross stepped away from them, rubbing his lips and blinking fast. "I'll call you," he said as he practically ran for the bedroom door. They stood together amid the mess of the nights before, not talking for a long time after that.

Chapter Twenty-Three

One month later

"I have to go back to the brewery." Austin tossed the mail onto the kitchen counter. "I gotta figure out what the hell is wrong with the—" He stopped and stared at her. Evelyn sat gazing out of the huge wall of windows onto their yard as the snow fell. She had her hair pulled up, exposing the long line of her neck.

She chewed at her lip, a line of worry between her beautiful blue eyes. Austin blew out a breath. Dear God, but he was a lucky man. In love with the woman of his dreams, albeit one who did not always make things easy.

He leaned on the counter a minute before she noticed him. He grasped the improbability that the two people he loved most in the universe were both emotional cripples. He grasped it and welcomed it because he understood he had provided them with the emotional catalyst they both required. Even if the thing with Ross had ended on a somewhat ignominious note.

His fault, he knew, but something she'd sensed and ended for them before it went pear-shaped. Ross had faded as Austin knew he would. The guy could switch it off and on like a light bulb, thank God.

Evelyn had a photo of the three of them in her hand. The one snapped when they'd received their award at the festival that weekend. Tears dripped onto it. He took it from her and knelt between her knees, laying his head in her lap.

"Where have you been?" She threaded her fingers through his hair. "You need a haircut. Dinner's ready. I was just tired all of a sudden. Jesus, I could use a nap."

He pulled her to her feet. It took all he had not to lay her back on the couch and take her right now. "I can't shake this cold or flu or whatever…" She looked up at him. "Oh shit, Austin, I'm late."

"Late for what?"

She frowned. He gripped her arms as panic stole across his psyche.

"Don't be obtuse," she ground out.

They'd been putting in long hours together, pushing their staff to its limit, he knew. But no one complained. He'd started the company on a basis of emotional ownership for all his employees, giving them leeway to make decisions and take on projects well beyond the norm. So far it had worked great.

But now that they faced a year filled with financial uncertainty, he'd been short with everyone, stressed beyond belief. Evelyn sucked in a breath and he knew she was trying hard not to cry. "Sorry. I'm just tired."

"No, I'm sorry. How late? I mean, what? Oh, hell." He sat, staring at her. They'd spent a long vacation between Christmas and New Year with Ross in Mykonos, a long stretch of sun, surf, food, beer, and some of the most amazing sex he'd ever experienced. Until he'd caught them post-intercourse that morning, and he'd been about five seconds away from punching Ross into oblivion before the whole thing had dried up and drifted away leaving nothing but intensely erotic memories in their wake.

There had not a condom in sight for the days they'd spent together, either.

The fact that Evelyn might very well be pregnant thanks to Ross and not himself penetrated his exhaustion.

Kids were not part of his personal agenda and never had been. Something about having a child with Evelyn made his ears ring with a fresh round of anxiety. God damn but it was shitty timing. They couldn't…or shouldn't. He sighed.

She stood, and he put a hand on her stomach, trying not

to let the exhaustion and stress make him say something really stupid. She sighed and let him hold her for a second. "I don't know. It's probably stress, anyway."

He led her to the bedroom and tucked her in, then sat, watching her drift off. His heart clenched with delight, worry, and terror all at once. His cock stirred, giving him a different message. Struggling with the urge to wake her, fuck her, own her all over again, knowing she'd not protest, he stood, adjusted himself and turned off the light.

He did need to get back over to the brewery. Truth was, he had to keep busy. Nervous energy forced him to action nearly around the clock. Knowing the best thing would be to crawl into bed with her and get a decent night's sleep, he ate standing up, then drank yet another cup of coffee. Ignoring the funny buzzing in his fingertips, he chalked it up to lack of sleep and too much caffeine. He headed back out into the wintry night.

* * * *

Evelyn sat in the dark room, hand on her stomach, her heart doing flips in her chest. The snow fell, quiet, col, and beautiful on the other side of the giant window. She watched it, not realizing she'd fallen asleep again until the phone buzzed by her ear nearly two hours later. She fumbled for it, knowing, the second she answered it, it would be bad news.

"It's Dad." Austin's voice was muffled. Evelyn sucked in a breath. "He's dead."

"Oh God, honey, where are you?"

"Heading to their house. He just dropped to the floor. Massive heart attack."

Thoughts of funerals, plans and of what would be expected of him now made Evelyn clench her jaw. But she had to be supportive. "Okay. Um, do you need me to do anything?"

"No. I'll—I'll be home soon, I hope."

She lay back, absorbed the overwhelming turning point of this moment then called Ross.

"Wow," he exhaled. "That is not good news at all." His soft German-tinged English made her smile in spite of her stress.

"No, it's not, Captain Obvious."

"Captain whom?"

She stood and started pacing the bedroom. "Never mind. Sorry."

"Well, what happens now? What about the family business?"

Evelyn sat, her legs shaking with stress. "Well, funeral and stuff first. After that, who knows?"

"*Ja.*"

They sat, quiet. Until she finally told him she should go. "Thanks."

"For what, my love?"

"For being you." She hung up and climbed into the shower, figuring sleep could wait.

Chapter Twenty-Four

Austin stood by his mother, greeting everyone, doing all the right and proper things one does at the funeral of a patriarch, a pillar of society, a guy who managed to take his own father's business from small to colossal in one generation.

It was, in a word, brutal.

His mother rose to the occasion, all social energy and putting on a good face. He watched as she greeted the governor's wife, the mayor of Grand Rapids, and pretty much every single successful businessman in the Midwest.

His parents' marriage had been a farce as best Austin could tell, from the moment he'd been able to sort out such things. His mother started drinking every day at five, and his father had had a string of affairs with younger women for years. But they'd stayed together.

He put a hand to his head, which had started to pound in an ominous way. The last three days had been the worst kind of nightmare between dealing with his mother's incessant demands on his time and the ritual of handing over something like thirty thousand dollars to throw a funeral. When his revived efforts to locate Brock failed, it sent him even further down into a spiral of frustrated regret.

Evelyn had been amazing. A rock of stability. He smiled, catching her eye across the room as she sat with the brewery staff. He'd told Ross to stay on the west coast, that they'd catch up after all this necessary family drama subsided.

"Valerie!" The sound of his mother's delighted high-pitched voice made him shiver with annoyance. He turned and saw her, the woman who'd been his girlfriend and lover for the better part of three years before he'd met Evelyn. Their history went back even further, since they'd grown up together, vacationing with their families on Lake Michigan and down in St. Bart's. She'd been his prom date their senior year, when they'd clumsily surrendered their virginity to each other before parting ways for college.

She smiled, her face no longer a mask of anger. And he relaxed.

Every hair Evelyn possessed stood on end at the sight of that rich bitch Valerie Masterson with her arms around Austin. Their easy familiarity did something ugly to her nerve endings. She averted her gaze, trying to pay attention to whatever conversation was swirling around her from the brewery staff. When she chanced another look, Austin was smiling, his hand on the woman's arm still. The expression on Valerie's face was one any normal woman with a hot boyfriend, fiancé, or husband would recognize immediately. It made her suck in a breath and rise to her feet.

At that moment, Evelyn caught Austin's mother's eyes on her. The evil smirk on her face-lifted countenance sent a clear message just before she hooked one arm under her son's elbow and the other under Valerie's and led the two of them into the crowd.

Evelyn stood in the middle of the circle of chairs, her face on fire. "I have to go," she said to everyone and no one. The group stared at her. She stumbled past them, around the clots of famous, rich and otherwise important people in the room and found the front door.

"Evelyn." The sound of her name froze her in place. She turned and came face to face with Virginia Fitzgerald, in all her glory. Evelyn figured she must have left Austin and Valerie somewhere so she could come seek her out. Virginia was herself an heiress to an automotive fortune on the east side of the state, and had married the wealthiest man in Michigan. The sum total of Austin's parents equaled this woman now, however. His life, the one he'd spent the majority of his years living, was one more familiar to Valerie Masterson, and Evelyn knew it. The old, long-buried self-loathing came roaring up, familiar and evil and loud in her ears.

Panic bloomed in Evelyn's chest as she caught herself actually missing the elder Fitzgerald's neutralizing presence.

"Dear." The woman's simpering face made Evelyn want to smack her, hard. "Thank you so much for coming."

Evelyn gulped. "Of course. I'm...so sorry for your loss."

The woman stepped closer. Chanel No. 5 nearly choked her as Austin's mother put a scrawny hand on her wrist. "We must have lunch. Once all of this unpleasantness is over. I do want to get to know you better." She made a point of staring straight at Evelyn's engagement ring.

Evelyn gaped at her. Virginia's face was open, guileless. She let herself relax. "Um, sure. I mean, next week is sort of..."

"Thursday after next. At the club. Eleven-thirty? See you then." She pressed papery lips to Evelyn's cheek then glided away, already greeting more people, leaving Evelyn to stare after her, amazed, furious and flabbergasted by the way the woman had railroaded her with minimal effort.

She took a breath and tried to find Austin, dreading the moment she'd find him with Valerie still dangling from his arm. The whole thing felt off to her now, and not only because of the obvious segregation in the room between the brewery people and everyone else. She bit her lip then headed back to her seat, surrounded by Fitzgerald Brewing staff. Awkward tension suffused the room.

She saw him, just as she figured, with the thin form of his ex-girlfriend attached to him like a parasite. Evelyn gulped and blinked back tears. A hand settled on her shoulder. Austin's ancient secretary, Mrs. Richardson, leaned down to whisper in her ear. "Don't let them upset you, dear. He loves you. Nothing will change that."

Evelyn nodded, mute, as she watched the continuous parade of the Midwest's rich and famous give their condolences to Austin, his mother, and the woman who, if one did not know better, could be his wife, judging by the way she stood so close, her hand resting possessively on his arm.

"I should go," she muttered, suddenly feeling peevish and blind with jealousy and self-doubt.

"No, you should not." Mrs. Richardson kept a firm hand on her. "I've been with this family for nearly thirty-five years, young lady. And I will not allow you to let her" — she leveled an arthritic finger at the tableau near the casket — "make you feel bad or out of place, or anything other than the woman her son loves." She patted Evelyn's cheek. "Buck up now, honey. Austin is your man. Start acting like it."

But she sat, glued to her seat, it seemed. And endured the rest of the gruesome visitation hours ritual, observing as Austin leaned into Valerie's slim shoulder one time too many for her taste. By the time the room had cleared she'd worked herself into a frenzy. Resignation, regret, and the hint of a future unhappiness tinged the edges of her raw emotions. She wandered out of the large chapel in a daze.

"Evelyn." Austin glanced up when he saw her in the doorway of a room full of dainty desserts, coffee and tea. He held a double bourbon in one hand. "Where have you been?" He took a sip, his expression tired, but guileless. Evelyn experienced a tiny thrill of anger at him for not seeing straight through his mother's and Valerie's little show.

Valerie's high-pitched laughter made her blink and turn. The woman held out a hand to Evelyn. "Hello. I'm Valerie. And you must be…"

The woman left just enough empty air after her last words to make Evelyn understand that her name and her position with Austin were forgettable. Her face flushed. "I must be going."

Austin held out the empty glass. Valerie took it from him, her eyes full of sympathy. "Another?" she asked, her scrawny hand on Austin's dark-suited arm.

"Uh, sure." He stared at Evelyn. "Where are you going? I told you we had the dinner—"

She cut him off. "I'm not going to that." She gestured to the refreshed drink the simpering Valerie held out. "You're pretty well covered, I'd say."

He didn't try to stop her and she knew it was childish. But she'd be damned if she stood there another minute like a stupid peasant watching the nobility and observing that bitch hover around her man.

Your man, Evelyn. Don't walk away from him. He needs you.

She threw her Mercedes sedan into reverse and backed out so fast she nearly ended up in the front room of the sedate, expensive funeral home. All the way home, she reminded herself that she was wearing Austin's engagement ring. She slept with him every night. They shared everything—from their morning coffee, to dinner, to towels. Everything up to and including the sort of wildly awesome sex life some women could only dream about.

But the voice in her ear, the one she'd successfully muffled for the past few months, kept up its yammering.

You don't fit in. You can't understand his life. You never will.

Tears rolled down her face as she parked under Austin's building and sat, gripping the steering wheel and regretting anything nasty or bitchy she'd ever said to him.

Chapter Twenty-Five

Austin's mouth felt like the Mojave Desert and his gut did sickening flips as he contemplated his new reality, sitting in the office he'd inherited. His father had left everything tidy and clear. Once the will had been read to them by the family's attorney, a mere two days after the funeral, it had been revealed that he, the only acknowledged son to the Fitzgerald fortune, would be CEO of Fitzgerald Brands.

He, Austin, now owned and operated a multi-billion-dollar food supply business. He, Austin, now had five giant warehouses, leased a fleet of semis, managed payroll, insurance and pension plans for nearly three thousand people, and supervised logistics delivery of restaurant-grade food and paper products to something like eight thousand locations in seven states.

He, Austin, had two personal assistants and a giant office…plus a possibly pregnant fiancée who'd more or less stopped talking to him.

He groaned and sat up on the couch of his new office and grappled with this destiny.

It had only taken a week for his mother to insert herself into his life as if he'd never left his boyhood home. She called, dropped by the office, and generally took over in ways he wasn't equipped to cope with, much less deny. He hadn't had a decent night's sleep in over a week. Or a real conversation with Evelyn. Forget about getting laid. He groaned and flopped back, the huge window reflecting a perfect West Michigan summer's day, as if mocking how utterly miserable he felt.

He glanced down at a text message, hoping it was Evelyn.

She'd been put in full charge of the brewery since they'd found Max Fitzgerald cold and dead on his kitchen floor. He didn't doubt for a second that she could handle it. He also didn't doubt that she'd been using their respective busyness levels to ignore him, even though they slept side by side every night.

The text was from Valerie.

She'd been invaluable this last week, being hands-on with his mother when he couldn't and generally buffering the woman for him. His feelings about her were straightforward. He considered her a friend and nothing more. But she could handle Virginia Fitzgerald's bursts of emotion and bouts of depression better than anyone, it seemed.

I'm in the building. Brought lunch, she said in her message.

He smiled when she appeared within seconds, a bag of delicious-smelling food in one hand and her phone in the other.

"Thanks." He rose and stretched, his chest still tight at the memory of Evelyn's gaunt face and her continued silent treatment. He was batting a thousand with her, no doubt. And it made him nuts. But he had zero energy to do anything about it. *I should call Ross,* he thought, even as he smiled at Valerie, taking in the slim line of her black skirt, creamy silk shirt and high heels in a fairly typical male fashion.

"You look terrible," she said as she set out the sandwiches and drinks. "I know you miss working at the brewery." She sat, crossed her legs, and gave him a searching look.

Austin suddenly wanted nothing more than to talk to someone who would talk back. He hadn't had time to really connect with Ross in the last two weeks, although he knew Evelyn had filled him in on what had happened. At that moment, nothing seemed more perfect than dumping it all on a woman he'd known for years, one of his oldest friends.

After nearly forty minutes of telling her pretty much

everything, including Evelyn's potential, but ultimately non-existent pregnancy and their new dynamic with Ross — since Valerie had known about their relationship in Germany — he felt a thousand times better. She remained quietly sympathetic, offering a few comments, mostly just listening. Eventually, she got up and cleared away their mess.

When she came around the desk and stood a bit too close to his chair, he did a mental double take, realizing he probably had said too much. But she put a hand on his shoulder, leaned down and brushed his cheek with a kiss, grabbed her purse and started for the door.

He sat, a little dumbstruck by the whole scene. Visions of Evelyn, her bright blue eyes and smart mouth that likely would have a few things to say about his whiney diatribe, passed through his brain. Valerie turned, her thin frame encased in designer names from head to toe. "I'm here for you, Austin, whenever you need an ear. I'd like to be more for you again. But I understand I can only be a friend, so please count on me."

He nodded, wondering what had just happened. Then Assistant Number One stuck her head in the door, reminding him of his next meeting and his brain clouded over at the crushing weight of unwanted responsibility.

After hours spent with a consultant, the human resources director, and his father's trusted attorney, he felt even worse. He groped for his phone, needing to hear Evelyn's voice, even if she were still pissed at him for whatever reason.

His pockets were empty. "Excuse me a second, gentlemen." He stood and took deep breaths to calm his nerves as he walked back to his office. The damn thing was nowhere to be found. "Jill!" he barked at Assistant Number Two.

She looked up from her computer screen. "Yes?"

He ground his teeth. "Have you seen my phone?"

* * * *

Evelyn stared at the woman across the elegant, cloth-draped table and let the humming in her ears that signaled major angry meltdown deafen her for a few more seconds. She sipped her iced tea then patted her lips with the crisp linen napkin as the sounds of a busy country club restaurant ebbed and flowed around her, mocking the innocuous... thing Austin's mother had just suggested to her.

Virginia mirrored her, all the while keeping her evil smile fixed in place as if she had not told Evelyn to get out of her son's life — in exchange for an obscene amount of money.

An envelope sat on the table between them, an embossed and heavy reminder of just how her life had been reduced to a mere number with a dollar sign attached to it.

The horrible woman's words kept coming, assaulting her in spite of her effort to not care. "I understand." She patted Evelyn's hand. The feel of her ice-cold skin broke Evelyn's silence.

"No, actually I don't think you do." Her face flushed hot and she recognized the familiar onrushing fury. She let it loose, keeping her voice low. "Your son is the one who wanted to marry me. He had to ask me five or six times before I agreed to it. And I just figured out why it took me so long to agree to it." She stood, a little wobbly but resolute.

Austin's mother merely looked at her, as if a scene was exactly what she had expected from his down-market fiancée. "Dear. Please sit. You need to know all of it. This must be a shock after all the...time you have spent together. But poor Austin couldn't bring himself to tell you himself. Bless his heart. He and Valerie are back together."

Evelyn picked up the envelope and tore it in half before shoving it in the remains of her soggy tuna salad.

"I thank you, Virginia, truly. For finally showing me the light." She kept a smile on her face at the cost of actual physical pain since what she wanted to do was dump the woman's expensive wine on her head. "If you are so fucking evil that you would punish your son, make him miserable just to further your own agenda, well, that's a family I want no part of. Because, I promise you, he will hate you for this." She stepped closer and leaned down to the woman's powdery-smelling ear. "I feel sorry for you. I wouldn't waste a good hate on someone as pitiful as you."

Her chest constricted as she made her way out of the chilly room and out into the parking lot. "Shit, shit." She dropped her keys to the pavement, then cracked the back of her head on the side mirror, bringing tears to her eyes.

She pulled to the side of the road before she had an accident, and hit Austin's speed dial. If she could only hear his voice, she'd know this whole thing was bullshit. He'd laugh, make some stupid joke out of it, and they'd be fine. She realized she'd been distant since his father's death, but that, on top of the pregnancy scare, plus her new role as head of Fitzgerald Brewing Company had turned her into a jittery mess. The fact that she hadn't allowed him his own frustrations, hadn't listened when he'd needed it hit her right between the eyes.

She'd fix all that now.

This whole thing was another one of Virginia's manipulations. He'd set her straight.

"Hello?" a woman's voice answered Austin's phone after one ring.

Evelyn gripped the steering wheel. "Jill? It's Evelyn. Is Austin around?"

"Oh, this isn't Jill. It's Valerie. I'm sorry, but Austin's a little busy at the moment..."

Evelyn stared down the tunnel that had just opened up in front of her vision, and threw the phone out of the window.

By the time she eased the car into the underground parking garage of Austin's building, Evelyn had calmed. She was so calm, it alarmed her. But she went with it, letting her non-racing pulse and her non-pounding heart guide her forward to the next obvious steps.

She turned the key, listening to the expensive German-made motor fade as her grip on the soft leather steering wheel tightened. But her breathing remained calm and tears didn't threaten as she glared out of the windshield at the dull gray concrete wall.

Sucking in a huge breath, hoping to force her hands to release, she got a lungful of expensive car interior. Glancing over to the passenger seat, still unable to move, she took in the small, tasteful bag. The interior light caught the metal on the understated, elegant designer watch. Her sunglasses chose that moment to slide off her hair down to her nose. A bright light seemed to pierce her eyeballs, making her wince. All of this—the cars, jewelry, accessories, condo, vacations, every ounce of food and drink she'd consumed for the last few months—was his. Not hers.

How had she allowed herself to get to this point? This dependent on a man—a man who had claimed he loved her. But was apparently just another cheating asshole, mama's boy.

A film seemed to cover her eyes. She glanced down, confused by the fact that her linen pants legs were damp. She touched them, honestly not even realizing that she must have been crying for the last ten minutes or so. She was that numb.

Evelyn Benedict, her inner, better self insisted, *this is all a huge misunderstanding. A giant one, to be sure. But Austin loves you. Why would you think otherwise? You're being overly dramatic. Just tell him what his mother did, laugh, then drag his ass to some wedding-planning events. It's what you want, and your endless need to play poor little poor girl is getting old.*

She pressed a hand to her forehead to shut the stupid, logical bitch up.

Now, now, it kept talking. *You know I'm right. That Valerie must have his phone because…*

Evelyn let out a primal scream and beat her fists against the steering wheel. "Well?" she cried out to the empty car interior. "What's your answer to that? Why would Valerie be answering his goddamn phone? Huh? Well?"

217

The voice shut up.

So she climbed out of the car, rode the elevator to the top floor, used her key in the lock, all the while marveling at the everydayness of this moment. She stood in the foyer, taking in the familiar, yet utterly strange, tasteful furnishings. The sight of her threadbare white robe draped over the leather couch glowed like a beacon of inappropriate, out-of-place tackiness.

At that moment, a massive cramp hit her belly. She marched grimly to the bathroom, where her suspicions about a pregnancy were realized.

Just a scare. Nothing to worry about. Move along with your lives.

Once she'd cleaned up, a firm resolution came over her. She headed toward the closet where she'd stashed a couple of broken-down boxes from a few years ago. Those, plus three of the oh-so-expensive pieces of luggage he'd bought for their last vacation would do quite nicely.

She threw them onto the huge bed, then started yanking her clothes off their hangers and out of drawers. All the while holding back tears. She would not cry. She refused to give him the satisfaction.

A drop of blood hit her hand. She licked her lip. She'd been biting on it so hard she'd made herself bleed.

Jesus.

Her knees shook and her hands trembled.

But she would not cry.

She heard Austin open the door, his keys hitting the bowl where he kept them, his footfalls echoing as he walked into the kitchen. She heard him open a beer. But she stayed frozen in place, incapable of movement.

Her heart chose that moment to speed up so fast her chest hurt. He knew she was here. They parked side by side so he would have seen her car. He must be figuring out how to break it to her. That he and that…that…skinny cunt of a debutante were indeed back together.

No, Evelyn. Go to him. Let him explain. Tell him exactly what happened today. Give him a chance to make it right before you temper tantrum yourself straight out of this amazing relationship.

"Shut up," she growled to herself.

"Honey?" She heard him making his way down the hall, the Turkish rug muffling his steps. She stared at the floor, trying to figure out what to say that did not involve screaming, cursing or thrown objects. "Hey, what's all... this?" His voice faded.

She looked at him, slumped in the doorway. He'd lost weight—couldn't manage to eat from stress, he claimed. Tears threatened but she bit them back and set her jaw.

"This is me. Leaving."

"I gathered as much." He kept his voice light. His usual method of dealing with hysteria on her part involved keeping it calm, cool, and collected. The bastard could pull it off in pretty much every circumstance.

"Well, if you'll excuse me?"

Tell him, Evelyn. Tell him...

"No. I won't." He grabbed her arm.

She yanked out of his grasp. "Spare me. I get it. I delayed the wedding too long so you turned to the junior varsity squad and plucked out a new player."

He stared at her. His eyes flashed with anger. "What in the hell... Are you drunk?"

"Fuck you, no. I'm not."

"Then what in God's name are you talking about?"

She sighed, slumped against the wall opposite their— no, scratch that, his—bedroom. She had to get out. Get away from him. This was too much. "Look, Austin, I get it. Valerie is a better fit for you all around. I'm too volatile. Too emotional. Too...down-market. You guys should be together."

Austin's jaw dropped, then he threw his head back and laughed so hard she feared for his sanity. Finally, he stopped and leveled his gaze at her. "What happened, Evelyn? I know you went to lunch with my mother. What in the hell did she say to you?"

"Why does it matter?" Her brain was buzzing now. The voice demanded that she tell him. Let him explain. But she just could not. And his next words sealed that deal for her.

"Because, frankly, if after all the time we've had together, all the conversations about her manipulation skills, and the months I stayed away from them for your sake can't convince you that I love you no matter what...well—" He ran a hand down his haggard face. Her heart clenched. "Maybe you should go." His eyes hardened, which made her react in kind. "I am so sick and tired of trying to reassure you. To make you believe that you are beautiful, talented, and deserving of everything that our life together means to me. You've resisted so hard for so long I'm exhausted."

"Fine." She shouldered past him. Slamming the suitcases shut, she stayed dry-eyed, to her amazement. Turning slowly, she crossed her arms over her chest. "But just so you know, the amount of money your mother was willing to pay me to get out of your life meant nothing. I walked out of her snotty country club lunchroom fully prepared to tell you about this. Until, of course, I called you."

He shook his head and rubbed his eyes, as if not understanding what she meant. "Wait, what? What money? When did you call me?"

"Why does any of it matter?" She made a valiant attempt to pick up both boxes, and grab one of the suitcases. And managed to dump the contents of both cardboard containers onto the floor. That breached the dam of tears. She slumped to the floor, face in her hands. Austin was at her side in a second, kissing her, holding her close.

"Shh, my Evelyn, please don't cry."

But no amount of his coddling or comfort meant anything to her anymore. She had no business here, with him, in this life. It was over. Valerie's chipper voice on the other end of the phone was simply one hint too many.

Don't be stupid, Evelyn. You love him.

Yes, she assured herself. But I can't do this anymore. Can't pretend he won't always be thinking about her. *About the woman who for whatever reason answered his damn phone today. After his mother had claimed her son and his old girlfriend, she of the chipper "No, this is Valerie and Austin is busy," were 'together'.*

Austin felt encased in a sort of deafening cotton batting. Noises were muffled and his vision fuzzy around the edges. He held her, let her cry it out, but he sensed the small bit of control he had over his life slipping out of his desperate grip. "Shh," he crooned once more. But he wasn't shocked when Evelyn wrenched out of his arms.

She crawled to the boxes and started throwing all her shit back into them. He watched, his arm resting on a bent knee, as if observing someone else's woman packing up to leave.

He had no words. The weird moment between him and Valerie earlier still rattled him. The extreme stress of the last weeks piled on, heaping more tension on top of the quivering ball of nerves that wore his suit. He barely recognized himself in the mirror anymore.

She stood. He stared at her with what must have been a dull look on his face. He didn't have the energy to fight her. Everything he had was wrong now. His brewery, his love life—all of it. All vanished in the blink of a single loose blood clot that had felled his once powerful father. He shut his aching eyes, willing it all back the way it was, as if he had that power.

"I'm not pregnant. So you don't have to worry about child support or anything," she stated.

He clambered to his feet. "Stop. Stop it right now, dammit. This is ridiculous. Put this shit away. Let's eat something and calm down." His heart pounded, ramping up the dull daily ache in head a thousand-fold.

"No, Austin. It's not ridiculous. It's just reality. I'm glad I figured it all out now. Before I really got hurt."

"Wait!" he yelled, but it only came out a whisper. "I love you," he said to the closed door, then fell back on the bed, more exhausted than he'd ever been. Sleep. That was what he needed. A few hours, then he'd find her.

He'd figure all this out.

He'd make it right.

His dreams were a cacophony of emotions, swirling with the faces of the people he loved. He woke with a start, thinking he heard a baby cry. He reached for his phone. He needed to call Ross. He would talk sense to her. But then he remembered his phone was lost, missing or something. He flopped back on the pillow as the migraine exploded across his weary brain, sinking its hooks in nice and deep.

He'd sort this out tomorrow. He was certain of it.

Chapter Twenty-Six

One month later

You again?

She typed out an answer when Ross dinged her on Skype for the thousandth time. She had tried to spare him the lame, useless way she'd spiraled downward since losing Austin. But the damn man would not leave her in peace.

Who else?

What is it?

She stretched her arms up and contemplated yet another day filled with work, home, sleep, lather, rinse, repeat.

Just wondering if you had heard the latest.

About what?

I'm the new brew master at Fitzgerald.

Great. Enjoy it.

And I've convinced Austin to hire you back.

Her skin prickled.

I have a job. Walked back into Tri-City Distribution with a promotion, as a matter of fact.

It was a solid five minutes before he replied.

Why won't you talk to him, Evelyn? He's miserable.

His misery is no longer my problem. It's Valerie's.

What the hell happened anyway?

She bit her lip, conjuring a reason to keep holding the whole thing back. And came up short.

They were together just after his father died. His mother took me to a lovely lunch to tell me because he couldn't do it.

How do you know that's really what went down? You know how his mother is. Did you even give him a chance to explain?

The blinding rage she'd felt that day, when Valerie's smooth voice had answered Austin's phone, rushed back into her aching chest. She shut her eyes, attempting to stay calm.

The day she'd driven out of the underground parking garage, she'd gone straight to her friend Melody's place and cried for two solid days.

She'd taken off the ring, canceled all the wedding planning crap, driven his stupid, expensive car over to his stupid, expensive condo and left it with the ring in the glove compartment, the key with the doorman. What hurt most was leaving her set of keys to Fitzgerald Brewing in the ashtray with a note, indicating that she'd told the management team she'd be on a leave of absence, indefinitely.

What he did about that damn place was now also solely his problem.

Ross, I delayed marrying him for a reason. And his mother gave me one. Let it go. I'm guessing he isn't exactly pining for me.

What I do know is I need you to help me get the brewery straightened out again. I can forgive you a lot, because I realize the inherent asshole-ish tendencies of men, but walking away from the brewery? Leaving it high and dry? You have to come back and fix it with me.

Listen to me, Ross. I don't care. I have a job. You have a life. Go live it and leave me alone.

She logged out before he could respond and sat, staring out of the window of her new office at Tri-City Distribution. She needed to get home and pack. It was beer fest week again in Denver and her role as beer manager for a distribution company meant a whole different set of tasks for that event.

She'd tried to get out of it, knowing the memories would likely kill her. But Grant had insisted. He was getting a little insistent about other stuff, too. She shifted in her chair, recalling the fairly forgettable kiss they'd shared late last night in his office.

God, she so did not want him. But the man she loved would never be hers. That much was crystal clear. Her silly fantasy life had popped like a soap bubble, right in front of her eyes. And it was partly her fault, to be certain. Thinking she could have two men? All to herself? What a load of crap.

Melody had insisted that she stay in her extra bedroom for the time being. Evelyn had never been more grateful to have such a friend in her life. They were well-matched — even in their tendencies to keep a polite distance from each other's personal lives. They both worked at Tri City — Melody in the business and logistics department, picking up extra cash bartending at Top of the Hops, one of the newer, trendier craft beer joints in Grand Rapids. Plus, the woman was a total beer fanatic and an expert the level of which Evelyn wished she could be.

Evelyn sat up nearly all night after getting her stuff ready for the early flight, staring at nothing and wondering how she'd gone from loved and loving to alone and miserable.

The fact that she knew she could shoulder a lot of the blame didn't make her feel any better.

* * * *

Austin glared at the computer screen, exhaustion making his vision dimmer by the minute. While on the one hand he was beyond relieved that he'd convinced Ross to dump his west coast gig so quickly and come run Fitzgerald for him while he managed his father's food company, on the other, the thought of Ross working alongside Evelyn without him made his teeth ache. He had no doubt Ross would convince her to come back. She was meant to run a brewery, not to be some sales manager flunkey at a distributor.

But the fact that she wouldn't return his calls, texts, emails, and that she'd dumped the Mercedes in the parking garage of his condo building, chock-full of every last stich of clothing, accessories, and electronics he'd given her, and, of course, the engagement ring, spoke volumes about his chances trying to make her see sense.

Once he'd clarified with his mother that she was no longer welcome anywhere near his office or the business and told Valerie to hand over his goddamned phone and get the fuck out of his life — again — he'd settled into his new reality.

Work, work, and more work, each day ending with a half a bottle of bourbon or a six-pack of beer and him passed out on the couch, rarely even making it to his bed.

With a groan, he rose and stretched out the kinks in his lower back. He'd put a lot into his plea to get Ross to come run Fitzgerald Brewing Company. And he hoped it would be worth it. As much as Evelyn claimed she wanted nothing more to do with him or his brewery, he knew she'd have a hard time resisting Ross' offer to come back and run the place.

Ross said he'd go out to Denver on their behalf. Claimed he'd find Evelyn and force her to talk to him, that he would get it sorted out so Fitzgerald Brewing, at least, would have her back.

Man up, Fitzgerald, and forget her. Live this life you've chosen for yourself. Or one that's been chosen by fate for you.

But he couldn't. Evelyn's voice, face, body, laughter, and smartass attitude rose in his head daily, sometimes hourly. Hence the booze and the passing out every night, and the huge hole full of shit that he raised his head from daily, suited and ready for work. How he'd gone in the space of a mere twelve months from last year's incredible discovery at the beer fest to this year when he'd have to watch from afar, miserable and alone, he had no earthly idea. But he was bound and determined to make one thing happen— to get Ross and Evelyn running his brewery the way they were meant to do.

Chapter Twenty-Seven

Denver, Colorado
Two weeks later

The buzz in the huge Denver convention hall reached deafening levels. Evelyn tried not to look too obvious glancing around yet again. She hadn't seen Austin in a while. But nothing had softened the harsh edges of her longing for him. Even painted with a bright red coat of anger, the need to see him, touch him, and hear his voice, choked her most days. She nodded to the media guy still talking to her, no longer listening to anything he said.

Her head-splitting hangover and extreme disbelief that he'd really not show competed for attention in her brain. When a sudden shift in the crowd allowed her to catch a glimpse of a familiar set of broad shoulders and long blond hair, she narrowed her eyes.

Before she could blink, Ross had a strong arm around her waist, his deep German-inflected voice in her ear. She stiffened, nearly gagging on the glut of memories his touch engendered.

She closed her eyes and let him hold her as the crowd moved around them.

"Let's sit." He gestured for the media gaggle to disperse and led her to a couple of chairs near the aisle. As the place filled and got even louder from the fans at the back who had to stand to see the awards ceremony, she remained acutely aware of his touch.

When his hand landed on her leg, she shifted. It didn't budge. She kept up the inane conversation, completely unaware of whom she spoke to or what she said. Her head spun with too much beer, emotion, and now no small measure of something she reluctantly identified as lust.

She took a second to glance up at the tall blond specimen who had his hot palm parked possessively on her thigh.

"You're a day late." This was not an auspicious start to a working relationship. She let anger replace the renewed sexual tension he'd created, despite them being in the middle of a huge crowd. She'd made a decision somewhere in the depths of yet another sleepless night. She would come back to Fitzgerald, work with Ross, and get the brewery back on track. She'd said as much to him in a two a.m. Skype message, then turned the thing off.

She'd been miserable at Tri-City. The challenge of marketing the brewery had been immense, but much more satisfying. The next day they'd finalized their employment negotiations, and Ross had promised Austin would stay away, let them make all major decisions together and not interfere. She'd made him swear that Austin wouldn't be around — at all, for any reason. Because actually laying eyes on him would kill what was left of the human in her. She could be the marketing director and wanted to be that again, but not if it meant she had to interact with him in any way.

Melody's words as she'd headed out of the door one morning had torn it. In a somewhat typical fashion, she'd grabbed Evelyn's briefcase handle and glared at her. "Go back to Fitzgerald," she'd said, her dark eyes blazing. "You owe it to yourself, and to what you started there, Austin be damned."

Evelyn had stared at her, amazed and not a little bit annoyed. "Tell you want, Mel. I'll do that. Only if you promise me you'll answer Trent's endless calls, emails and text messages. The poor man's sent everything short of smoke signals. Seriously." She looked around their shared space, full to the brim with flowers, thanks to Trent's efforts to communicate with Melody.

Her friend had let go of the briefcase and stepped back, rubbing one bare arm with her other hand, "That's...not your business."

"Oh no?" Evelyn re-shouldered her purse and crossed her arms. In her head, she was already formulating her resignation from Tri-City. It was an inauspicious time to do so but she'd offer to help out in Denver if they wanted her to, one last time. "It's no more my business than mine with Austin Fitzgerald is yours, I guess."

Melody smiled, her deep olive-toned skin fairly glowing in the hallway's weak light. "Deal," she said, holding out her hand. "I'll make up with Trent—or try to, and you make up with—"

"Hold on right there. I'm not making up with anyone. But I will..." She stopped and swallowed hard. "I will go back and work with Ross."

She'd resigned from Tri-City, turned the beer fest tasks over to her assistant. She and Ross had agreed they would announce the new arrangement out in Denver at one of the many parties.

And now she glanced down at Ross' palm that was practically caressing her leg. On impulse, she covered it with hers, swallowing the sudden rush of alarming desire. She picked up his hand and put it firmly back on his own leg. "Surely you didn't mean to do that."

He smiled, not meeting her eyes. "Yes. Actually, I did."

She frowned, staring straight ahead. The man was too charming for his own good. She'd forgotten how much. But this was *her* moment. She had to convince this crowd, the media, her colleagues, that Fitzgerald was back and better than ever, despite the yawning absence of its handsome, charismatic founder.

Her heart raced, but she couldn't figure out whether from excitement or fury at Ross' behavior. She refused to make eye contact with him and instead watched the announcer on the stage as she ground out, "I needed you here yesterday."

"Don't be angry." His lips brushed her ear, made her skin

pebble. "I've got an alibi. Things are going to be looking up for Fitzgerald Brewing. You can call me your master brewer and your walking press release." He clutched her thigh once more, claimed it as his territory while his voice rumbled in her ear. "We need to talk later. Alone."

Her entire body zinged at his words. He had no business changing the tenor of their newly forged professional relationship. She tried to focus.

She must have blocked his gorgeousness from her memory banks. Tall, nearly six foot four, the broadest shoulders she'd ever seen on a man, long blond hair tied with a strip of leather, square jaw covered with light, reddish beard and those eyes—the term lethally blue floated through her foggy brain. She shook her head and kept frowning, blocking out the rest. Even as the memory of his incredible body, talented lips and hands, and his face beneath her, curtained by the fall of her hair, almost choked her with their clarity.

The pressure on her leg eased. Ross stood, put a finger to her cheek and gave her a knee-melting smile before going up to the stage.

What the hell?

Ross? National Brewer of the Year?

She gulped, clapped, and acknowledged the congratulations of those all around her while her eyes locked onto his amazing denim-covered ass moving down the aisle. Her entire body broke out in chills.

The crush of media and fellow brewery owners afterward separated them, resigning her to yet another evening shaking hands, drinking too much, and falling into her hotel bed alone. Tears burned behind her eyes.

"Evelyn! Hold up!"

She turned and came face to face with him, closer than was necessary, but suddenly she didn't care anymore.

"Can I talk to you a minute?"

The immediate crowd around them fell silent. She frowned as her scalp tingled.

Shit. Get control of yourself. He's just being nice. He probably has some size-two skinny-bitch fan club waiting somewhere. How could he not? He couldn't be interested in her anymore. They were friends now, at her insistence. Just that. They were colleagues, nothing more or less.

Besides, the extra pounds she carried around now put her firmly out of serious consideration as sexy.

She lifted her chin, resisted the urge to tug on her too-tight shirt, and gave him a look she prayed he'd interpret as cool and aloof, not panting and horny.

Horny? Jesus, where did that come from? She tried to move away, keep her balance, maintain her distance.

"Congrats, Ross. A celebrity now, eh? Glad your salary negotiations are done already." She frowned when he took her arm and guided her firmly away from the cameras, his lips inappropriately close to her ear.

"Remember, we need to talk. In private."

Staying silent, she let herself be led out of the cavernous hall filled with increasingly drunken idiots, past the line of security, and into a darkened hallway. Once they were alone, she pulled her arm out of his grasp.

"What the hell? We need to be in there, Mr. Walking Press Release." Her throat closed when she made the mistake of meeting his eyes. The deep sapphire snap of his gaze held her, bringing back way too many memories of their time together with Austin. She repressed a groan at the long-blocked images racing through her skull.

Reaching out, she ran trembling fingers across the tight red curls on his jaw, unsure why she wanted to touch him, but needing it more than she needed anything at that moment. He closed his eyes. Time seemed to stretch between them. She remembered his reticence when it came to anything resembling emotion and decided to speak first.

"I have no idea what you're doing right now, but…" Her voice barely registered in her own ears. The pounding heart she'd sustained all day grew louder. "I should go." She took a step to the side.

Go. Now. Before you make a giant mistake.

He mirrored her, letting his tap handle-shaped trophy fall to the floor with a loud *clank*. He cradled her face in his huge hands. "I don't know either, but—" He swallowed, looked up at the ceiling, then back at her. "I'm going with it, if that's okay with you." His lips hovered over hers. She could barely breathe. The sounds of the fest echoed down the empty hall. Familiar odors of stale beer stung her nose. "Because if I can't kiss you in the next five seconds, I will make a huge, embarrassing scene." His infectious grin forced a smile and a sigh when he finally touched his mouth to hers.

It started out tentative but picked up urgency. Once he parted her lips with his tongue, he kissed her so hard her ears rang. He kept his body separate at first, but by the time he'd swept into her mouth, she had no more qualms.

She wrapped her arms around him, clutched him close, and moaned when he pressed her against the wall. Tearing herself away, she struggled to get control. He touched his tongue to her cheek, tasting her tears. "I can't," she murmured, eyes tightly shut. The unmistakable heat of his erection pressed against her. "I. You— This is…" Austin's face wafted across her vision.

"Shh, my love." He nipped at her earlobe. Keeping one hand propped on the wall, he ran the other hand down her back and cupped her ass. She sighed and repressed thoughts about the extra padding on her body. After the disastrous breakup, she'd gone into a spiral of ice-cream-and-booze-addled grief, and the twenty pounds she'd added to her frame refused to budge.

"You are perfect. Exactly as a woman should be." He made a low hum in his throat. His mouth found the dip between her collarbones and he cradled the swell of her breast. "I have missed you, so much." His soft German accent ramped up her libido. "And I'm not waiting any longer."

She shifted, allowing the thigh he shoved between her

legs. He dove into her mouth once again, his hands all over her ass, back, breasts. Her nipples ached, requiring contact. Her clit pulsed against the inside of her soaking-wet panties.

He yanked her T-shirt out of her jeans, shoved it up, and pulled her bra aside. Lowering his lips to one rock-hard nub of flesh, he sighed against her skin as if in relief.

She threaded her fingers in his hair, tugging it free of the leather tie and relishing the silky strands in her eager, shaking hands. "Harder," she ground out. "Please, Ross." She couldn't believe the words coming from her mouth, but she let them flow. "I need it, ah, Jesus!"

In one smooth motion, he had her jeans popped open and his hand down into her panties. The rich smell of her arousal enveloped them. It had been so long she'd honestly believed she would never feel this way again. But it all came rushing back in a whirl of erotic recollection.

She cupped the impressive bulge in his jeans, the memory of what lay underneath the denim taking her breath away.

"No," he growled against her breast and pinned both her wrists over her head. He sucked her nipple so hard it brought more tears to her eyes and dampness between her legs. "I'm touching now. You must wait." She angled her hips, eager to get him deeper. "Oh God, Evelyn, I want to taste you." His eyes sparkled in the darkness. "But, in the meantime, I must hear you come."

He stroked her clit with his thumb and plunged two fingers inside her. Capturing her mouth once more, swallowing her groans, he slid his fingers in and out, all the while grinding his cock against her leg. She gripped the bunched muscles of his arm.

She spread her legs, needing more. He sank his fingers in deeper. Her body flushed, the hallway closed in on her, and the orgasm bowled her over her so hard she cried out, heard his name escape her lips. Loudly.

Wave after wave of ecstasy drowned her senses, shutting off all noise, all vision.

Ross had offered her the most erotic experiences of her

life a mere twelve months ago. But she had cut him off. Like she had Austin. A tiny flame of regret blazed in her soul. She'd been so quick to judge. So eager to think the worst of the man she had loved.

"I've missed the sound of your voice so much." He hovered just out of reach. He nuzzled her neck. "I want to hear you cry out my name again and again. Dear God, I have missed you, Evelyn. Everything about you." Grasping the back of her neck with his free hand, he slanted his mouth over hers once more. The kiss spoke volumes about his neediness and the last of her defenses slipped away.

Face stinging from so much contact with his beard, knees on the verge of collapse, she stared up at the ceiling. As if sensing her need for space, he pulled his fingers out of her body and sucked them into his mouth, eyes closed with reverence, then owned her mouth with his again, giving her a taste of herself. She threaded her fingers in his hair once more. He broke the kiss and gazed into her soul.

"I need you," she whispered. He smiled—a lazy, sexy thing that made her nerves do another erotic tap dance. She mentally smacked herself. Why would she say that? Other than the fact it was true.

Keeping his gaze on hers, he zipped up her jeans, tucked her brewery T-shirt back in the waistband and cupped her ass, grinding his erection against her. She leaned in and bit down on the skin of his neck, tasting his sweat. His hips thrust against her. She smiled. "Now. If not sooner."

"I am all yours. But later. As you said, we should get back. And we still need to talk. About Austin." His hands' slow journey from her ass, to hip, to waist, breast, and then her face made her tremble in anticipation. Damn, if she wasn't ready to drop trou and jump him right there in the hallway. His mention of Austin's name did nothing to quell her desire. His next moves didn't help.

"I want you to think about this." He nipped her neck. "And this." He ran a thumb across her stiff nipple. "And this." He put her palm against his straining zipper. "Because—"

"Ross! You down there?" a deep voice echoed through the space.

Evelyn jerked away from him, logic flooding her brain. Ross didn't move, his incredible blue gaze locked on hers.

"*Ja*, who wants to know?" He put a palm against her flushed cheek. She shook her head to clear it. This man was her colleague now, for God's sake. She nearly wept with embarrassment.

Ross' gaze darkened. "What the fuck do you want?" he shouted at the disembodied voice.

Unmistakably male footsteps echoed down the hall. He sighed and stepped back from her, adjusted the bulge under his zipper, and grabbed the trophy where he'd dumped it before kissing her. She fled, face burning with embarrassment.

Ross watched her go, jaw clenched at the deep ache in his gut. He didn't like holding off, delaying his own satisfaction, and his balls declared their unhappiness loud and clear. He closed his eyes and took a deep breath. That amazing experiences they'd shared had haunted him, especially when she'd cut him off after the disaster with Austin. But something about her that made him protective and horny all at once had flared today, forcing him to act.

"Don't ask me about it, all right," Austin had insisted when Ross had asked, angrily, what he'd done to ruin things with Evelyn. "I mean it." And Ross had to respect the finality of that. He'd never been one to dig too deep, emotionally speaking, so who was he to insist anyone else act differently?

But it had confused him, hurt him all over, recalling the intensity of the love Austin and Evelyn had shared. All he knew of the break-up was what Evelyn had told him. And no matter how many times he tried to insist that Austin was not with Valerie in any way, shape or form, she refused to listen.

He was in for some interesting times ahead, that much

was certain. He put his fingers to his lips, smelling and tasting her again, which rendered his efforts to soften the massive erection straining his jeans somewhat moot.

This is a mess, Ross. Stay out of it.

But he was incapable of that, and he knew it now.

"Is she, I mean, uh," he'd said to Austin, trying to decide the best way to determine exactly where things stood between them the day he'd agreed to leave the west coast and run Fitzgerald Brewing.

"Do whatever you want with her," Austin had said, his voice devoid of emotion. "She and I are finished."

But Ross knew damn good and well that was not the case. Unfortunately, at that precise moment, all he wanted was her. And he would have her, that very night. Austin's apparent screw-up with her be damned.

Chapter Twenty-Eight

"No, no, really, guys. I'm exhausted." Evelyn motioned for the check. Her head swam with gin and remorse. She'd allowed herself to be corralled into an after party once the day's expo work was done and the last drunken beer taster had been ejected from the convention center. "I'm calling it."

Amid congratulations and promises of rain checks, she made her slow way down the narrow steps to the surprisingly luxurious restrooms.

She liked staying at the Oxford when in Denver, more out of tradition than anything else. A little shabby, but cool as hell, it boasted the best martini bar in the city. And she didn't risk reminders of Austin too much since he always preferred the downtown Marriott with its huge suites.

She glared in the mirror over the sink. The same five-foot-nine-inch, former happy fiancée of the most amazing man in the world, now twenty pounds overweight, with a desperation in her eyes that made her ill, female met her gaze. She hated the image of herself lately.

The echo of Ross' rough German-accented voice made a blush rise from her cheeks. *"I want to taste you."*

What a colossal mistake. How could she have done that with him earlier? Groping and dry humping like a couple of teenagers at a house party. Ugh. She made herself sick.

Austin's face danced across her vision. She'd nearly gotten past the throat-choking agony that usually brought. But it all fell in on her again. That amazing moment with Ross at the convention center had somehow brought back Austin's memory as bright and sharp as a razor's edge.

Biting back more tears, she looked down, trying to regain her composure, hoping she could hold it together for the rest of the festival.

When a large hand dropped onto her shoulder, she flinched and turned. Ross stared at her for a split second, then pulled her to him before she could protest, crushing her against the hard warmth of his chest, silencing her with a tongue-tangling kiss.

She let go of the final vestige of propriety, the last little bit of logic, and wrapped her entire body around the huge, gorgeous man who'd apparently followed her into the restroom with one thing on his mind.

Shoving away her inner protests, she reached down to release his cock, humming in her throat at its familiar velvety-skinned steel in her hand. When she wiped her thumb across the pearling moisture at the tip, he gasped with pleasure, then pushed her back against the wall and had her jeans down and off within seconds. All thoughts of her failed relationship faded. Her focus now zeroed in on the man she'd had once as lover and a friend, needing a connection with him so badly her throat had closed up with emotion.

"God, Ross," she gasped as he shoved up her shirt and lowered his lips to her nipples, tugging at them as he ripped her damp scrap of lace panties into two pieces.

"*Ja*, my darling, my Evelyn," he muttered into her flesh. As she reveled in the tumble of blond hair between her fingers, he started crooning softly in German. She leaned her head against the wall, her emotions tangled with chaos, but her body locked in on a single goal, namely satisfaction and renewed connection.

"Wait, do you have…?"

Damn, she was out of practice.

Ross raised his face from her breasts, a rubber packet in one hand. He ripped it open with his teeth and handed the latex circle to her. She shoved his shirt up as he braced himself against the wall, sighing with pleasure while she licked her way down his pecs. She flicked his nipple with her tongue then made her way down and sucked the head of his thick cock into her mouth, reveling in the salty deliciousness of him. His hips thrust forward, his fingers wound in her hair. On her knees, she licked down the length of him, cradling his heavy balls in one hand.

"*Ach.* Stop, you are going to—" He yanked her to her feet. "Put that thing on me." His eyes twinkled and he lowered his amazing lips to hers while she rolled the condom down his length.

She sighed as he lifted her, forcing her legs around his waist and held on. He turned them so her back was against the wall as he slipped inside her one incredible inch at a time.

"Hold on, my lovely," he muttered into her hair, his voice husky and low. "Ah…you feel just like I remember." He pressed deeper, then retreated, before burying himself in her, reaching up high and grinding his pubic bone against her clit.

The hard wall against her back, Ross holding them up, the sensation of his body in and out of hers all combined to bring her to the brink of orgasm in a heartbeat. She could hear Austin crooning to her, encouraging her to release her fantasies to him that first weekend.

Ross moved faster, pinning her once again with his intense blue stare. Their combined labored breathing and the musky scent of their shared desire wound around them. His hips rocked against her, bringing stars across her vision.

"Dear God," he breathed into her neck. "Come, my darling. I can feel how much you want to." He shoved harder, going deeper than ever, grunting with the effort. She held on, letting him take her, in public, against the wall like some kind of horny teenager unable to find anywhere else to fuck but in the bathroom.

"Oh! Yes!" The orgasm scorched up her spine, enveloping her, blurring her vision. She locked onto his lips, needing that connection. His tongue swept into her mouth. His hips took on a harder, faster rhythm. He kept kissing her, moaning into her mouth, his entire body shaking with energy as he came.

He broke their kiss and gave a massive shudder.

When she put first one, then the other leg down, she was surprised when her knees gave out. Ross grabbed her before she hit the floor, pulling her close for a deep kiss. Trembling, holding back tears, she allowed the intense memories through the brick wall she'd built over time — let them wash over her, drowning her in so many emotions she couldn't pin them all down.

His scent — all man, with an undercurrent of ever-present malt and hops and yeast — made her wobbly and brought everything she missed about Austin roaring back, along with her long-suppressed desire to be right there, in Ross' arms.

Shaking her head, unwilling to meet his eyes, she tugged her clothes back into place. She started to speak, to protest, to apologize. He lifted her face up to his.

"You are so beautiful." The same words he'd spoken to her the first time they'd made love. He kissed her with a tenderness and longing that spoke of something more than the moment they'd just shared.

"I'm far from that, trust me." She ducked away, her face hot with embarrassment. Surely the man was drunk or something. What could he possibly want from her? "I'll, ah, see you around, okay?"

He looked puzzled. When he touched her face, she refused to lean into his hand.

What did he think? They'd toddle out of there together, to his or her hotel room?

Her whole body reacted to that lovely possibility as she opened the door without a backward look and ran out and up the stairs, her heart thudding, the pulse between her legs nearly as loud.

Dear Lord, she was a sad-sack, desperate cliché. She had let a man fuck her standing up in the women's room. Not just any man, either. The magnitude of what she had done bowled her over, blinded and deafened her.

She shoved the old-fashioned key in the lock and slammed the door behind her. "Shower. I need a shower." She turned the water to the hottest possible setting and crawled under the spray, shivering and berating herself nonstop. Shampoo poured down her body, as she attempted to scrub away the embarrassment, the delicious scent of Ross, the abject mortification at her behavior.

How the hell can I face him now? She braced herself against the black and white tile as her tears mingled with the shower water. "Oh God, what have I done?"

"You've done nothing a healthy, beautiful woman wouldn't do." The soft voice made her scream and clutch the shower curtain around her naked self. Ross' blue eyes gleamed. His grin stood out stark white against the red of his beard. "If she's been pulled into a hallway and practically attacked." He stood, arms crossed, watching her. She frowned at him as fury replaced fear.

"Get the hell out of here, Ross. Seriously. How did you —" He held up a key and stayed put. She clutched the shower curtain tighter, resisting her body's purely chemical reaction to his presence. "Well, it won't happen again, I assure you." She flipped the water off and started to step out, reaching for a towel.

His voice stayed low. "I'm sorry. Truly. Sometimes I don't think with the correct brain. Do you know what I mean?" She snorted. "But we had something once. Something I want to talk about with you."

"Whatever. Get out. You had your fun." She shouldered past him. She had no time for this. Wouldn't allow it to happen. When he touched her bare, damp shoulder, she closed her eyes. "Get out." She moved farther into the room, anything to get away from him before she did something utterly stupid. Like throw him down on the bed that dominated the small room like an omen and climb all over him.

He pulled a bottle from behind his back. She eyed one of her absolute favorite Imperial IPAs. The bastard. He grinned, cracked it open and poured some into a glass, holding it under his nose. "Mmm. Smells nice. Sure I can't stay?"

She had to turn away so he wouldn't see her smiling. The presumptuous asshole. "Yes, I'm sure. Ross, we can't." She dropped into a chair.

He poured a glass. She took it, letting the amazing, perfectly balanced hops and malt concoction ease her throat, allowed the alcohol to warm her from head to toe. She glared at the tall blond man taking up so much sexual energy in the room, the man who now sat casually propped up against the headboard, sipping his beer in silence.

Fine. Two could play at that game.

She let the unspoken words spin out between them, taking on a life of their own. Strangely enough, the silence seemed comfortable, which prompted her to speak. "Austin would have filled the room with mindless chatter just now." She cocked her head and observed Ross. "I miss him so much."

He looked at his empty glass. "Rumor has it he misses you too."

"Whatever." She suddenly needed to be alone. No matter the extreme temptation of the man lying on her bed.

"He wants you back." Ross sat on the edge of the bed and reached over for her to refill his glass. "Rumor has it."

"Not my problem." She shifted in her seat, as exhaustion stole through her again. "I'm tired. Get out of my room."

Suddenly, he stood, unzipped his jeans, stepped out of them, pulled his shirt over his head, and looked at her, in all his lip-smacking, knee-knocking, naked glory. "I came to talk. And we will talk, but first I need to finish what we started."

She turned away. She wouldn't be manipulated by him. "Ross, this is completely inappropriate, no matter what we think we want. This is not what we—"

Before she could finish, he had her on her feet, her towel

still between them, mouth slanted over hers until she was lightheaded with the force of his kiss.

Oh, God. I can't.

In spite of the inner reminders, she wrapped her arms around his neck, hooked a leg around his waist, and pulled them both down on the bed. Their teeth clicked together, tongues tangling with urgency. He ripped the towel from between them, and she tried not to whimper when he broke their kiss.

He loomed over her, that lovely, long shaft warm against her body. "I said earlier I wanted to taste you."

She nodded, speechless.

He paid careful attention to each peaking nipple, aware on some level that he'd effectively sidetracked her attempt to have an actual discussion, but unwilling to stop him now. He had released his long hair and she threaded her fingers through it with a sigh of satisfaction.

"Mmm." His throaty growl made her scalp tingle. He dipped his tongue into her navel, nuzzled the sparse bit of blonde that covered her mound, then crouched between her legs, focusing on her sex — but not touching, just…looking at it.

She shifted. "What? Is there a problem down there?" In her early, utterly numb weeks without Austin, she'd not only put on extra pounds, she'd let other things go, too. The Brazilian wax she'd gotten before heading to the festival made her nervous, worried it looked funny. Plus, she was about to orgasm under his gaze, he had her built up so.

"No. Everything is perfect. Touch yourself. Let me watch."

She reached down and flicked her clit. She needed the release badly enough not to feel self-conscious as she rubbed faster and arched up on the bed. Wrapping both legs over his broad shoulders, she proceeded to make herself come, hard, pinching her own nipple, stroking her clit.

Ross' breath came in harsh gasps along with hers as she rubbed herself to orgasm, the amazing erotic sensation of his nearness sending her over the edge. Once she'd calmed, she stretched her arms up, keeping her legs hooked over his shoulders.

As Ross watched Evelyn's beautiful, amazing, lush body writhing and climaxing under his gaze, he struggled to maintain control. He'd been half in love with this woman for a year now. Her soft curves, sexy laugh, gorgeous blue eyes, beer-business savvy — she'd always turned him into a walking hard-on any time she'd been around.

When he'd caught sight of her in the lobby earlier, her face a mask of sadness and barely concealed fury when he'd shown up a day late, he'd known he had to act. He'd ducked behind a column then, not ready to face her. The compulsion to touch, kiss, treat her the way he knew his friend Austin had had pulsed so strong he'd had to bite it back.

Something about this day had felt right. So, he'd acted on it and now, nothing seemed more perfect in his universe than to have Evelyn Benedict — former fiancée of his good friend, and newly appointed head of the brewery where he'd be working — spread and ready for him. All those hours he'd spent staying away, giving her space, but always recalling her classic beauty, her smile, her lips — he'd done more fantasizing about her than he cared to admit.

That weekend this time last year, when they'd consummated an undeniable mutual attraction, stayed etched in his memory like a never-healing scar. He fully acknowledged it probably did him no good to obsess over her. But today, he'd fulfilled a long fantasy with this woman and would keep doing it the entire weekend if he had any say in it.

He groaned at the irony, lowering his face to her flesh to lap at the juices flowing down the inside of her thighs. His brain buzzed with sexual energy and tension. Making his way up, he captured her hard clit between his lips and sucked, forcing another ecstatic cry from her lips.

His cock jerked and leaked even more at the sound and

smell of her. He closed his eyes but opened them when Austin's dark stare appeared. The other man's deep green gaze had always been mesmerizing when they were together. Ross pushed the memory aside as she shuddered, coating his lips with yet more of her delicious fluid.

He climbed up between her legs and captured her lips once more. Her moans suffused every inch of him, suffusing him with happiness than he'd felt in months. He grinned and flipped onto his back, bringing her with him, grabbing the condom he'd pulled from his pocket earlier, fumbling and clumsy in his eagerness. Damn things were no more comfortable than a dick girdle, but given how much he'd played around since he'd been with her, he wasn't about to put her at any risk. She lifted her hips, poised herself above him, her lush breasts inches from his face.

"Please," he choked out in a rough whisper. He ached to be inside her. The connection they'd shared in the bathroom wasn't enough. The memory of her, with Austin, the three of them together, crashed around in his psyche. He gritted his teeth.

Ross wanted to fuck her silly, fall asleep with her in his arms, then wake and start all over again. He'd walked the planet for forty years, screwed countless women, a few men, and fallen hard for only two people.

As she lowered herself onto his cock, enveloping him, he sucked her nipple into his mouth, tugging on it, before he pushed her up, wanting that angle, needing to see her face.

"Please what?" She rocked against his body. He groaned at the sweet sensation of her glove-like grip on his shaft.

"Please. Do that." He thrust up. "Please do exactly what you're doing. Please don't stop. Please fuck me. Please make me come." She leaned down to flick the dark pink circles of his nipples with her sweet tongue, making him move faster.

"Hmm. Aren't you the polite one?" She grinned and brought her face to his, her long blonde hair cascading around him. He cupped her neck, tugged her close. Her body held him, clutched tight again, milking him, pulling him toward the inevitable. At that moment, he saw him.

Austin.

Pictured him behind her, poised to, oh fuck. He thrust faster, harder, his fingers digging into her thighs.

"Ross!" she yelled. He groaned, letting her body take him over the edge while her pussy clutched and pulsed around him. He held her, blinking at the emotion flitting through his brain. When she lifted herself off and flopped down beside him, Ross' breathing slowed, his body absorbing the climax and pushing him toward sleep.

But he couldn't get the vision from his head. There had been a brief moment, when three had been a perfect number, at least for him. He would have gladly carried that relationship on forever. Something about both Austin and Evelyn had fulfilled him more than anything he'd ever experienced. But now, lying here with her, the new possibility of happiness emerged. One without Austin, granted, but one he now wanted, and was determined to keep.

Chapter Twenty-Nine

Four months later

The mantra running through Ross' brain resembled something like *wrong, wrong, totally, completely wrong.* Sweat dripped from his hair. His shoulders and biceps seized up from the brew day's effort.

Strong odors of the wet barley grains from his latest concoction filled his nose, distracting him from the one thing he'd fought for the last month, ever since returning from Denver and admitting how ass over elbow in love he now was with Evelyn Benedict. It strangled him, kept him up nights with a bizarre combination of guilt and terror.

Terror she would figure out that she still loved Austin.

Because he knew she did.

He clenched his eyes shut and pictured her face the night before, when anxiety had worked its cold-shower magic on his dick. "Oh, honey, it's okay," she had soothed him, her lush body enveloping his. "I'm sorry. I mean, you always make sure I'm taken care of. Seems unfair."

Ross had leapt from the bed and pulled his jeans on before stomping into her kitchen to slam some water and get a grip on himself. One of the best things about their relationship so far, besides the near constant mind-blowing sex they had in pretty much every corner of the brewery, the bar and her place, was her ability to leave him the hell alone when he needed to be left alone. Her understanding that his natural reticence about 'feelings' was part and parcel of Ross. But he figured it couldn't last much longer, this patience.

They had progressed from random, illicit sex to sleepovers

pretty quickly. The fact that whenever he woke up without her in his arms, he honestly felt unhappy alarmed him.

She'd followed him to the kitchen. The look in her eyes when he'd turned to face her held something he couldn't place at first. He fully realized that they were in dangerous emotional territory. Years spent alone, staying aloof, even when faced with the extreme irony of their shared connection, were crashing in on him, making him want to do crazy shit, like buy her jewelry. Or, even more insane, make her pregnant.

He truly had gone around the bend.

"So, you gonna pout all night or come back to bed?"

He ran a hand down his face. "I should probably go home." Absolutely the very last thing he wanted to do, of course. With a flash of self-awareness, he accepted that what he needed was for her to ask him to stay.

She raised an eyebrow. "Don't let me keep you."

Closing his eyes once more at the feel of her of soft, warm body against his, he heaved a deep sigh. If he let himself, he could love this woman. But something seemed off, and he knew it had to be his problem, not hers. Their relationship had been intensely physical from the beginning — something they both agreed they needed.

The night he'd been named Brewer of the Year, he'd given in to some sort of base urge, and their relationship ever since had been physically fulfilling. He smiled into her hair, pulled away, and tilted her face up to his. It truly did feel right to have her there in his arms.

If they were identical emotional cripples, so be it. They'd had the support they both needed in Austin. Perhaps without him they could forge a bridge with baby steps. And plenty of arguing, it would seem. Austin had been right about her on many levels, including the one about her always needing to be right. "Then again, maybe I won't go."

* * * *

Evelyn lay awake in the early morning hours, watching Ross sleep, her body languid with satisfaction. He'd rallied — and then some — proving once again that he was better at physical than emotional. She sighed, brushing a strand of his hair back behind his ear. He stirred and opened his eyes, shocking her all over again with their brilliant sapphire hue.

"Morning." He pulled her into his arms. "Want coffee?"

"Sure." She followed him to the kitchen and sat, observing him as he moved around and made them breakfast. Ross had to be the most emotionally constipated man on the planet. But one she knew in her soul she could never live without.

What had begun as a purely physical release had become a phantom link to Austin and, she believed, held something much deeper. Every day that passed with Ross should have forced Austin to fade. But a maddening sensation of ever-present loss never really faded, leaving behind remorse and a gut-deep longing for him.

Was it possible to love two men equally?

It was something she had wondered once, then let go. But it was back, almost as strong as her need to see Austin again — to ask him the same thing.

Her fear that the Denver hookup had been just that had dissipated within twenty-four hours of their return as she'd settled into Austin's old office above the brewery floor. The very first Monday she'd had a Skype conference with her 'Brewer Twenty', a group of fellow west Michigan breweries who compared notes on the expo and talked about the various challenges they all faced. By the time she'd fired up the computer and stood looking out into the darkened brewery from her office window, Ross had materialized and had his hands all over her, threaded in her hair, his amazing lips on her neck and shoulders.

"Shh," he'd whispered. "Have your meeting. I have plenty to occupy me." And he'd proceeded to fuck her silly, standing up from behind, forcing her to switch the Skype audio off.

Now that she had him near night and day lately, she would admit that she needed more.

She had Ross.

She wanted Austin, too.

And the whole mess could have been avoided if she herself had been willing to talk to Austin that horrible day.

Time, distance, and plenty of beer-fueled late-night tear-stained discussions with Melody after Evelyn had procured her own place to live had convinced her that Valerie had conspired with Virginia to ambush the man emotionally the same day Virginia told her off at lunch. The one time she'd allowed herself to listen to one of Austin's late-night drunken voicemails had given her the first hint.

He'd lost his phone that day. Had wanted to call her after Valerie had done a subtle number on his nerves over lunch. The day he'd lost the phone had been the day Valerie had answered for him. She must have taken it.

"You're a stubborn cow," Melody had said once she'd copped to this realization. "But I get it. I am, too. And besides, that Viking you're fucking day and night ought to keep you plenty occupied." She'd raised a dark eyebrow as she sipped the last of her beer.

One of the first hires Evelyn had made once her own employment contract was finalized — with Austin never making a personal appearance at any of the negotiation sessions — was Melody Rodriguez as the Fitz Pub manager. The woman had already instigated dramatic changes designed to drag that side of the business back into the black.

Evelyn would admit to some selfishness with the move. She wanted her friend around. Luckily, Melody was, hands-down, the best possible choice for manager. And they got to share a beer nearly every day before Evelyn headed home — their therapy sessions, they called them.

"This whole friends-with-benefits thing with Ross is nice, but it's making me edgy and miss Austin more. The three of us should be here, working in the brewery together," she said one evening, staring into her full glass of perfectly hopped amber liquid. She shoved it away, alarmed at the way her stomach churned at the smell.

"Hmm...well," Melody said, staring over the bar, observing her staff at work. "Pretty much only you can do anything about that. Ross tried. Maybe it's your turn to try."

"No," Evelyn. "No way. I am not about to beg Austin Fitzgerald for anything." She got up and shouldered her purse. "Besides, my Viking is enough for me."

"Don't want it?" Melody indicated the full beer. Her phone buzzed across the bar. Evelyn snagged it before she could. "Hey!" her friend said.

Evelyn held up a hand and looked at the screen. Trent was calling. And once she let the call go to voicemail, she noted that Trent had called something like a dozen times in the last few hours, plus sent a half-dozen text messages. Frowning, she studied the increasingly frantic tone of the missives from the hunky older man who owned the beer store where she and Austin had had their first hookup.

And who, if memory served and she thought it did, was into some seriously kinky shit. Evelyn shivered at the memory — and at the way Melody was ignoring him. Trent had not shown her much of anything but his Super Alpha Dom side. Which had been something that intrigued her, once upon a time. Their break-up had been mutual. And she had a ton of respect for the way he played both parents for his young daughter while building his liquor store empire.

"You have to tell me what happened. Please, Mel, I'm sorry. But I have to know."

"Stay out of it, boss lady," Melody muttered. Evelyn handed her phone over. "Not your business."

"Just tell me one thing," Evelyn said, pointing to the phone now in her friend's hand. "Are you okay? Really, truly, okay?"

Melody's huge, brown eyes filled with tears. But before Evelyn could reach for her, or say anything, a voice called from the kitchen. Melody jumped to her feet, swiped her eyes, and gave Evelyn a quick squeeze. "I'm pregnant," she whispered. "But I'm taking care of it. Now go on, beat it. Find Austin. Or Ross. Or both of 'em. But do something, all right? All this bitching and whining is getting old."

Evelyn blinked, taking in the force of her friend's words — all of them. "Do you need me to…?"

"Yeah, maybe, I'll let you know more tomorrow. I have some thinking to do." When the voice called again, Melody rolled her eyes and shot Evelyn a jaunty salute before heading down the bar so she could duck behind it and deal with whatever required her attention.

Evelyn headed to her car in a daze and sat for a good long while, contemplating her hands on the steering wheel. Austin's continued, distinct absence from their once well-balanced triangle was not working for her. And it was making Ross more and more irritable, she could tell. She owed it to herself to talk to Austin again.

But she couldn't do it. It had been too long and was probably too late, anyway.

* * * *

"Hey, Evelyn." Her assistant's voice cut through the cobwebs that kept invading her brain lately.

Evelyn leaned on her hand, staring out of the window of the raised office complex inside the brewery. The irritating mental loop of the moment she'd walked away from Austin ran again. It so often did when she found herself watching Ross. She followed his tall form making his way around the twenty-thousand-square-foot space filled with a state-of-the-art brew house and the newest one-hundred-barrel fermentation vessels she'd just purchased.

His broad back flexed under the brewery T-shirt while he did his usual berating of the brewery boys. As brew master, he'd made changes Austin would never have instigated. The level of tension tinged with camaraderie he'd developed amongst the staff was the polar opposite of Austin's style. Some thrived under it, but it pissed off almost as many staff members as it pleased.

"It's Sean, from Standard Beverage. Line one."

She rolled her eyes and prepped herself for an argument with one of her less-motivated distributors.

She could practically hear Austin's calm voice in her head. Those soothing sounds had been her touchstone for a long time. She'd loved that man so much that losing him made her hate waking up every morning. Having Ross back in her life had certainly helped. But she'd risen that day and made a decision. She needed to get some distance from him. She had to sort out how she really felt about Austin before sinking any deeper with the tall, handsome brewer.

By the time the day had eased into late afternoon, exhaustion had taken over. Between expansion plans and personnel issues, the thought of facing a huge beer dinner crowd later that night made her ill. But then again, a lot of things had made her ill lately.

Frowning, she sat up fast, making her head spin as she did a quick mental calculation, in the way of women since the dawn of time. With a curse, she checked her phone's calendar. Evelyn had never understood what it meant to feel the blood drain from her face, until that moment. Knees quaking, she dropped into a chair near the window, which let her keep staring down at Ross' broad shoulders and back.

Ross, the man who'd soothed her, loved her, lusted after her, cooked her delicious, gourmet-level meals, made her laugh and, at times, forget her gut-deep need for Austin back in her life. And now, the man who would be the father of her child. Evelyn closed her eyes as a rush of acid-laced nausea hit her throat, forcing her to her feet and into the hall toward the bathroom. Once she'd emptied her stomach, she gripped the edge of the sink, glaring at her flushed face and her wild, tear-filled eyes.

A baby. But a baby with Ross?

And how, exactly, would that help anything?

Recalling her last pregnancy scare made the acid lurch into her mouth again. She ran for the toilet, but experienced nothing but a series of painful dry heaves for a few seconds. Tears burned her face as she sobbed her way back to the sink and splashed her face and neck with ice-cold water.

A sudden loud shout made her run out of the bathroom. Gripping the railing, she stared down onto the brewery floor, terrified someone had been injured. Not seeing anything from that awkward angle, she took the four steps up to her office and stood at the window, peering around for disaster, or blood, or anything that would take her mind off her current, unwanted, terrifying, condition.

She watched Ross stomp away, leaving another other man standing with his back to her, arms crossed. Heart racing, she put her palms against the cool glass.

It was Austin, dressed in an expensive blue suit, looking good enough to eat—his dark hair close cropped, the familiar span of his shoulders making her palms itch with the need to touch him until she clenched her hands into fists to keep from pounding on the window, from yelling at him to come upstairs, to talk to her if nothing else.

Ross turned again. He pointed at the large fermentation vessels. She watched as Austin responded just as heatedly, but silent, as he waved his arms, obviously furious about something. She swallowed hard, observing the man who'd rocked her universe for the last few months take the five or six steps separating the two men, haul back, and punch his friend in the nose.

She gasped, unable to stop watching, unwilling to admit what was happening right in front of her. Austin staggered, then came at Ross, fists flying. The energy in the room that permeated the entire space made her face flush and her knees wobbly. She sat, her gaze still on the fray. An assistant brewer had stepped in and separated them. They were glaring at each other, noses dripping blood, chests heaving, eyes glaring.

Frustrated rage at her own impotence in this situation made her face hot. Her palm landed on the first thing it encountered and she flung it against the tall bookshelves that lined one wall of the office.

The crash of glass from the shattered pint made it worse, as she pictured the calm way Austin would simply clean it up and leave her to her tantrum. While Ross would rise to it, meet her halfway, encouraging her screaming, yelling fury. She acknowledged the utter absurdity of being angry at Austin for merely being himself even in her hazy fantasy of him at that moment, but the scene with Ross burned holes in her brain. Her throat ached, as if it had only been days, not months since she'd last seen him, in this very office when she'd officially resigned and he'd let her walk away without a word of protest.

* * * *

Ross could not believe it. That son-of-a-bitch Fitzgerald was yelling at him across the empty brewery floor, furious that he'd let the amber lager get exactly one and a half degrees too warm a day early.

What the fuck?

He crossed his arms, watching as Austin's broad-suited back retreated, his gaze drawn unconsciously to the other man's ass. He quelled the urge to call him out, to ask why he'd hired him if he was going to do this sort of micro-managing bullshit. When he opened his mouth to speak, Austin whirled around and pointed at the fermenters.

"You'll be responsible if that entire fucking batch is ruined. Do you hear me?"

"Austin, Jesus, both you and I know that isn't going to happen. What the hell — "

Before he could finish, the guy moved up in his grill, tight, too tight. Ross' body reacted in a primal fashion. His fists clenched. His muscles tensed for action.

"Why are you here, Austin?" His voice was barely a

whisper. "You told me, you made me promise her, that you wouldn't do this. That you wouldn't come here, remember?"

Austin seemed so stressed, so miserable, it made Ross' body clench in sympathy.

"So I hear you're fucking her plenty," Austin said, shocking Ross out of his sympathy fugue. "I hear you guys are like rabbits around here. Nice work, Hoffman. Way to play to type."

A roar of inner fury split Ross' brain in half as he hauled back and landed a hard punch to Austin's face. "Do not talk about her like that, you fucking asshole," he said, ducking to avoid Austin's thrown left hook, only to catch an uppercut to his solar plexus. His breath rushed out in a whoosh.

"I'll talk about her any way I damn well please. She's mine. Not yours."

"Really," Ross said, as they circled each other, seeking an opening. "Maybe you should act like it for a change."

"I tried," Austin yelled, landing a hard right to Ross' eye socket. "You know I —"

"You didn't *try* hard enough," Ross said, getting in his own hard left to Austin's, which would leave them with matching black eyes for days. "She deserved better. Better than you gave her."

With a roar of anger, Austin launched himself at Ross, half punching, half wrestling until a brewery assistant managed to separate them.

"Answer my goddamned question," Ross ground out before he spit blood into a floor drain. "Why are you here?"

Austin glared at him in silence. Ross felt his heart breaking for this, for him, for his budding relationship with the amazing Evelyn. Because it was over. He knew that. He'd known that all along. But he was going to put this right if it killed him. He shrugged out of the assistant's grip and got up in Austin's face. "You are in very real danger of starting something I'm gonna finish. Right here. Right now." He grabbed Austin's shirt in one fist. "If you don't want that, you'd better get the hell out and leave this to me."

Ross heard the sounds of the brewery shutting down for the night. More lights flickered off, plunging them into darkness. Austin sighed. "I can't do this."

"*Ja*, so step away from me, Austin. You don't know..." Ross swallowed. "I mean, you should know, we, Evelyn and I we have been together. We are together."

Austin barked out an ugly laugh, interrupting him. "Of course you are. Jesus." He ran a hand through his hair. Ross stayed silent. What could he say, anyway? The guy had effectively cut both Ross and Evelyn off, putting them in place to run the brewery and leaving them alone, as he'd promised.

Ross stared at his friend. "She's upstairs in the office. Go. Talk to her. You owe each other a discussion."

Austin shook his head, started to back away. "No. I'm not here to make up with her."

"Excuse me but that is bullshit." Ross crossed his arms and shoved the ugly jealousy away. Evelyn was not his — she never had been. She and Austin were meant to be the couple, he merely the third wheel, the spare, the extra — but he didn't care. He loved her and couldn't stand another minute of her misery.

"It may be. But it's true. Tell her I came by if you want. Or not. Enjoy the ride with her, Ross. I know I did." He started to turn but Ross had had enough. A sudden surge of anger and anticipated loss propelled him across the short distance, made him grab Austin's arm and spin him around, shove him up against the wall.

"You are the most lame-ass motherfucker on the planet, Fitzgerald. You really don't deserve her. But I'm gonna give you one more shot. Then all bets are off. Get up the steps to that office. Talk to her. Tell her how you feel."

"Why?" Austin pushed him away. "She's the one who won't talk, remember?"

"She will. Because I'll tell her to. C'mon. It's time to get this shit back together again. The way it belongs."

Ross had no idea if he could make it happen, but he was damned if wasn't going to try. Even if it meant he was the third wheel again. The people he loved were miserable without each other and it was within his power at this moment to shove them together into a room and force them to talk.

Chapter Thirty

Footsteps sounded outside her door, hard to miss on the metal walkway, followed by a loud knock. "What?" she called out.

Ross opened the door, Austin on his heels.

"Go away."

"Evelyn." Austin's rough voice seared her nerve endings. She shook her head. But he kept talking. "I'm sorry."

She whirled on him, unable to stop herself, her relief at seeing him quickly subsumed by long-repressed rage. "Sorry for what, Austin? For letting your mother railroad you or for letting Valerie con me? For giving up on the brewery, nearly letting it collapse under its own weight? For pretending you don't care? Or for living a lie?"

"What lie?" he asked, his expression blank. "I'm not the one living a lie, Evelyn. You are."

"Bullshit," she spat out, backing away from him, her eyes burning, her gut churning with the new reality of her life.

"Every morning when you wake up, look in the mirror, and claim you don't love me," he said, hitting the nail so firmly on the head it made her furious and dizzy and, dare she think, hopeful. "That lie."

He leaned on the door frame, his tall body relaxed, his face calm. She worried her lower lip. He let her spin the anger out, reach its logical conclusion, then wait while she climbed down off the ledge herself. Just like he always did. Something about this pissed her off even more.

"You do not get to stand there and pretend all this time hasn't passed since you've talked to me." Her throat was tight, making her voice high and stressed.

He frowned and walked toward her, making her gasp when he gripped her arm and glared at her. "I tried talking to you. I called, texted, emailed – shit, I stood outside your goddamned door all night once. Or has your selective memory erased that?"

She started to speak, but he put a finger over her mouth. "No. You didn't want to talk then. You just packed up your shit and left me, remember? No explanation, no nothing. So, I moved on. But I'm perfectly miserable because the one woman on the planet I want is a stubborn, self-centered bitch."

Her hand stung and his face reddened, the loud smack of skin on skin echoing around the giant office. She glared at him and words shot out of her she'd been thinking for so long she couldn't snatch them back. "Well, I have news for you. The one woman on the planet you want to please will never, ever be happy with you. Her name is Virginia Fitzgerald and she took me to lunch a few months ago and informed me you were back together with Valerie. In case you've forgotten this other detail, I'll remind you that she tried to give me a huge check. The woman tried to pay me to leave you. So you and Valerie could be together."

Ross gasped behind her. But she kept her gaze on Austin, hand still raised from her blow to his face. He grabbed it and held her wrist tight, eyes flashing with fury. "And you actually believed her? After all we had been through, had done, you let thirty minutes over a limp country club salad with a woman you hated convince you that you couldn't trust me?"

Her ears rang. "I…"

"No." He let go of her, dropped her hand as though it were a poisonous snake and turned away. "You're the one with the problem, Evelyn. Not me. You finally got to justify that giant fucking chip on your shoulder, didn't you? The evil rich bitches conspiring to ruin the poor little poverty-stricken girl's life? You let Valerie con you, Benedict. If you'd had the balls to just ask me about it that night, we could have skipped all this. But, no, you got to feel all righteous about those lame-ass excuses you gave for not marrying me?" He pointed at Ross. "And him? What is he to you now? A way to keep flagellating yourself? Reminding yourself of what we almost, but not quite, had?"

"I'm pregnant," she blurted out, before clapping her hand over her lips. Tears rolled down her face nonstop as she watched their respective reactions. Ross, his jaw gaping, then closed, then clenched, his fists the same at his sides. Austin, his eyes wide, then narrowed, his hands shoved into his suit trouser pockets. "Yeah, so, I guess he and I will need to do some talking now. Since what *he* is to me now, is the father of my child."

Austin and Ross glared at each other.

Her head pounded. She dropped into the large leather chair, face in her hands. She sensed him near, could feel his presence as if they'd not spent all the past months apart. She rose and pushed him back. "Get out of my office," she croaked. "Both of you. Just leave me alone."

She moved to the bank of windows and tried not to faint, willing them away. When she turned, they were gone.

* * * *

Ross went through the motions of the beer dinner, doing his usual commentary, making recommendations about pairings and other random crap, the chill coming from Evelyn's side of the pub palpable. On the one hand, his whole body still buzzed from the encounter with Austin and Evelyn. On the other, he found it hard to take a full breath. He held the bridge of his nose, willing the pressure out of his skull.

A baby. He was going to be a father. Something in him seemed to rise up and want to beat its chest every time he thought of that. His baby, with her, Evelyn, his goddess, his friend, his lover, the woman who loved another man more than she loved him.

Dear Lord but he had to fix this now.

"What's that?" He looked down at the woman asking him another question about his background. She smiled at him in a way that indicated she'd like to know more about the background of what lay behind his zipper.

He suppressed a groan of frustration and launched into the same old story. It wasn't that he minded telling it. It was that, at this particular moment, he would rather be talking to Evelyn, alone.

He glanced at her, admired the sexy curve of her waist, the delectable swell of her hips in his usual knee-jerk fashion. She seemed sexier to him now, knowing what he knew, if that were possible. Even though the memory of Austin's haunted eyes as he ran from the office then stumbled down the metal stairs were etched in his brain.

Clearing his throat, he excused himself behind the bar. His damn cock was rock hard at the sight of her. But more alarming was the ache in his heart. He knew he loved her. And owed it to her to come out and say it. But after that scene in the office, he knew that Austin loved her just as much, still. And he had no idea what to do about any of it.

"Hey, Ross!"

He nodded a greeting and got pulled into yet another beer conversation. Usually his favorite topic without a doubt — but not today. He glanced across the room and locked eyes with Evelyn before she glanced away.

He caught Melody Rodriguez staring at him, her intense, Latina glare like a physical knife at his temples. As if she had room to judge. Last he'd heard, she'd left Trent Hettinger, the perfectly nice dude who owned a bunch of successful liquor stores and just opened a hot new beer bar in Kalamazoo, high and fucking dry, the bitch.

Goddamned women.

He shook his head and forced himself to focus on the crowd who'd paid perfectly good money to come here and listen to him run his mouth.

* * * *

Evelyn tried like hell to avoid Ross. She knew she had to keep her distance, that he deserved her cold shoulder for trying to force her and Austin's confrontation. But found herself drawn to him like a magnet, requiring his presence to soothe her rattled psyche. By the time the last table had been cleared, they sat shoulder to shoulder at the bar, sharing coffee. He had a finger of one-hundred-year-old Scotch in a glass in front of him and had made a huge deal out of not pouring her one.

"God, my throat is killing me." Her face flushed when she realized her clumsy use of words. "Oh hell, you know what I mean." She put her head on Ross' shoulder.

She shouldn't be this comfortable with him. The man remained utterly incapable of giving her anything but his body. But their usual familiarity came with a new undercurrent of awkward she didn't have the energy to deal with tonight. She needed him as a friend, perhaps as a lover, but mostly as a companion—the man who was helping her save the brewery from Austin's forced neglect. The man who'd be with her through her pregnancy, delivery, beyond. The thought of losing that made her nearly blind with terror.

"Relax." Ross put an arm around her and his lips hit her ear, his German accent doing its usual number on her libido. She clenched her thighs together.

"How do you know I'm not?" She leaned away from him, until he pulled her close again.

"Because you never change." He heaved a huge sigh. "I'm sorry Austin's mother and Valerie did that to you, but you know he's right."

He bit her earlobe as if he were seducing her and not saying things she didn't want to hear. Of course he was right. Austin was always right. And she'd let that very chip on her shoulder grow to such proportions it had become an insurmountable wall between her and the man she loved.

"Okay, lovebirds, I think this puppy is ready to shut down for the night," Melody said as she grabbed Ross' glass and drained it for him. "Behave."

"Wait, don't go yet," Evelyn said. But her friend looked wrung out, so exhausted she might pass out behind the bar. "You all right?"

"Fuck no, I'm not and you know it." Melody leaned her elbows on the bar's slate top and grabbed Evelyn's arm in one hand and Ross' in the other. "You guys need to get your shit together. The company can't withstand all the drama in the front office." She muttered something in Spanish, then tightened her grip on them. "Get Austin back. I'm pretty sure between you, you can manage that? *Jesu*," she said.

"I'm pregnant...too," Evelyn admitted, her voice small and helpless sounding. Ross did a double take, realizing what she'd just revealed about Melody.

"Well, shit, we can do Lamaze together then, I guess. Now get off your collective asses and get Austin Fitzgerald back here where he belongs." She gave them both light smacks on their cheeks before stomping away, muttering a mile a minute in her native language.

"Well, I guess she told us," Ross said mildly, as he poured himself another splash of amber liquor.

If it were any other day, any other night than the one where she'd been confronted with such a shitty reality, she knew she and Ross would be heading back to her house, no questions asked. But now, she had no idea what to do or say around him.

She would have the baby. Of that there was no doubt. But did she want to be married to Ross Hoffman? Her doubts and second-guessing about that for the past few hours had made her even dizzier than the pregnancy.

She put her palm on his thigh, felt the muscles bunched there, and tried not to squeeze, to encourage like she normally would. He scooted forward, the way he had when they'd connected in Denver last year, bringing his crotch closer to her touch.

Her heart ached and her eyes burned with the memory of the two men together. She had to release him. He had to go, back to the west coast, or Germany, or someplace and live the life he deserved. The one that did not involve her, her wounded heart, and her messy mistakes. But her body kept clamoring for him in a familiar, not-to-be-ignored way.

She leaned into his ear and whispered a set of words for the final time. "I'm going to my office. Need to wrap some stuff up."

It was a code they shared. 'Going to my office' from her lips usually meant 'get up here and fuck me' to his body. And today had been no exception. Ross had no reason to think the fantasies dancing around in his head since she'd revealed her pregnancy had any hope of seeing the light of real day. He, Austin and Evelyn, back together, the images would — should — remain that. Fantasy.

The fantasy of a home with them in it, with a child — their child — growing up safe and loved by the three of them. Ross was nothing if not fully cognizant of his own failings. He didn't feel in any way equipped to be a husband and father, not the sort Evelyn deserved. No, she and Austin had to be together, a married couple. But for the first time he allowed himself a space in that future — one of beloved uncle, Fitzgerald master brewer, friend to two of the most incredible people in the universe.

But from a distance from now. His time as Evelyn's lover was over.

He watched her go, admiring for the millionth time the sway of her hips, the way her long hair swept her shoulders. He licked his lips, knocked back the booze, and leapt off the bar stool.

He smiled, remembering the first time she'd used the code. He'd been outside in the hall, studying the expansion blueprints when she'd looked out of her door, crooked a finger and beckoned him inside. She had been gloriously naked behind the door and he'd fucked her over the desk, twice, as the brewery had shut down for the night under their gaze.

Dear God, she was insatiable. And he adored that about her. Among other things — like her voice, her smile, and her passion for the business he held dear.

And now? They were at a major turning point, to put it mildly. The moment Austin had confronted her and she had broken her news, the flash of realization about what he wanted then had terrified him. And damned if he wasn't frozen to the spot, unsure how to proceed, until he heard the words, *I'm going up to my office.*

He grabbed his phone and tapped out one of the hardest messages of his life to Austin. "She's upstairs. This is your last chance." With a sigh, he poured more whiskey and stared into the darkened bar. "She's all yours, my friend," he said to no one, but of course to Austin. "Don't screw it up this time."

He was already planning where he might land next.

Chapter Thirty-One

Evelyn shuffled papers around, pretending not to listen for the sound of Ross' work boots on the metal stairs. She had used their code on purpose. And planned to give him what they both wanted—a perfect physical release.

Before she released him completely.

Her body thrummed with a strange energy. Her brain kept up the loop of Ross and Austin—Austin and Ross—she'd seen on the brewery floor. Unwilling to admit exactly how that had affected her, she sat down before the turmoil of the situation she found herself in became too overwhelming to contemplate any longer.

She'd had everything once. And now? She'd thrown a perfectly good life away with both hands, with the sort of childish energy Austin had finally called her on.

And now, she had another set of responsibilities looming—the most important kind. The kind that meant more than running any brewery ever would. She put a hand on her flat stomach and closed her eyes, focusing on that future and how she'd forge it alone, with no one but her child, because that was simply how it had to be now.

"We can do Lamaze together," her friend Melody had said. Evelyn set her jaw against the tears.

When her computer's soft incoming message *ding* hit her ears, she glanced at the screen, unwilling to engage in work but unable to not check and see what required her attention. As she took in the sender and the subject line, she gasped and sat up, mouth hanging open in shock.

BFitz@gmail had sent a message.

Coming home, was the subject.

Hi, Evelyn, I'm Brock, Austin's brother. I'm guessing you've heard about me. I wanted to let you know that I'm headed home this week and was hoping we could talk about a position for me at the brewery. This is pretty weird, I know, considering I don't know exactly what he's told you about me, but I promise to clear it all up when we meet. I'll be in on Saturday and can be at the brewery around noon. I hope to hear from you. I understand that you're the one in charge there, since Austin took over our father's company. He's a dumb ass for doing that, but that's just my humble, prodigal son-style opinion.

Sincerely,
Brock Fitzgerald.

Holy shit.
Brock.

The brother Austin was convinced had either OD'd in some heroin den or jumped off a bridge — anything but this. The six-year-long stretch of remaining hidden and silent, letting his family think that about him made her furious at the man, then relieved, then terrified at the fact that he'd reached out to her for a meeting.

When she met Austin's deep green eyes she truly wasn't surprised. She closed the laptop, took a deep breath, and nodded at him.

"Um, Evelyn, we need to talk."

"You think?" She crossed her legs, kept her gaze on his face.

"Yeah, I do." He parked himself against the work top, arms crossed. Her body tingled. And his proximity did not help.

He ran a shaking hand down his face and she noticed for the first time how gaunt he was. His jeans and button-down shirt hung on him. Relief and sadness poured off him in nearly visible waves. Unable to resist, she walked to him and put a hand alongside his face. He grabbed it and pulled her close so fast she yelped. "Thank God," he muttered into her hair.

269

She disentangled herself, uncomfortable with how much she wanted him back. Convinced she could live without him, she'd returned to this job, jumped into bed with Ross and had come close to even dumping him in an attempt to regain some control over her life. Even as she faced an even scarier set of circumstances, thanks to her inability to be consistent with condoms.

Austin put his hands in his pockets but stayed slumped against the work table. "I'm such a mess." He shrugged. "Sorry. I won't bother you again." He rose and walked straight into her personal space, pulling her close. "After one more kiss."

Before she could protest, he slanted his lips over hers and the familiarity of his body made her gasp and nearly faint. He held her tightly, parted her lips, slid his hands down her back and she met him halfway in a tongue-tangling, teeth-clicking urgency that made every inch of her skin burn with need.

The need for his flesh against hers, to regain the intense connection they'd shared, made her pull her lips away and yank his shirt open, sending buttons flying around the room. "That's not gonna cut it for me, Austin," she said, lust making her voice low and rough.

He grinned and her entire world shifted back into focus at the sight of it.

"Good. Me neither." He yanked her close again, shoving her skirt up. But he stared at her, put his other hand to her cheek. "I'm not interested in some kind of mercy fuck, Evelyn. So, don't kid yourself. We do this and all bets are off."

Her scalp tingled at his words. "No mercy about it, Fitzgerald," she whispered as she slid his zipper down.

Austin had never felt more complete the moment his lips touched hers. Although he'd convinced himself to stay away, to leave Evelyn and Ross to their own lives, especially in light of the pregnancy news, in the end he'd let his heart lead. He had to. He'd wasted too much time in his life listening to the practical voices in his head. It had denied him the happiness he'd found with her, and with Ross, and he was done with that. Even if she rejected him again, he had to try once more.

And now, this split second of time, between the *Should I kiss her?* and the *Hell yes, what are you waiting for?* he felt like his old self again. The happy Austin, the one who'd owned and run a brewery with the woman he loved by his side and with an amazing third in their lives. Ross, with his passionate, artistic, temperamental nature, who'd completed them like the most perfect puzzle piece in the universe.

He sighed into her neck and yanked her shirt over her head as he maneuvered them over to the large desk where they'd done this very thing so many times.

She tasted different to him, richer somehow, and he groaned against her nipple at the realization of why as she leaned back on the desk's surface, propping one heel-clad shoe on the chair. He had not had sex for months, after explaining not too kindly to Valerie that she could dream on about getting anywhere near him. She'd cried, fumed, pouted and called his mother.

Which had convinced him he was right to tell her exactly that.

But the lack of outlet for a guy used to getting laid on a regular basis made him pant and grunt when she fisted his cock. "It's not gonna take long for me, baby. I'm sorry. Oh, God," he moaned when she yanked up his undershirt.

"No, I'm sorry, Austin," she whispered between kisses as he slid into the perfect glove of her body in a long, deep stroke, making them both sigh with satisfaction at the same time. "I'm so sorry for not loving you like you deserved."

He thrust in deeper, his brain on fire. She gripped his shoulders and bent one leg up against his chest, giving him an even better angle. Her voice coiled around in his brain like smoke. "I love you, Austin. I never stopped loving you and I should have trusted you. I… Oh, yes," she hissed as he pounded into her hard, nearly blind with it, and the climax roared up his spine, exploding across his vision. Now he knew why they called it fireworks.

"I'm gonna…" he grunted, his knees getting wobbly as every drop of blood he had filled his cock, making it even harder as the entire world narrowed to the two of them.

"Austin!" she whispered and the glorious pulse of her orgasm grabbed his cock milked him toward his own monster release.

He shuddered, cried out, and the last weeks and months of misery dissipated like sun-struck fog. He shivered as his body released into hers, seemingly forever. She held on to him as tears slicked her face and he kissed and kissed her, laying his mark on her, knowing he would never let her go.

The sound and feel of her breath on his skin made him shiver. He kept his hands on her thighs, unwilling to stop touching her for any reason even after he pulled out of her body. She ran her hands down his chest, back up, cupped his face, her brilliant blue eyes full of meaning. "I mean it," she said. "I am sorry. You deserve so much better than me."

He zipped himself up, then helped her put her shirt back on and straighten the skirt she'd not even removed. Then kissed her once more, thinking he would never get enough of her lips. "Evelyn," he whispered around her skin. "I need to ask you something."

She stiffened, but he kept going. He had to, or he'd be lost forever.

"Evelyn, will you please—"

He stood, his ruined shirt in a puddle at his feet, arms crossed, watching her try to avoid his eyes. He grabbed her arms and pushed her up against the wall, propping his hands on either side of her head. "Evelyn. Will you put this back on?" He pulled her engagement ring from his pocket. She smiled and slid it on her finger. "And will you please never, ever leave me?" He ran a thumb over her trembling lower lip and smiled when she shook her head.

A noise from the doorway made them both turn their heads. Austin smiled and held out a hand for Ross.

"That is to say, will you never leave us?"

More books from
Totally Bound Publishing

From international bestselling author Sierra Cartwright

He will have her…

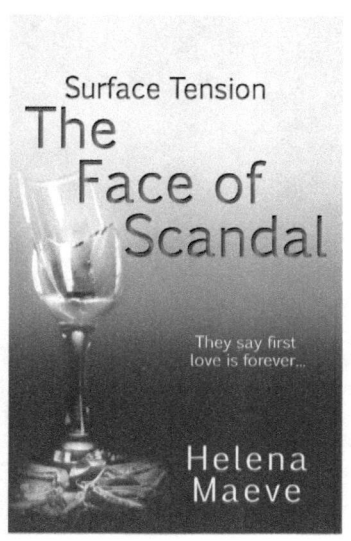

Surface Tension
The Face of Scandal

They say first love is forever...

Helena Maeve

Book three in the Surface Tension serial

They say first love is forever. They don't say that sometimes it's against your will.

Part of the Totally 5 Star collection

Who knew lies and billionaires were an explosive combination?

Shy and serious by day – insatiable by night.

About the Author

Liz Crowe

Amazon best-selling author, mom of three, Realtor, beer blogger, brewery marketing expert, and soccer fan, Liz Crowe is a Kentucky native and graduate of the University of Louisville currently living in Ann Arbor. She has decades of experience in sales and fund raising, plus an eight-year stint as a three-continent, ex-pat trailing spouse.

With stories set in the not-so-common worlds of breweries, on the soccer pitch, in successful real estate offices and at times in exotic locales like Istanbul, Turkey, her books are unique and told with a fresh voice. The Liz Crowe backlist has something for any reader seeking complex storylines with humor and complete casts of characters that will delight, frustrate and linger in the imagination long after the book is finished.

Don't ever ask her for anything "like a Budweiser" or risk bodily injury.

Liz Crowe loves to hear from readers. You can find contact information, website details and an author profile page at https://www.totallybound.com/

Home of Erotic Romance